hot asset

OTHER TITLES BY LAUREN LAYNE

I Do, I Don't

Ready to Run

Runway Groom

Stiletto and Oxford

After the Kiss

Love the One You're With

Just One Night

The Trouble with Love

Irresistibly Yours

I Wish You Were Mine

Someone Like You

I Knew You Were Trouble

I Think I Love You

Love Unexpectedly (stand-alone novels)

Blurred Lines

Good Girl

Love Story

Walk of Shame

An Ex for Christmas

The Wedding Belles

From This Day Forward (novella)

To Have and to Hold

hot asset

LAUREN LAYNE

Montlake
Romance

Text copyright © 2018 by Lauren Layne
All rights reserved.

Published by Montlake Romance, Seattle

www.apub.com

Amazon, the Amazon logo, and Montlake Romance are trademarks of Amazon.com, Inc., or its affiliates.

ISBN-13: 9781503901063
ISBN-10: 1503901068

Cover design by Letitia Hasser

Cover photography by Wander Aguiar

Printed in the United States of America

For Kristi Yanta—
for bringing out my best writing as an editor
and bringing out my best self as a friend

1

IAN

On paper, I'm a douchebag. Yeah, I said it so you don't have to.

Don't believe me? Here's a crash course in Ian Bradley:

The charcoal-gray suit I'm currently wearing costs more than my first car. I'm six foot two, black hair, blue eyes, and I work out every day, so I wear that suit *well*, if you get what I'm saying, and you know you do.

At thirty-two, I'm an investment broker—director level, thank you very much—for Wolfe Investments. And let's just say, *work hard, play hard* is basically the unspoken company motto.

I've got a corner office, a seven-figure salary, a swanky apartment in Manhattan's Financial District, and I never sleep with the same woman twice—because I don't have to.

Did I mention I went to Yale? Managed to graduate top of my class *and* get all the usual college bad decisions under my belt. Achieving both a thriving social life and summa cum laude at an Ivy League is no easy task, let me tell you.

So, like I said—I'm basically the poster boy for "Wall Street dickhead."

But don't hate me just yet, because here's what that Ian Bradley poster *doesn't* say:

Unlike the rest of my fraternity, that Ivy League education didn't come courtesy of a trust fund and four generations of Yale alumni to get me in the door. More like three jobs, an academic scholarship, and a shit-ton of financial aid.

As a kid, my spoon was plastic, not silver, and was provided by a cranky but kind gas-service attendant in South Philly because most of my foster parents didn't give a fuck whether or not I ate.

That cushy corner office I just told you about? Mine came from sheer force of will and about a decade of no sleep.

And while that seven-figure salary puts a swanky Manhattan roof over my head, it also provides college education for Philly foster kids who are willing to work for it.

Have you started a mocking slow clap yet? Yeah, that's fair.

But the point is there's never been a damn thing I worked for and didn't get through relentless hard work and hustle.

Until her.

And that's where my story *really* begins.

Week 1: Monday Afternoon

It's three o'clock on "Merger Monday," and I need more caffeine.

Monday is the day of the week where a shit-ton of mergers between companies is announced. For my colleagues and me at Wolfe Investments, that means a lot of time staring at the list, making phone calls, trying to figure out what's *huge*, what's *pay attention*, and what's *who cares* among the deals.

In other words, it's necessary but mind-numbing, especially after a late night, and, well . . . they're *all* late nights in my world.

I step out of my office for a Starbucks run, and the second I do, the office door across from mine opens, and a stunning brunette in a tight red dress gives me a slow smile. "Hey, Ian."

I smile back at my colleague. "Joss."

She leans against the doorframe and strategically crosses her arms to emphasize her cleavage before giving me a slow once-over. "Busy?"

Subtlety's not her strong suit. Hell, it's not any of ours here at Wolfe.

"'Fraid so."

Her eyes narrow. "I haven't seen you around."

She's seen me around plenty. She just means she hasn't seen me naked since the gin-fueled mistake last week that I have no intention of repeating. Not because she's not hot, but because I don't *do* do-overs.

The moment the challenge is over, so's the appeal.

I'm not proud of it, but it's always been that way—faulty wiring, I suppose.

"Sorry, been busy." I give her a wink, then turn to head down the hall.

"Is Kennedy around?" she calls after me.

I smirk a little at the too-obvious question. If she's trying to make me jealous, she's wrong on both counts. I don't do jealous, and Kennedy Dawson doesn't do office hookups. Even if he did, my friend doesn't touch my leftovers. Wall Street has a guy code.

"No clue," I call over my shoulder.

I'm texting my Monday Starbucks barista to let her know I'll be there in five (no point waiting in line when a twenty-dollar tip has your drink waiting for you) when a pair of *excellent* female legs in the break room catches my attention.

I slow, trying to see what I'm dealing with here. I don't recognize the calves. Not the ass or slim waist, either, and I'd definitely remember the long blonde ponytail that's got just the right amount of grown-up cheerleader fantasy going on.

Hot. Very hot.

Still, I've got shit to do, and I'm about to pass on by when I hear the woman talking to herself. "How are there *eight* milk options?"

I smile at the genuine bafflement in her voice. Shoving both hands into my pockets, I step into the kitchen to see firsthand if the face is as great as the body. "Well, I'm no expert, but off the top of my head, whole, two percent, skim, soy, almond unsweetened, almond sweetened with vanilla, coconut . . ."

She whirls around at my voice, and my head snaps back a little when I see her face-to-face.

Not because I know her but because I *want* to know her. For one bizarre-ass moment, the woman feels meant for me.

The kicker? She's not even my type.

I like my women with flirty smiles, quick laughs, great bodies, and a solid understanding of what I'm looking for: a good time for one night only.

This woman . . . I'm not entirely sure she'd know a good time if it swatted her on the ass. Her blonde hair is parted down the middle, pulled back away from her good-girl features. She's not particularly well endowed up top, and though the flare to her hips is worth a second look, her blouse and prim skirt are all business, her bra probably white and cotton. Or worse, *beige* and cotton. I won't even get started on her purse, which is huge and brown and ugly.

Nothing about her, save the great legs, explains why I'm itching to unravel her inch by inch.

Except the glasses.

Yeah, it's definitely the glasses that do it for me.

Sexy black frames with a vaguely naughty-librarian vibe that are pure fantasy material. They enhance the sexy punch of her wide blue gaze that's thoroughly . . .

Suspicious.

She's holding a file folder in one hand, and she taps the corner against the palm of her other, saying nothing as she gives me a once-over.

When her gaze slides back up to mine, I'm expecting the admiring smile I usually get from women, but she looks . . .

Bored?

Which leaves *me* feeling off-balance. So off-balance that instead of a smooth pickup line, I find myself nodding at the machine on the counter. "You need help with that?"

Her eyebrows lift. "Do I need help with what? Pushing buttons?"

You can push my buttons anytime.

Her eyes narrow, and I get the sense she's read my unspoken words and found them lacking. I'm annoyed. And intrigued. It's been far too long since I've had a challenge.

I ease a step closer to her, moving toward the espresso machine. She doesn't get the least bit flustered by my proximity, so I lean against the machine, patting the top of it with my hand. "Just say the word. Happy to mansplain this to you, little lady," I say with an exaggerated drawl.

She responds in kind, fluttering her eyelashes, the glasses making the gesture even more mocking. "Oh, *could* you?"

I smile, enjoying her more than I expected. "What are you drinking?"

"Coffee."

I roll my eyes. "What kind?"

"Caffeinated," she says, pulling out one of the company mugs, setting it beneath the spout, and punching the standard drip-coffee option.

"Boring," I declare.

"Classic," she counters.

I give her a slow smile. "I'm headed to Starbucks. Let me buy you a real drink."

She lifts her mug. "I'm good with this."

"You could be better with something else," I say, lowering my voice.

She surprises me by laughing, and not a flirty, breathless laugh but an *at* me laugh. "Seriously? Do these lines usually work for you?"

"Honestly?" I give a small smile. "Yeah."

"Well "—she sips her coffee—"let me know when I'm supposed to fake the swoon."

You wouldn't be faking anything with me, sweetheart.

I reach out my right hand. "Ian Bradley."

She ignores the hand and nods. "Nice to meet you."

I lean forward and whisper, "This is the point where you give me your name."

She leans forward and whispers back, "This is the point where you take the hint that I'm not interested in what you're offering."

Challenge accepted.

She starts to move around me, clearly planning to walk away, but I'm not about to let that happen. I step forward. "Have drinks with me."

"No, thank you." She sounds almost amused in her rejection.

"Why not?" I keep the question light, but truthfully? I want to know. It's not often a woman tells me no, even less common that I care. But here I am fantasizing about her naked, and she could not look more disinterested if she tried.

"Oh, so many reasons," she says with a sly smile, as she uses her folder to gesture at my neck. "That fresh hickey, for starters."

I resist the urge to cover the mark with my hand. *Damn the little vampire-inclined bartender from last night.*

"Hmm," I muse. "You sure it's a hickey? Maybe it's a bad reaction to whatever my dry cleaner did to this shirt."

The mystery blonde lifts her cup of coffee. "Well now, that's another reason. I don't like a guy with a rash."

I laugh, more intrigued than ever by her sharp tongue. "Who are you?"

"Someone you're going to regret asking to drinks," she says with a small *I've got a secret* smile.

"Why—"

"Ian."

I turn toward the interruption, tamping down my annoyance when I see it's my assistant, Kate, who looks . . .

Horrified.

I straighten and forget about Blondie for a moment. "Kate, what's up?"

She swallows, shooting a nervous look at the woman beside me. "I've been looking everywhere for you. You're not answering your phone . . ."

"Shit, I forgot to take it off 'Do Not Disturb' after my last meeting," I say, pulling my phone out of my pocket. Sure enough, I have four missed text messages and three missed calls, all from Kate.

I feel my stomach drop out at her first text; my heart skips a beat at the second.

I look up at Kate, now understanding her horrified expression. "The SEC's here?"

Holy hell.

The Securities and Exchange Commission is the government's guard dog against financial crimes, only it's not a badass, useful guard dog.

Nope, the SEC is like a yipping little lapdog, determined to bite ankles, shit all over the place, and ultimately be a huge pain in the ass while providing zero value to anyone other than their own plus-size egos.

"Who're they after?" I ask.

But I already know. I've worked with Kate long enough to know that look on her face, to know when something's wrong.

They're after *me.*

And when the nameless blonde behind me takes a casual sip of her coffee, suddenly it hits me why Kate looks so horrified.

It's not just because an SEC investigator is investigating me . . .

It's because I was just flirting with one.

I slowly turn and face the woman, and she doesn't even bother to hide her amusement as she tucks the folder under her arm and finally extends her hand to introduce herself.

7

I shake her hand out of habit, even as ice settles in the pit of my stomach as our eyes meet. Gone is my fantasy good-girl librarian, and in her place is my nightmare: the Securities and Exchange Commission.

She smiles wider at my obvious discomfort. "Nice to meet you, Mr. Bradley. I'm Lara McKenzie with the SEC. Here to inform you that you're under investigation for insider trading."

2

LARA

Week 1: Monday Afternoon

Is it wrong that I enjoyed that so much? Maybe.

Is it right that I want to celebrate it with champagne?

Not if I don't drink alone.

I pull out my phone and text my best friend / roommate, who's not only always up for champagne but whose freelance model schedule means there's at least a fifty-fifty chance she'll be free at three thirty on a Monday.

Happy Hour? I text, adding the champagne emoji for good measure.

Gabby responds immediately. Who is this, and how did you steal my best friend's phone?

I roll my eyes. It's me, Gab.

Prove it. How did we meet?

Tampon passed under the bathroom stall at Boca.

Super or Light?

Omg, do you want to grab drinks or not?

This is the first time you've EVER texted me for drinks
before six p.m. You understand my skepticism.

She has a point. My job as an investigator for the Securities and
Exchange Commission doesn't exactly allow for flexible hours and day
drinking.

In fact, if I'm being honest, it's quite possibly the least sexy job
on the planet. But I'm good at it, and it's a necessary step on my path
toward my endgame:

The FBI.

The bureau runs in my blood—Dad's an agent; Mom's an agent.

I *will* be an agent, just as soon as I do my time with the SEC.
See, while Dad's National Security and Mom's Science and Technology,
neither "in" is particularly helpful for my own career aspirations.

I want to be part of the white-collar division. I want to deal with art
theft and Ponzi schemes and those slick criminals who turn thousands of
lives upside down every day without even a flicker of guilty conscience.

But . . . I want to *earn* my spot there—not have Mom or Dad put
in a phone call. Doing my time at the SEC's as good an "in" as any; I
just need my big break to get Quantico's attention.

And rumor has it around the SEC that the Ian Bradley case is going
to be the one to change everything.

Hence the champagne.

Gabby and I agree to meet in thirty at a wine bar around the corner
from our Lower East Side apartment.

I slide my phone back into my purse, still smiling at the unexpected
perk of seeing Ian Bradley's face when he learned the news. I know that
sounds awful, relishing in someone else's *oh shit* moment, but here's the
thing. These Wall Street guys . . . it's like . . . I don't even know how to
explain.

It's like they're not real.

Objectively, of course I know they breathe oxygen and bleed red. (Although I wouldn't be surprised if some of the ones I've met out on a Friday night bleed single-malt scotch.)

They're just so dang confident, so convinced that they live on a different plane from the rest of us.

Here's an example:

Last week, Gabby went home with a broker who had a Steinway concert grand piano in the living room of his penthouse. When Gabby asked if he played, he said he's never even touched the keys. His decorator had recommended the piano to him as a "statement piece."

Sorry, but can we pause on that for a second?

There are people in my own city whose "statement pieces" cost more than double my annual income.

I get that it's reverse snobbery, but *come on.*

Anyway.

I don't *officially* kick off my investigation until later this week, but statistically speaking, Ian's probably every bit as guilty of insider trading as our source claims. He's one of the biggest names at one of the biggest firms. That means the most money. The most money means the most to lose . . . and the most to win. Which means the most temptation to cheat.

Ian's also exactly what I'd expected. The guy's pic on the company website is pretty much the stock photo equivalent of a Wall Street broker—expensive haircut, expensive teeth, expensive suit, expensive tan.

In person, he was even more . . .

Well, he was just . . . too much. Too tall. Too charming. Too masculine.

Also . . . gorgeous. Really, ridiculously, *hurts your eyes* gorgeous.

But he knows it.

Even if I hadn't been investigating the guy, I'd have dodged his come-ons. Guys like that just aren't for me. I don't have the patience for their flash and dazzle and strutting, and they don't have time for my rules and structure.

So is Ian Bradley hot? Yes. Very. But I don't need hot. I'd settle for someone a little plain, even a little boring, just so long as he's loyal. Someone who won't mind when I geek out over a new case at work or spend my Saturdays updating my Quantico application.

Professional life first, personal after. It's a little pact I've made with myself since acknowledging that apparently I'm incapable of juggling both.

I'm just starting toward the subway when I hear a masculine voice calling my name.

I turn to see Ian strolling out of Wolfe Investments' revolving doors and heading right toward me. I press my lips together, not loving the jolt of surprise that has me freezing instead of continuing on my way.

I don't like surprises.

Usually the people I'm investigating avoid me at all costs. The fact that he's breaking the rules already does not bode well for the investigation proceeding predictably.

And I *do* like predictability.

Still, the job is the job, so I paste a professional smile on my face, even as I feel a strange flicker of awareness as he comes closer. The Ian Bradley in the office had been all quippy one-liners, superficial charm, and playboy confidence. This Ian, though . . . let's just say I can understand why Ian Bradley and his crew at Wolfe Investments are nicknamed the Wolfes of Wall Street—they're wicked hot, insanely rich, and known for getting exactly what they want, consequences be damned.

Ian slides on sunglasses, hiding eyes that I know are piercingly blue. He stops in front of me, a hair closer than he needs to be, but I refuse to step back.

God, he smells good. Manly and expensive. How annoying.

"Hello again," I say, giving him my most generic "SEC smile."

He doesn't smile back, and even with his sunglasses on, I'm more certain than ever that I'm dealing with a very different version of Ian Bradley from the one I met ten minutes ago. A more dangerous version.

"Was it good for you?" he asks in a low voice.

My smile drops. "Excuse me?"

"Your little game back there." He tilts his head toward the office. "You have fun?"

"Actually, yes," I say, lifting my chin defiantly.

He steps closer, and I can feel the anger radiating off him. "Where the hell do you get off? Coming into my office, flirting—"

"Flirting?" I interrupt, furious. "*I* was just trying to get a stupid cup of coffee. *You're* the one who was acting like freaking Don Juan."

"I'm not going to apologize for asking an attractive woman to drinks," he snaps.

I snort. "Save the flattery for someone who's interested."

He shakes his head. "You've got a sad-ass love life if you think that was flattery, Ms. McKenzie."

His barb hits a little too close to home, but I swipe away the sting and step closer. "Let's get one thing straight, Mr. Bradley, for both our sakes. You think you're the first Wall Street suit who thinks I'll be so dazzled by broad shoulders and a well-played line that I'll lose my little female head and overlook any wrongdoing? You think you're the first one to think this is a game to be won by slimy seduction?"

His mouth drops open. "What the—? Slimy seduction, my ass!"

I ignore his protest and continue with my tirade. "Being a woman in today's world is no easy task, and being a woman in the SEC is that much harder. But here's the part I want you to listen to very closely, Mr. Bradley. I love working for an agency that seeks justice. I love the fact that when it comes to the world of trades and stock and money, nobody's above the law. Not freaking Martha Stewart and most definitely not you."

He takes a small step back and crosses his arms. "Guilty until proven innocent, is that how this works?" I can't see his eyes through the dark shades, but I feel the heat of his glare.

I open my mouth to retort, but his comment slices into my conscience like a very thin paper cut. He's maybe a tiny bit right. In my experience, rumors of insider trading are almost always true, but that doesn't mean I can assume.

"My job is to find out the truth," I say through gritted teeth.

"And what if the truth isn't what you want to hear?"

"Meaning?"

He leans toward me, and I can see the faintest bit of dark stubble against the decidedly stubborn set of his jawline.

Damn it, he really does smell good. What is that, sandalwood? Cedar? George Clooney's sweat?

"Meaning, I think you *want* me to be guilty," he says in a low rumble.

"Why would I want that?"

"You've got a hero complex," he continues. "You're determined to save the world, even if you have to invent your own villains."

I scoff. "That's ridiculous."

"Is it?"

Is it?

I've known this guy for all of three minutes, and somehow, he's made me doubt myself twice. The feeling is unfamiliar and highly annoying.

Much like the man in front of me.

I give him a cool, dismissive smile. "Ah. I see. Asking me to drinks didn't work, so now you're trying to twist this around. Get in my head."

To my surprise, he grins, all traces of his former intensity vanished. "Is it working?"

"Getting in my head? Nope."

"What about the seduction?"

I spread my arms to the side, resisting the urge to roll my eyes. "Again, no signs of imminent swooning. Suspected criminals aren't my type."

I expect him to growl at me, but his smile merely widens, though there's a sharpness to it. "Then I look forward to the day you have to look me in the eyes and tell me I'm innocent."

"If you're innocent, I will surely do that," I say.

"But you don't think I am."

"I told you, it's my job to find out."

"Great. So when this thing goes my way, maybe you can buy *me* a drink."

"Oh, absolutely," I say, making no effort to hide my sarcasm.

He rubs his jaw and studies me, then he shakes his head and turns away. "See you around, Ms. McKenzie."

I'll deny it to my dying day, even to myself, but I'm disappointed that he doesn't turn and glance my way, because I can't seem to remove my eyes from his retreating back.

A back that's too broad, too muscular, too . . .

Gah!

I pivot on my heel and march away, more in need of that champagne than ever.

A drink with Ian Bradley, indeed. Can you imagine?

Even if he's not guilty, it won't happen.

And if he is . . .

Let's just say I'm totally not visiting him in prison, even though I know he would look *really* good in an orange jumpsuit.

3

IAN

Week 1: Tuesday Morning

"Ian. Ready for you."

Well, hell. That makes a first—the first time in my life I've ever hated hearing a woman tell me she's ready for me.

I stand and manage a flirty wink for Carla, the longtime executive assistant of Wolfe's CEOs. She winks back, but it does little to ease my nerves as I enter the office.

It's not that I mind bosses. I don't know that I even have trouble with authority—that's more my friend Matt Cannon's gig. And as far as my superior goes, the guy I report to's a good one. Joe Schneider, my MD (managing director, not the doctor kind), is a hard-ass, but he's decent. Granted, he's the type of guy who nobody particularly likes at cocktail parties because he doesn't know how to talk about anything other than work. But in the office, he commands respect, and that's good enough for me.

However, today I'm not dealing with Joe. Or at least, not just Joe. Today, I'm dealing with his bosses—the CEOs of the company.

I've met Sam and Sam Wolfe (yeah, you read that right) several times. The CEOs love me. I'm their hottest asset. They know it, and I know it. Between holiday parties, fund-raisers, and quarterly meetings, I've gotten plenty of face time with the higher-ups.

This time, though, is entirely different. There's no shooting the shit, no clap on the back, no grin at my arrival. I'm all too aware of their somber faces, the way the room smells like tension.

As it should. The SEC likes to give the illusion it's got Wall Street by the balls, but Wolfe's got a rep for steering clear of their attention—mostly. I hate like hell that I'm the one to put Wolfe on the SEC's radar for the first time in years.

Most annoying of all, I don't even know what the hell this is all about.

I had an opportunity to know—to go into this meeting armed with the details of the case and maybe even a strategy for how to fight it. All I had to do was play Lara McKenzie exactly right when I cornered her on the sidewalk yesterday.

I'd fucked up.

Not only had I not coaxed the details of the case from her, I'd forgotten to try. Those big eyes behind her glasses drove me fucking crazy. Add in the smart mouth, the tight skirt . . .

Someone clears his throat, and I nod at Joe as I sit across the table from the two Sams.

They're a scary duo.

For starters, they're married.

Just days after inheriting the CEO title from his dad, Samuel Wolfe Jr. married Samantha Barry, a partner at a competing firm, thus creating one of the world's richest power couples.

There's a long moment of silence, then Sam—female Sam—stands. "Screw this. Who wants a whiskey?"

Whiskey, gin, whatever. She could have offered me a damn white wine spritzer and I'd have said yes.

Joe and Samantha's husband nod affirmatively for the drink as well. Apparently, I'm not the only one stressed out.

Four generous pours of bourbon later, they get right to it.

"We think they're after J-Conn," Samantha announces.

It takes me a second to register what they're talking about, and it's with equal parts irritation and surprise when I do.

J-Conn is a tech company that went tits up and screwed plenty of people out of plenty of money. But not me. Or my clients. I'd sold my J-Conn stock before it all went to hell and hadn't gotten kicked in the balls like everyone else.

As you might imagine, there'd been a lot of "How the hell did you know?" thrown around, but nobody outright accused me of getting a tip.

Until now.

Joe shares my incredulity. "J-Conn? That was nearly a year ago. Why now?"

My mind is reeling.

I get why people had to ask about J-Conn back when it all went down—even Matt and Kennedy had gotten screwed by that one, and they're the best in the business.

In that particular case, I was just . . . better.

After months of waiting with everyone else for J-Conn to make the rumored "groundbreaking" technology announcement, I'd called bullshit. I'd sold when everyone else was buying high.

Risky as hell, but it had been a risk that paid off.

Call it intuition, call it brains—hell, I'll even take dumb luck. But what I won't accept is cheating.

"We can only assume the SEC's received new information," Sam says, seeming to choose his words carefully without looking at me directly. "We don't know for sure that it's J-Conn, but there've been whispers about Ian and that deal for months."

"Nothing but playground gossip," I snap. "There's no new information, because there's no information to be had. I didn't—"

Samantha quickly holds up her hand. "Stop right there." She blows out a breath. "Ian, you're one of our best, but if we were to have to testify . . ."

I close my eyes. *Testify.* This can't be happening.

"I get it," I say quietly. "Plausible deniability."

We're not there yet, but . . . we could be, and that's what worries me.

The only silver lining in all this is that the SEC is still at the informal investigation stage. If they weren't, Lara McKenzie would have come at me with a subpoena yesterday instead of a courtesy call. Informal is good, in that it means they don't yet have the evidence they need to launch a full-blown case against me.

But it's also bad, in that they don't *have* to tell me the details of my "crime."

I run my hand through my hair. "J-Conn?" I ask again. "Seriously?"

Samantha sighs and shrugs, managing to pack a wallop of disdain into the small gestures. If I had to describe Samantha Wolfe in a word, it'd be hard-ass. She's fiftysomething, attractive in a polished, perfect-lipstick kind of way.

Her husband's the opposite, at least in looks. He's got a small stature, balding head, and, no matter how straight the tie, how expensive the suit, he always manages to have a slightly rumpled quality about him.

Sam clears his throat. "We'll know for certain soon enough. You know how these things go. We'll be able to tell what she's after by the people she talks to and the questions she asks."

"We've guaranteed Ms. McKenzie our full cooperation. I'm sure you'll share our policy of cooperation," Samantha continues with a pointed look at me.

The instructions are clear: *Play nice.*

I run my hands over my face. This fucking blows. Objectively, I know the SEC has a job to do. I understand their function; I can even respect it. But this feels like a goddamn witch hunt. That they can come in here, ask us to cooperate, all without telling us why or when or what . . .

I don't want to play nice.

I want to fucking fight it.

Joe seems to read my thoughts. "We need to let this die before it's a formal investigation, Ian. The best way to do that is to—"

"Roll over? Hand them whatever they want based on their unfounded accusations?" I don't bother to disguise my anger.

They don't bother to calm me down.

There's a pregnant pause before anyone speaks again.

"Ian, you've been with us a long time," Sam says, taking a sip of whiskey. "We like you. Consider you a friend."

"Likewise," I grunt with a nod.

"We've got the best attorneys in the business," Samantha says. "They're here to protect the company and everyone in it, and that includes you."

I meet her gaze. "But?"

"*But*," she says with the faintest smile, "if it comes down to you or the company . . ." She looks at her husband.

"You've got to get independent counsel, Ian. For your own sake," Sam says.

It's sound advice. No matter how good Wolfe's lawyers are, if the SEC decides to pin something on me, the company would—and should—cut ties with me, thus severing access to their lawyers.

I need my own.

I've known this. I've known it since the second Lara McKenzie said the words "SEC" and "investigation." But hearing it from my bosses makes it all the more real. And serious.

Joe thumps my shoulder in solidarity, but it's an empty gesture. I'm not sure what grates more, the fact that none of them is confident I'm innocent or the fact that I'm getting the distinct sense they'll hang me out to dry if I'm not.

Sam clears his throat, and I realize that the meeting's over. They've done all they can do, said all they can say. They've also covered their own asses while giving me plenty of fair warning, which I guess I can appreciate.

I set my glass aside and stand. "Thanks for the time. And the whiskey."

"We'd say the same thing to anyone in this situation," Samantha says, standing and leaning across the table to shake my hand.

I nod, shake her hand, as well as Sam's.

"I'll stop by your office later," Joe says, clearly intending to stay behind to talk with the Sams.

"Sure."

"Ian." I turn back again to Sam, female version. "We've given Ms. McKenzie full access to the west conference room on your floor for the course of her investigation. It'll work in your favor to make her like you."

I don't bother to respond to that. It's not until I get back to my office, door closed, that the anger sets in.

Not at either of the Sams. And not at Joe.

No, my anger has a very specific focus. A blonde, bespectacled, SEC kind of focus, and the lying asshole who set her after me in the first place.

I squeeze my eyes shut and try to ward off the panic. I can't fight this when I don't know who I'm fighting or why. I haven't worked this hard, haven't gotten this far, only to have it crumble around me because some blonde ballbuster has a liar whispering in her ear.

My phone buzzes in my pocket, and I have every intention of ignoring whomever it is, but then I see the name, and it's the one person I've never been able to ignore.

I take a deep breath to calm my storming emotions, then answer. "Dave. Hey."

"Hiya, boy."

I smile. Nearly two decades have passed since Dave Coving took me in when I was fourteen, but I've only ever been "boy" to him.

"What's up?" I ask, lowering to my chair and spinning to look at the rainy morning. Of course it's raining. All we need is an ominous clap of thunder, and I'd be inside one of those damn Netflix dramas.

"TV broke."

I rub my forehead. "Did something hit it?"

He coughs, the sound devolving into a nasty smoker's hack that has me wincing. "A bottle," he says when the cough settles.

I roll my eyes upward. *Shocking.* "Phillies lost, huh?"

"They're in a slump," he grumbles. "Lost my temper at a bad call."

I stifle the sigh. Let's just say this isn't the first time Dave's lost a battle against his temper, and a bottle of beer and the TV paid the price.

And I pay for the TV. All of them.

It's the least I can do. The man put a roof over my head for four years, a place to come home to during Christmas break from college, and he never lost his temper with me, which is more than I can say about the six foster homes that came before him.

"I'll get you a new one," I say, already reaching for a pen to make a note of it.

"Thanks," he says gruffly. "I don't need big and fancy. A little cheap one's fine."

"Sure." We both know he'll have the biggest flat-screen that can fit into his mobile home delivered tomorrow.

"So, what's new with you?" he asks.

I hesitate. To Dave's credit, he usually only calls when he needs something, but he doesn't hang up the second he gets it. He stays on the phone long enough to check in. And what the hell, I let myself pretend he actually cares.

Usually I give him the highlight reel, sticking to my latest job coup or describing my box seats at Citi Field. Today, though, I hear myself giving him the real deal.

"The SEC's on my ass."

"The Ess-EE-What?"

"SEC. It's an acronym for . . . let's just say they're Wall Street's watchdog."

"What'dya do?"

"Wish I knew," I say, rubbing a hand over my neck. "Supposedly I got an inside tip on a tech company a while back, but it's news to me."

Dave grunts. "So, nothing to worry about."

"There is if whoever's making shit up about this 'inside tip' is a better liar than I am truth teller."

"Bullshit," Dave says on another round of hacking. "Since when do you just grab your ankles when shit gets rough?"

I wince. "That's nice, Dave. Very introspective."

"Intro-what?"

"Never mind." I pinch the bridge of my nose.

"Look," Dave says with a hefty sigh. "I ain't your family. I got no right to lecture you, but you're the most stubborn son of a bitch I know. You always got everything you ever wanted—haven't you?"

Almost. Almost everything.

I don't say it, though. I'm not sure there'll ever be a good time to tell Dave how much I used to long for him to adopt me.

I smile a little at the memory. I was a stupid kid, thinking if I just talked a good game and never gave up, I'd be worth the adoption hassle.

Nope.

It's cool, though—we've got a good thing going on.

"Hello?" Dave asks grumpily.

"Yeah, still here."

"So you gonna fight this SPT or what?"

I smile. "SEC. And yeah, I suspect she'd like nothing more than a good fight."

"*She?*" Dave laughs, a cackling, dry sound. "Hell, boy, why didn't you say so? There's not a woman alive you couldn't get to do exactly what you wanted and have her thinkin' it was her idea. Doubt this one's any different."

"She is," I mutter, spinning idly in my chair. "She fell for exactly none of my bullshit yesterday."

"Yesterday. You gave up after one day? Ain't like you. You've always been stubborn as a mule, digging your teeth in, lighting a fire under every bush . . ."

I go still at his words, letting them sink in. Mixed metaphors aside, Dave's got a point.

Persistence is my ace in the hole—the thing that's gotten me where I am today.

Have I gotten so lazy, so complacent, that I'm giving up after a single afternoon of getting shot down?

Fifteen years in the foster system couldn't keep me down. Nor could the Yale legacies who'd tried to make it clear I didn't belong.

I get what I want by fighting for it. And what I want right now?

Lara McKenzie on her knees, begging me to forgive her for the false accusation.

Well, okay, the *on her knees* part is a different fantasy entirely. One I'm not completely ready to give up on.

"Dave, you're a damn genius."

"Yeah, yeah. So when'll the TV be here?"

I shake my head with a grin, telling him I'll get right on it. I hang up, then grab my desk phone to call my assistant.

Kate picks up on the first ring. "How'd the meeting with the Sams go?"

"'Bout like you'd expect."

"Did they—"

"I'll fill you in on everything later," I promise, interrupting. "But first, any chance I can talk you into getting Dave another TV by tomorrow?"

"Oh, jeez," she says, and I hear the efficient *clack* of her keyboard. "What happened this time? His favorite hockey player get traded again?"

"It was a baseball emergency."

"Mmm. Okay, I'm on it. What else can I do? I feel useless, and you *know* that's not my jam."

I smile. I do know. Kate Henley's been my assistant for five years, and I've learned that her tiny, tidy package hides an administrative powerhouse.

"No, nothing yet . . ." I break off. "Actually, yes. If you were trying to sell someone on the magic of overpriced Starbucks beverages—"

"Mocha Frappuccino, extra whip, extra chocolate shavings," she says without hesitation. "You can't go wrong. Your Tuesday barista's Karen, right?"

"Yeah, but I'll take care of it." This is one challenge I need to undertake on my own.

"But—"

"If you're fishing for shit to do, Matt started trying to manage his own calendar again. He's got himself triple booked for three o'clock but is too scared to tell you."

"Are you freaking *kidding* me?" Kate makes a hissing noise. "Okay. I'm on it."

Kate hangs up on me, as I knew she would, and I text Tuesday barista Karen, ordering two mocha Frappuccinos.

Lara McKenzie thinks she saw Don Juan yesterday?

She hasn't seen nothin' yet.

4

LARA

Week 1: Tuesday Afternoon

I'm pulling my stapler out of my box of office crap when there's a knock at the conference room door.

I glance up, lifting my eyebrows in surprise when I see the last person I'd expect leaning against the doorway.

Ian Bradley's dressed impeccably in a light-gray suit, black tie, and holding two frothy concoctions.

I click my stapler twice and study him, trying to figure out his game. His expression's friendly, but his blue eyes are calculating.

"Mr. Bradley."

"Ms. McKenzie." He doesn't move.

"Would you like to come in?"

He grins. "Would you like to put that stapler down?"

The moment I do, he steps forward and, setting one of the drinks on the table, slides it toward me with a flick of the wrist. If anyone else did this, the drink would tip and fall, but Ian simply makes the cup slide perfectly across the table and into my waiting hand.

I lift the Starbucks cup and study it. "Really. Bribery?"

"Barista made two by accident. I could just give it to Kate . . ."

"Ah yes, your assistant," I say, leaping on the opening. I'd met Kate Henley yesterday, and my initial impression of the tiny brunette was that she has one of the best poker faces I've ever seen.

Verdict after trying to coax her into conversation today?

The best poker face I've ever seen.

"She said she's worked for you for five years," I say.

"Mm." He walks toward the window, looks down. "They gave you the shitty conference room. The other ones have a better view."

"I'm not here for the view."

"No, you're here because of J-Conn," he says, turning back around.

It's a predictable play, fishing for information. Granted, he's right. I'm here for J-Conn, and I'm not all that surprised Wolfe's already put that at the top of their guesses.

But this isn't my first rodeo.

I say nothing, instead watching him carefully for any signs of nervousness, finding none.

"Why now?" he asks quietly. "Why are you guys after me for a company that crashed ten months ago?"

"Didn't say that we were." He'll find out he's right the second I start asking questions, but that's not today. And I have no intention of playing this game on his terms.

Not that this is a game.

But the way he's watching me, and the Starbucks drinks . . . I can tell *he* thinks it's one.

"Okay, well let's say *hypothetically* you're here because of J-Conn," Ian says smoothly. "What would have to happen to put me on your radar?"

I set the cup aside without taking a drink. "*Hypothetically*, we'd have a source," I say, telling him nothing he doesn't already know. "Who's alleged you had insider knowledge of the company's future."

"Who's the source?"

I snort. "Really. You bring me an overpriced coffee and think I'll just tell all?"

27

"Or you could swoon," he says with a wink.

This time I roll my eyes. "I'd heard you were a womanizer, but I confess, it's really hard to picture."

"Yeah?" He crosses his arms and sits on the edge of the conference room table. "What have you heard? Maybe that I'm good with my hands? That when I'm with a woman, I always make sure she gets her—"

I hold up a hand. "Stop."

Good Lord, is it hot in here? I resist the urge to undo a button on my shirt.

He smirks, then glances down at my ignored beverage. "Try the drink, Ms. McKenzie."

"No thanks," I say briskly, trying to remind myself that I'm Lara McKenzie with the SEC, not Lara McKenzie, Ian Bradley groupie.

He gives an exasperated sigh as though I'm an uncooperative child and stands and walks toward me. He stops a couple of feet away and, without breaking eye contact, picks up the drink I've set aside and holds it out. "Try it."

"This caveman approach might work on other women, but—"

"Oh, I get it," he interrupts, starting to set aside the drink. "You're scared. You like your lines straight, your colors black and white, your coffee boring. God forbid you try something new, live a little—"

Before I can stop myself, I reach out and snatch the drink. My fingers brush his, and the contact is so unexpectedly electric I nearly drop the damn thing.

He shifts slightly closer. Not to crowd, or to intimidate, or to kiss, but for a whisper-quiet seduction that's about a million times more effective than his pickup lines so far.

For a hideous moment, I want to lean in to him, to brush my lips along my jaw, to . . .

Well, hell, I realize with a jolt. The man really may be as good as his reputation after all.

I can't let him know it. I *won't*.

I stay put, giving a little lean of my own, letting my eyes lock on his as I part my lips and put the green straw in my mouth. I take a sip of the cold, wonderfully sweet beverage, and I let out an *mmm* noise unlike anything I've ever made in my life.

His eyes flare with surprise, then desire, and for a long moment I have no idea who's seducing whom, who's one-upping the other . . .

Ian gives a slow smile that crinkles his eyes. "Well played, Ms. McKenzie."

"Back at you, Mr. Bradley." I take a victory sip—it really is delicious. "You want to play sexy cat and mouse, I can play right back, and I'll win."

I turn away to resume unpacking my box when I feel his fingers wrap around my wrist, gripping hard enough to get my attention but not enough to feel threatening. "You won't win, Ms. McKenzie. I've worked too damn hard to be found guilty of something I didn't do."

He's good and pissed, and I take advantage, going for a surprise attack. "I know you weren't in bed with Arnold Maverick," I say. "But it doesn't mean you weren't in contact with him."

Ian blinks. "Who the fuck is Arnold Maverick?"

Damn it, he's good. He's either a really good liar or . . . honest.

"Arnold Maverick was the CIO of J-Conn," I say.

He thinks for a moment, then drops my wrist as recognition settles. "He was in the news. The tech guru who committed suicide a couple of months ago. *That's* who you think tipped me off about J-Conn?"

I take another sip of my drink and let my silence do the talking. *I'll neither confirm nor deny . . .*

To my surprise, instead of getting pissed and defensive, he smiles, back to charming Ian once again. "Let me see if I've got this straight . . . an anonymous source, who you won't identify, is claiming that I got an inside tip from a J-Conn executive who's now dead and can't confirm one way or the other. Makes for a convenient accusation, doesn't it?"

"We're just following protocol, Mr. Bradley."

"Fantastic," he mutters, rummaging through my office stuff. "You know, I'm not the only one with lines. Mine may be of the pickup variety, but they're a hell of a lot better than your evasive SEC bullshit."

"That wasn't a line—"

"Sure it was," he says, grabbing a pen and a pad of Post-its. He scribbles something, drops the pen back in the cup, and hands me the sticky pad.

I look down as he stands. "What is—"

"My e-mail account information—work and personal. Eat your heart out. I have nothing to hide."

I'm still staring at the Post-it in surprise as he saunters away, turning back after he opens the conference room door.

"Oh, and Ms. McKenzie . . ."

I look up.

"My personal account has a few naughty pictures in there. Enjoy those." He winks.

Damn it. I hate knowing that I probably will.

5

Ian

Week 1: Thursday Morning

"Dude." Matt slows to an easy jog beside me. "When you asked if I wanted to go for a run, you could have mentioned you were trying to set an Olympic record."

"You've done four Ironmans," I point out, catching my breath.

"Exactly. Because I like the swimming and bike shit. If I liked the running part, I'd do a marathon like Prefontaine up there."

I slow my cool-down jog all the way to a walk. "Hey, Kennedy," I call out. "Slow your roll."

My other best friend doesn't glance back, but I know he hears me because he slows his damn sprint pace to a walk, then stops and waits for Matt and me to catch up.

Kennedy's not even breathing slightly hard, damn the man. We're all in good shape, but of the three of us, Kennedy's the runner. Matt's all about the competition, and me . . . well, to be honest, I just like a good old-fashioned gym session, preferably with a hot female trainer.

Today, though, I'd talked the guys into a run with me. I see them enough around the office, but today I need them as friends not coworkers.

And there are no better friends than these two.

Matt Cannon, Kennedy Dawson, and I all came up with one another at Wolfe. We started the same year and worked the bullpen together, even as we were competitors. Investment brokerage is an up-or-out business—you either make it to the next level, burn out, or are pushed out.

All three of us had made it. We're competitors still, fighting for the same clients, the same accounts, but friends in spite of it. Hell, maybe friends because of it. All of us are fighters in our own way.

Matt's the brains. Younger than both Kennedy and me, he's twenty-eight now, but everyone from the trading room floor up to the CEO penthouse still thinks of him as a boy wonder. The little shit skipped God-knows-how-many grades to graduate from Cornell at the age of nineteen, then took Wall Street by storm by twenty-two.

Lucky for Matt, the women of New York City know that he's all grown up now. Blond, blue eyed, charming, and clever as shit, the guy's almost as big of a manwhore as me.

And if Matt got here by brains and I did by sheer force of will and hard work, Kennedy Dawson's a big dick on Wall Street because it's just his damn destiny.

As dark haired as Matt is blond, Kennedy and his family have been in finance for *for-fucking-ever*, his trust fund big enough to ensure he could quit tomorrow and still have more money than Matt and I will ever see in our lifetimes, combined.

It's more than the bank account, though. Kennedy's old money, and it shows. His apartment's got a goddamn library, his mother wears pearls, he only drinks single-malt scotch, he belongs to two different country clubs, and he looks like one of the Kennedys (whom he was named after).

He's also a bit of a nerd. He gets way too into museums, and his idea of a wild Friday night is reading a philosophy tome *and* a World War II history book. When we do manage to drag him out on the town with us, I'm not sure he even notices the way women relentlessly chase him, swooning over the dimples that he thinks are ridiculous.

Matt drops into a stretch. "For real, what was with the double-time sprinting?" he asks me.

"If the SEC were on your ass, you'd be running, too," Kennedy says.

"I *was* running."

"Could have fooled me," Kennedy says, leaning against the railing along the Hudson, looking every bit as polished after a five-mile run as he does in the office.

Matt shoots Kennedy the bird, then turns his attention back to me. "So what's our plan? How do we clear your name?"

See that? Loyalty. Told you these guys were solid. Not once since this went down have they thought or implied I was guilty of anything other than shitty luck.

I brace on the railing and, dipping my chin to my chest, take a deep breath. "I don't know, man."

"Who's your lawyer?" Kennedy asks.

"Dunno yet."

"Damn it, Ian. You need a lawyer."

I look up in irritation. "Yeah, thanks for the brilliant words of wisdom, Dad. I said I didn't know yet, not that I wasn't going to get one."

"You found out about the investigation on Monday. Today's Thursday. What the hell have you been doing if not lawyering up?"

"Flirting with the SEC," Matt chimes in.

Kennedy snarls, "What?"

Matt gives me a shit-eating grin as I glare at him. "Kate filled me in. Dude, you bought her a Frappuccino? *That* was your grand plan?"

Kennedy braces both hands on his thick head of hair and turns in an agitated circle.

"We got off on the wrong foot. I was trying to make amends," I say, defending myself as we start walking back toward our respective apartments.

"Bullshit," Matt says. "You were trying to use the infamous Ian charm on her in hopes she'd go easy on your case."

Kennedy's arms drop. "Tell me he's joking. Tell me there's another explanation for why you haven't made time to find a lawyer that doesn't involve bringing the SEC whipped-cream concoctions."

"In Ian's defense, whipped cream has led me to many an interesting encounter with women," Matt says, lifting his hands above his head in a stretch.

Damn it. Now a vision of Lara McKenzie wearing only whipped cream and her librarian glasses has me biting back a groan.

"Grandpa here's right, though, about you needing a lawyer ASAP," Matt says, his face turning serious. "Kate's looked up every detail there is to know about this woman. She's good. Doesn't lose cases, doesn't miss a beat, doesn't screw up on a technicality. Doesn't back down. Ever."

"Sounds like someone we know," Kennedy says with a pointed look in my direction.

"Right, because you two are so easygoing," I snap, losing patience with the lecture. "Look, I'm working on it."

"Work harder. McKenzie will send you to jail if she can, man."

I rub a hand over my face as Matt punches Kennedy. "That's not what he needed to hear."

"He needs to take it seriously," Kennedy snaps back.

Enough already. "I *am* taking it seriously. I know I'm in deep shit. You think I've just had my thumb up my butt the past two days? I've got a dozen phone calls out—"

"Don't bother," Kennedy says. "You need Vanessa Lewis."

"Oh, definitely," I agree. "Just as soon as I capture a unicorn."

"You won't know until you try—"

"I *did* try. You think I didn't think of her first?" I say. Vanessa Lewis is the best white-collar defense attorney in the city, and everyone knows it. "Her office said she'd put me on the waitlist. You guys are good with numbers . . . Tell me, if I'm eighty-sixth on the list, how good are my chances?"

"A hell of a lot better if you got some help," Kennedy says.

"Good plan, Dawson. I'll just toss a few coins in a wishing well. Better yet, does anyone know a genie?"

"I was thinking more along the lines of calling the best fixer in the city," Kennedy says.

Matt groans. "No. Anyone but—"

"I didn't say *you* had to talk to her," Kennedy points out.

The three of us have been walking as we talk, so we're now outside my apartment building. I rock back on my heels a bit, contemplating Kennedy's suggestion. "It's not a horrible idea."

One I should have thought of first, if I hadn't been so distracted . . .

"It's a damn good idea," Kennedy says. "Call her. And for the love of God, do not talk to the SEC again until you get an attorney." Kennedy's already continuing at a slow jog toward his own apartment building a few blocks over. "Cannon, try to keep up."

Matt glares at Kennedy's back, then gives me a nod goodbye.

I lift my hand in farewell as I head into my lobby, grateful for the blast of air-conditioning. Grateful, as I am every damn day, to have a roof over my head to call my own—one I don't have to worry about getting kicked out of the next day when someone tires of me.

Yeah, I know. Foster-kid issues. You'd have 'em, too, though. Trust me.

The lobby's big and modern, the amenities state of the art. The building is fifty-eight stories. I live on the fifty-sixth. It's not the penthouse, but hey, as we've already established, I thrive on challenges.

I open the door to my living room and toss the keys on the side table. My apartment is pure bachelor pad—big TV, black leather couch, sideboard, bar cart, big bed, the whole deal.

I pour myself a glass of water, downing it in three gulps as I check my e-mail on my phone. There's one from a hookup a few months back that includes an NSFW subject line, a kiss-face emoji, and a picture of her on her bed. Naked.

I grin, remembering Lara McKenzie has access to my e-mail. That should blow her prudish little mind.

My cock twitches, and I realize my mistake—thinking of Lara and blow in the same sentence. Damn it.

What is it about her?

That I can't have her? That she doesn't want me?

I take a shower, in which I take care of business, if you know what I mean, picturing Lara McKenzie in nothing but whipped cream and glasses, then pull on boxers and an undershirt before heading into the kitchen to make coffee.

My phone buzzes. A text from Kennedy. Call her.

It annoys me, but he's right. I need to get a lawyer, and not just a good one. I need the best one. I need Vanessa Lewis.

Kennedy's also right that I need to ignore Lara McKenzie until I do so. I'd like to think I can stay out of any trap she lays for me, but I'd be an idiot to test my willpower with a woman who makes my blood hum like Lara does.

I scroll through my favorites until I find the number I'm looking for.

"Hey," I say the second she picks up. "I need you."

6

LARA

Week 1: Friday, Lunchtime

"So, do you think he did it?"

I tuck my cell phone beneath my ear so I can pull off my blazer. What started as a pleasantly warm morning has turned into a sweltering afternoon, and I'm keenly aware of my blouse plastered to my sweaty back.

"Too soon to say," I tell my dad, shrugging my arms out of the sleeves of the blazer and rolling it into a tidy bundle to stuff into my purse.

"What's the accusation?"

"Insider trading," I say, keeping my voice low, even though nobody's paying attention to me. The weekday lunch hour on Wall Street is everything you'd expect—plenty of suits and martinis and pretension. Nobody bothers to look twice at a woman in a boring blouse and four-year-old stilettos bought at Nordstrom Rack.

I don't really mind, but I'll confess that just once, I wouldn't mind one of those high-priced lunches instead of a mediocre café with cheap sandwiches.

Since today's lunch will likely involve a thrilling debate between dry turkey and boring tuna, I'm in no hurry to get off the phone with my dad. He's been working a big case, so we've been playing phone tag for a couple of weeks. It's good to hear his voice.

"Who's the tip?" my dad asks.

"Fantastic question," I mutter.

I practically hear my dad's frown. "You don't know?"

"Steve's keeping it quiet. Confidential informant and all that."

Steve Ennis is my boss. I've worked for the guy ever since I started with the SEC at twenty-three, and up until this case, I couldn't have asked for a better one. With the Ian Bradley thing, however, Steve's been cagey, and it's driving me *crazy*. I understand the need to protect witnesses in certain cases, but keeping the witness's name from the investigator is a whole other frustrating level of classified.

My dad apparently agrees. "But you're the investigator. How're you supposed to do your job?"

I lift my heavy hair off my neck, but there's no breeze today, so it does me no good. "Trust me, this is nothing I haven't already told Steve. But those were the informant's terms. We have to protect his privacy."

"So you know it's a him."

I smile, because it's so Dad—he's FBI through and through. "Yes. Apparently, it's a him."

"Well, that's a start. Surely with a little digging—"

"Dad," I interrupt gently. "I don't get paid to find the informant. I get paid to find out if he's right."

"Is he?"

I shrug, even though my dad can't see me. "I told you, it's too soon to tell."

"What's your gut say?" I hear the crunch of whatever he's eating for lunch, and my stomach growls.

"It says it's hungry. What are you eating?"

"Healthy crap with no taste. Now quit evading. What does your gut say about the case?"

"Who cares?" I say breezily. "Gut feelings can be wrong. My job is to find facts. Evidence."

"Don't discount intuition, Lara. If your mom and I've learned anything in the bureau—"

"Yeah, well, I'm not *in* the bureau, Dad."

I hear him blow out a breath. "Not this again . . ."

I shouldn't let my irritation show, but the more work experience I get under my belt, the harder it is to accept the wall my parents put up every time I mention my dream of joining the FBI.

They've always told me I can do whatever I set my mind to—that I can do anything any man can do, all that good, empowering stuff. Right up until the moment I told them I wanted to follow in their footsteps.

Instead of being encouraging, they've been . . . reluctant.

"I'm not asking you to get me into Quantico," I say quietly. "I want to get there myself, on my own merits. But you and Mom both change the subject every time I mention it."

"Lara, if you have kids someday, you'll get it. Your mother and I are just having a hell of a hard time thinking about our baby girl going through combat training and target practice."

"Skills I'll likely never need in the white-collar division," I point out. "The job will be pretty much just like the one I have now—"

"Then why not keep the one you have?"

I tilt my head back in frustration and gaze for a moment at the sky. It's an old argument and an exhausting one.

"The SEC's fine; it's been great training, but I want to be FBI, Dad. You know this has always been the plan."

"I know," he says grumpily, resuming his crunching.

"Is it such a bad thing?" I tease. "Having your only child want to follow in her parents' footsteps?"

"It is when our footsteps are dangerous."

"Exactly," I say, pouncing on the point. "You and Mom walk into danger every day, and I worry, but I'm proud of you. I want you to be proud of me, too."

There's a long moment of thoughtful silence.

"We're proud of you."

I stifle a sigh. I understand their protectiveness, but if I'm being totally honest, a little part of me wonders if they think I can't do it—that I won't be good enough. I'm not as whip-smart as my dad, not as hard-ass as my mom, and maybe . . . ah hell, I'm that girl. The one still trying to please her parents at age twenty-eight.

My thoughts are distracted as I see a familiar form crossing the street.

Ian's been avoiding me since our Frappuccino moment on Tuesday, and I'm sick of it. I can do only so much with e-mails and reports and meeting minutes. I need to talk to the guy. Read him.

And today, for the first time in days, he's without his guard-dog assistant.

Now's my chance.

"Dad, I gotta run. Talk soon, okay?"

"Keep me updated on the case."

"Will do."

I hang up the phone and tuck it in my purse, quickening my pace so I don't lose sight of Ian. A little stalker-ish, I know, but I am an investigator. Sometimes we get downright gumshoe for the sake of the job.

Ian crosses yet another street, heading toward the Hudson waterfront, which is . . . odd. The place is a hotbed for tourists and parents pushing strollers, not Wall Street elite. I'd have expected him to duck into one of the FiDi hot spots for martinis and caviar.

I don't have to follow him long. He walks into a cheesy-looking restaurant called Vincedi's that looks like its next New York health inspection rating will be questionable at best.

Definitely the type of place you'd meet with someone you didn't want to be seen with.

I give it a couple of minutes, then enter the restaurant.

"Just one?" the chipper hostess asks, holding up a vinyl menu.

I nod and follow her to the table, keeping an eye out for Ian and hoping I spot him before he spots me.

The restaurant's bigger than I realized, so it's not until I've been seated, alternating between scanning the room and feigning interest in their "gourmet burgers," that I spot him.

My stomach drops out.

As expected, he's meeting someone. But from the looks of it, his interest in her has nothing to do with J-Conn.

Ian's table is a corner booth, and he's whispering into the ear of the most beautiful woman I've ever seen. The red dress is fitted to her perfect figure and is low-cut enough to show off impressive boobs without being *yikes*. Her hair's long and black, her makeup flawless. She's hardly the type of woman to be hidden away in a crappy, off-the-beaten-path restaurant, which makes me wonder if she's married.

Why else would they be meeting so far away from the other beautiful people of Wall Street?

Then it hits me: I'm spying on Ian Bradley having a tryst.

I close my eyes in dismayed humiliation. *Someone kill me now.*

When I open my eyes, my stomach doesn't just drop, it turns into a freaking roller coaster.

He's looking right at me, eyebrows lifted in challenge.

For one of the first times in my professional career, I feel completely unsure of what to do. There's no way I can play it off as a coincidence—judging from the food I've seen go by my table, this place sucks. And it's not even cheap, so I truly have no reason to be here other than spying on him, which his smirk tells me he knows.

Is it possible to spontaneously combust from embarrassment?

I sneak a glance at the door, wondering if I can somehow escape with my dignity intact. When I look back again, Ian's smile widens, and I realize that's exactly what he's hoping for: me to make a humiliated retreat.

Fat chance.

Without breaking eye contact, I shove aside my embarrassment, greet the waiter who comes over to my table, and order a Diet Coke and a turkey burger. Then I pull out a notepad and pencil from my purse and sit back in my seat, as though prepared to write down Ian's every move.

I won't learn a damn thing from across the room, but I can tell by the way his smile dims and jaw tenses that my unexpected fortitude pisses him off.

For the moment, that's good enough for me.

7

IAN

Week 1: Friday, Lunchtime

"So that's her," Sabrina Cross says casually, taking a sip of her Chardonnay and unabashedly craning her neck to see Lara McKenzie watching us from across the restaurant.

"That's her," I say, finishing the rest of my Negroni. Apparently my idea of meeting my oldest friend at a diner-type place with mediocre food so we wouldn't see anyone we knew didn't account for the possibility of being stalked by the SEC. Go figure.

"She's pretty."

"Shut up."

Sabrina laughs. "So you've already noticed she's pretty."

And this is the pain-in-the-ass part of remaining friends with someone who's known you since you were eight.

Sabrina digs through the breadbasket on our table. "She's very bold. She's still watching us."

"Yes, I know." I can *feel* it. Somehow Lara McKenzie's gaze has more effect on my body than any other woman's physical touch. I've been in a constant state of want since our first meeting, with no relief in sight—I can't have her, and I don't want any of the women I can have.

I don't know what the hell the woman is doing to me, but I don't like it.

"She looks annoyed," Sabrina says, taking a bite of bread.

"She probably is. I've been avoiding her." Not that it's been easy. Staying away from her's been damn hard, but Matt and Kennedy are right—I'd be an idiot to tangle with the SEC before getting a lawyer on my side.

"I thought you said you were supposed to cooperate," Sabrina says.

"*You* go talk to her," I say, pointing a finger in Lara's direction. "You'll learn real quick she's not the *cooperative* type."

"Meaning she didn't fall all over herself when you flashed your smile," Sabrina says knowingly.

"Exactly," I mutter, both relieved and annoyed that she's getting a read on the situation so quickly.

In addition to Sabrina Cross knowing me like the back of her hand, courtesy of our long history, she also just knows *people*. Sabrina's a fixer. She's the person you call when you need help with . . . well, anything. Need a fake girlfriend? Call Sabrina. Someone to blackmail your wife so your wife will stop blackmailing you? Sabrina. Someone to sweet-talk a judge, put a rush on your passport, or get your delinquent kid into that prestigious school? Sabrina knows someone who knows someone who can help. For a price.

In my case, the price is friendship. Besides Dave, she's the one person who's as much a part of my new life as she was my old life. Sabrina's the only person who's ever really known both sides of me—the foster kid from Philly and the Wall Street hotshot.

Sabrina's been there through it all.

And for the love of God, please don't turn this into some grand romantic story. Aside from an awkward make-out session in freshman year of high school, which we both declared almost unbearably gross, it's never been like that between us.

Sabrina's one of the most gorgeous women I've ever seen, and yet there's not a lick of sexual chemistry between us. I love her like a sister. Hell, she even *looks* like my sister. We've got the same dark hair, blue eyes, olive skin, and shitty, shitty pasts.

Although, while my upbringing was somewhere between dismal and frustrating, hers was downright unbearable. Drug-addict mom, barely there dad, shithead brother. Made my foster parents and their blatant indifference seem kind.

"So let's hear it," Sabrina says, pushing her soggy Caesar salad around her plate. "You only drag me to this tourist trap with crappy food when you need to ask me for something and you don't want Wall Street to know about it."

I nod in thanks as the waiter brings another drink. He doesn't ask if my barely touched burger is okay, probably because he knows how overcooked it is, how stale the bun is, and doesn't want to deal with it. I don't mind. It's a liquid-lunch kind of day anyway.

"I need Vanessa Lewis."

Sabrina lets out a long breath. "Damn. You don't ask for favors often, but when you do, they're whoppers. If you think *I'm* exclusive with the clientele I take on, Vanessa's even more exclusive."

"Why do you think I called you? I've called her office; she won't give me the time of day, and I need her to. She's the best damn defense attorney in the city. If she got Ray Iris off charges of that Ponzi scheme, she can get me out of bogus insider-trading accusations."

Sabrina swirls her wine. "She only takes on clients she believes to be innocent. She likes to win, but only when she believes it's truly justice."

"Which is what this would be," says a newcomer.

Sabrina and I both glance up to see Matt Cannon plop down on her other side.

"How the hell did you find us?" I ask.

"Please," he says, reaching over, picking up Sabrina's fork, and taking a bite of her salad. "You always come here when you're in a mood. God only knows why." He points the fork at the salad. "That is disgusting." He washes it down with a sip of her wine.

"By all means," she purrs in a dangerous voice that generally means *die*. "What's mine is yours."

"Really?" he asks, turning toward her, his gaze dropping to her cleavage.

"Go ahead. Try it," she says. "I've been in a castration sort of mood lately."

I wince. "Can you two kids pretend to get along, just until the end of this meal?"

Matt jerks his chin toward my plate. "What's that?"

Wordlessly, I hand him the plate.

"Are we aware of the SEC agent at ten o'clock?" Matt asks, taking a bite of the burger without looking toward Lara's table.

"Yes. We're ignoring her," Sabrina says.

I nod in agreement, though, truth be told, it's taking every ounce of willpower not to glance her way. I refuse to give her the satisfaction, even if I'm starved for a look. Interaction. Anything.

It's been three days since we went toe to toe in the conference room with only a Starbucks Frappuccino between us. A day and a half since the guys told me to steer clear of her.

And I've been aware of every damn minute.

Partially because it goes against my nature to sit on my hands and bide my time, but also because the sheer challenge of her makes me feel alive.

"Ian wants Vanessa Lewis," Sabrina says, filling Matt in on our conversation.

Matt nods. "As he should. But I told him you couldn't get her."

I roll my eyes. He told me no such thing, but I know what he's up to. A bull with a red cape waved in its face has more restraint than Sabrina when Matt issues a challenge. They're two of my best friends, but their relationship with each other is contentious on a good day.

"It's *Vanessa Lewis*," Sabrina says in exasperation. "Her schedule's booked up for years—"

"Isn't that why everyone pays you the big bucks?" Matt asks, pulling her napkin off her lap and using it to wipe ketchup from his bottom lip. "Because you're supposed to be the best at getting people what they want? Get Vanessa for Ian."

"I *am* the best," she snaps. "But I don't just 'get people' because you command it."

Matt shrugs. "Sounds like you *can't* get her."

"I—"

"Guys." I hold up my hands. "This mutual hatred is exhausting."

"I'll make some phone calls," Sabrina mutters, pulling out the red leather book she carries with her everywhere and making a note. "But you need a backup list, Ian. Despite what Boy Wonder here thinks, I'm not a magician."

Matt nods. "Kennedy and I can help with a list."

I'm barely listening. I'd finally given in to the urge to look at Lara's table again, but she's gone.

I try to tell myself that what I feel is relief.

I hate like hell that it's not.

8

LARA

Week 2: Monday Morning

"It's like I told you," Kate Henley says in a smooth *go to hell* tone. "Mr. Bradley's unavailable at the moment."

"At the moment?" I ask in exasperation. "He's been unavailable for nearly a week."

"He's extremely busy."

"So am I," I snap. "I was assured by Mr. and Mrs. Wolfe that I'd have this company's full cooperation."

"And you have our full cooperation. What can I do for you?"

The words are pure honey and completely belie her *bite me* expression that tells me I'm being fed a line. I inhale for patience. "You can get me a spot on Mr. Bradley's calendar."

"Of course." She taps something on her keyboard. "How does next Thursday at four sound?"

"It sounds like a week and a half away."

She folds her hands on her desk and lifts her eyebrows in a clear *take it or leave it, but it's all I'm offering* gesture.

If I weren't so frustrated by the woman, I'd admire her. Actually, scratch that. I *do* admire her. Kate's not only Ian's assistant, she also works for Matt Cannon and Kennedy Dawson, and she manages the three bullheaded, egomaniac investment brokers with more aplomb than I've seen any other assistant manage *one*, all while looking like a grown-up schoolgirl.

Kate wears her dark-brown hair pulled back with a simple headband. Her eyes are wide and brown and makeup free. Her blouses are primly buttoned to the top, her skirts always just below the knee. Last week, she was wearing honest-to-god Mary Janes.

Her appearance is all soft sweetness, a direct contrast to her personality, which can best be described as hard-ass.

There's zero chance she'll meet me halfway on this.

"Next Thursday would be great," I say with a forced smile.

She nods and adds it to his calendar. "In the meantime, I'd be happy to answer any questions you have."

"Yes, because you were *so* helpful when we met last week," I mutter.

I'd sat with Kate for nearly an hour on Friday afternoon, and impressively, she'd managed to answer every single question with as few words as humanly possible.

You've worked for Mr. Bradley for five years? Yes.

Would you say he's a fair employer? Yes.

Have you ever known him to correspond with any J-Conn employees? No.

Has Mr. Bradley ever asked you to lie for him? No.

"What about Mr. Cannon and Mr. Dawson?" As Ian's closest confidants, they're at the top of my interview list but thus far have been proving just as difficult to pin down as Ian himself.

I get it. They're protecting one another. So I've been patient, biding my time by combing through every electronic and paper record with a fine-tooth comb last week.

I haven't found crap—not a single thing we can use to connect Ian and J-Conn. Not that I'm surprised. The man strikes me as brash but not foolish. He's not going to put anything incriminating in writing.

He might, however, say something to his best friends over drinks.

Kate is clicking idly on her keyboard. "I can get you on Mr. Cannon's schedule next Tuesday. Mr. Dawson . . ."

I suck in another breath for patience as she takes her sweet time checking her bosses' schedules. I've played this game just about as long as I can afford to. Any more of this and I'll have to go over all their heads, which I don't particularly want to do. The last thing I need is more hostility if I want to make any progress. I can play bad cop if I have to, but my record's what it is because I use finesse, not brass knuckles, to get my way.

Kate's phone rings, and she lifts a *hold, please* finger as she picks it up. I'm about to give her a finger of my own—a different one—when over Kate's head, I see a familiar brown head moving toward his office, white Starbucks cup in hand.

It's the opening I've been waiting for.

As Kate turns her attention to her computer screen, I dart toward the man, managing to step in front of him just before he can enter his office.

Kennedy Dawson's brown eyes are cold and bored as he looks down at me. "Yes?"

"Mr. Dawson," I say, extending a hand. "We haven't had the pleasure of meeting yet."

"Because there's nothing pleasurable about it," he responds, reluctantly shaking my hand.

Kennedy's a very attractive man. For one, he has dimples. Really, really great dimples. Not that they're present now, but I saw him laugh with Ian the other day outside the conference room. He wears glasses about half the time, like he is today, and it emphasizes the quiet, scholarly way he carries himself. His suits are classic, his ties never flashy.

My family's got a bit of a classic movie obsession going for us, so let me put it this way: if Ian's got Cary Grant's swagger, and Matt's got Paul Newman's charm, Kennedy's got the uptight brooding thing going for him, a little bit Humphrey Bogart meets Clint Eastwood. *Yum.*

In other words, I should *definitely* be feeling something when our palms make contact. Kennedy looks like every version of the one I've been dreaming about since I hit puberty. Quiet. Sensible. Safe. He's the opposite of Ian Bradley, and thus exactly what I'm looking for.

I wait for the expected feminine awareness, and . . . nothing.

Not a zip, not a spark, not even a flutter.

He drops the handshake as soon as he can without being rude, and judging from the near-sneer on his face, I don't think he felt anything, either.

"Can I help you?"

"Absolutely," I say quickly, before Kate can get off the phone and run her usual watchdog interference. "I'd like a few minutes of your time."

"To discuss Ian."

"To discuss your knowledge of Wolfe Investments' connection with J-Conn."

"Talk to my assistant to schedule an appointment."

He tries to step around me, but I sidestep with him, earning myself a glare. "I've tried, but I got the sense that you'll be booked out as far as Mr. Bradley and Mr. Cannon are."

"Well, there you go. If you'll excuse me . . ." Another step, which I match once again.

"What are you doing right now?"

"I've got a meeting." He's a good liar but not good enough. He waited just a heartbeat too long to answer, telling me it's an excuse.

I glance at my watch. "It's 8:51. I'm assuming your meeting's at nine, so I'll keep you company until then."

"Ms. McKenzie—"

"I could get a subpoena, Mr. Dawson. *Or* you could convince me I don't need one. For any of this."

He goes still, unapologetically studying me. "Five minutes."

"That's all I need."

He unlocks the door to his office and makes an exaggerated inward motion for me to precede him.

I have to hide a smile, because the office is exactly what I'd expected. While the common areas of Wolfe Investments are all sleek and modern, Kennedy's office feels like a step back in time to when men wore smoking jackets and the only corporate job for women was as a typist. His desk is a dark wood with ornate detailing. The chairs are mahogany leather with just the right amount of wear to be inviting instead of stuffy. Every nonwindowed wall is covered in bookshelves, and I've been in enough Wolfe exec offices in the past week to know they're a custom addition.

"Problem?" he asks, stepping around his desk and setting his coffee on a coaster.

"Nope. Just trying to figure out where you keep the globe and antique chessboard."

For a moment, I swear his eyes brighten in amusement, but he shuts it down, gesturing to a guest chair across from his own. "Five minutes, Ms. McKenzie."

Right.

I sit and cross my legs, wishing I had something to write with, but that's what I get for ambushing the guy. "Is Kate going to be pissed?" I ask, partially to ease him into the conversation but also because I really am curious just how much I'm going to pay for my little stunt.

This time he doesn't bother to hide his amusement. "Probably. Might be good for her."

"Yes, she's very . . . regimented."

"That's one word for it." He takes a sip of his coffee.

"She works for you, Mr. Bradley, and Mr. Cannon?"

"Yes. Which is something you could have found out without taking up my time."

"How'd that come about, her taking on all three of you?" I ask, ignoring his grouch.

Kennedy sighs, drumming his fingers on the desk. "When Ian, Matt, and I were each promoted to director, we were given the opportunity to hire our own assistants. Kate had already been working as an office assistant for some of us junior guys, and she was the best."

"And you all wanted her."

"We all wanted the best."

"So it was a competition thing?"

He gives me a bland look, takes another sip of coffee. "Did you come in here to discuss the hiring process of Kate Henley or to do your job?"

"This is my job," I say, not remotely insulted. I've heard worse over the course of my career. So much worse.

"I thought you were investigating Ian, not Kate or me."

"I am. And in order to do that, I need access to his world. Best I can tell so far, that's you, Ms. Henley, and Mr. Cannon."

"Impressive. A week on the job, and you've already cracked the code," he says sarcastically.

I lift my hands in surrender. "Fine. You want to get to it, I can do it that way, too. Do you know anyone from J-Conn?"

"Yes."

I sit up a bit straighter. "Who?"

He shrugs. "My dad plays golf with one of their senior directors. Ray Clouse. He came over to my family's house for dinner back in the day. My sister dated a guy who worked on their product development team. I met him once or twice. First name's Brian, I'd have to dig around for the last. One of my college buddies was on their sales team. Curtis Linder. I think that's it."

"Did Mr. Bradley ever meet any of these individuals through you?"

"No."

"Did any of these individuals at any point indicate the company's dire straits in the days leading up to their bankruptcy announcement?"

"My clients lost millions when they folded. What do you think?"

"I think that's not an answer to my question."

"No," he snaps, with a pointed look at his watch. "Nobody told me shit; I haven't talked to any of them in years. Your five minutes are nearly up."

"We both know you don't have a nine o'clock, Mr. Dawson, so you might as well settle in. It's in Mr. Bradley's best interest that you do."

His brown eyes narrow on me. "Why are you after him?"

"I'm simply following through on a lead. It isn't like I've got a personal vendetta against the man."

His thumb slides slowly up and down his Starbucks cup as he studies me. "You sure about that?"

"About what?"

"That this isn't personal." Kennedy's voice is low and calm, but the jab couldn't have hit more directly if he'd shouted it.

I've never been anything but 100 percent professional on a case, but I'm dangerously close to letting personal motivations creep in on this one. Not just because it could be my ticket into the FBI, but because I honestly can't say that my opinions on Ian Bradley are solely work-related.

Still, I'm not about to admit that here, so I keep my voice impassive. "I was assigned to the case. I'm following up on the allegations that were handed to me by the SEC."

"What about the accuser?" he says.

"I'm sorry?"

"You said you knew the allegations. But you don't know who made the allegations, correct?"

"I can't answer that."

He smiles in victory. "You just did."

I bite my cheek to keep from reacting. *Get it under control, Lara. You're better than this.*

I skip right over what Kennedy thinks he knows. "Would you say Mr. Bradley's skilled at his job?"

"Yes."

"Better than you?"

"No."

I lean forward. "And yet, you lost money over J-Conn. He didn't. Why do you think that is?"

"Because that's how this business works, Ms. McKenzie. You win some, you lose some. You want me to pull up a list of stocks I made out on when Ian lost? I can. Other companies he benefited from that I didn't? I can do that, too. The only thing different about J-Conn is the scope of the loss."

"It's a big difference, though. You said yourself you lost millions. How did your clients feel about that?"

"Really fantastic, thanks for bringing it up," he says with a bored look over my shoulder, as though I'm wasting his time.

I very well may be. God knows this is shaping up to be a waste of mine. Hell, for that matter, this whole case is starting to feel like a waste of time, and I really need it not to be. My boss has all but assured me that frying a fish as big as Ian could be the coup I need to make Quantico admissions notice me.

Only the fish and his fleet aren't cooperating. Either they're a pack of damn impressive liars, more adept at destroying evidence and covering their tracks than any company I've come across so far, or the tip we received is bogus.

It's not that I think Ian's incapable of breaking the law. It's that I think he's too close with the people around him not to confide in one of them or have them put the pieces together. And while Kate and Kennedy, and I suspect Matt, too, would definitely cover for Ian . . .

I don't get the sense that they are. They're too genuinely ticked by my very presence.

Still, I try for one more question, knowing my time is limited, his patience at its end. "Mr. Dawson, I realize Mr. Bradley's a friend as well as a colleague. I respect that. Which is why you need to understand that the best way you can protect him is to be honest with me about any connection he may have to J-Conn."

He's silent for a moment. "You want me to be honest."

I nod. "Yes."

"You want me to tell you anything about him that might be useful to you."

I resist the urge to roll my eyes. "Yes, absolutely."

"All right, then. Maybe this will be helpful . . . I don't think I've ever seen him so pissed off."

"When?" I ask, leaning forward.

"Right now."

The gruff statement isn't Kennedy's. It comes from behind me, and even if I didn't already hear that voice in my dirty dreams at night, I'd know exactly whom it belongs to by Kennedy's growing smirk.

Taking a deep breath, I stand and turn to face a very irate-looking Ian.

9

Ian

Week 2: Monday Morning

"My office. Now."

I don't bother waiting to see if Lara follows me—I know she will. She's been panting after a meeting for days now and stalking me at lunch. She'll follow.

My office is on the opposite corner of our floor from Kennedy's. My long strides mean I beat her to it, but I stand by the door until she enters, slamming it shut and moving toward her until she's backed up against it.

I don't mean to. I'm not the sort of shithead who uses my title or build to intimidate people, but intimidating is not my angle here. I'm pissed.

Pissed that she followed me to lunch last Friday. Pissed that she's interrogating my friends.

Pissed that of all the SEC investigators, I have to get one who makes my dick hard.

We're both breathing heavily, and my gaze drops to her mouth just as she speaks.

"Step back, Mr. Bradley," she says, her tone ice-cold as she glares up at me. "Now."

I mutter a curse, slamming my hand on the door behind her head, then use it to push back away from her to a safe distance where I won't want to press her against the wood and slide my hand beneath her skirt, seeing if her skin's as smooth as it is in my fantasies.

"You've been avoiding me," she says, coming farther into the office. Her tone is cool, her face impassive. Only the slight shake of her hand as she runs a palm over her ponytail belies that she's as impacted by me as I am by her.

"Yup."

"I had your company's assurances that you'd cooperate, and I got the impression last week in the conference room when you brought me coffee that you were planning on doing exactly that. What changed?"

I realized I couldn't be in the same room as you and not want to fuck you, that's what changed.

I run my hands through my hair. "I was advised to get an attorney before speaking with you further."

"Prudent," she says, running a finger along the edge of the desk. "And did you?"

Much as I'm looking forward to seeing her face when she learns who my lawyer is, I decide to bide my time and ignore her question. "You get what you need harassing my friend?"

"I assume you mean Mr. Dawson. Yes, I had an illuminating interview with your colleague."

I note her phrasing, chosen carefully to counter mine, and I roll my eyes.

"I've learned he's fiercely loyal to you." She gestures at the office. "And that you have incredibly different tastes in décor."

I glance around my swanky office. It's basically another version of my apartment—awesome view, sleek and modern furnishings. It's exactly what people expect my office to look like. It's also entirely replaceable. A tornado could wipe out the place, and I wouldn't give a shit. That's something I learned bouncing around from foster home to foster home—there's no point in getting attached to things. Or people.

She nods, then points to a table behind my desk. "Is that real? The orchid?"

I glance over. "Yeah." Her surprised look pisses me off again. "What?" I snap.

Lara blinks. "Nothing. You just don't strike me as the type to have an orchid. They're notoriously finicky and require a bit of coddling."

"I can coddle." As soon as the words are out of my mouth, I realize how ridiculous they sound and shrug. "It was a Christmas gift last year from Kate. She and Kennedy have a bet going over whether or not I can keep it alive an entire year."

"Which way did she bet?"

"Let's just say she checks on it about ten times a day and has forbidden Kennedy from doing anything to keep the damn thing from dying."

She walks over and studies the flower. "Looks like you haven't killed it. Yet."

"You like orchids?" I ask, noting the wistful smile on her face.

Other than her boring taste in coffee, it's one of the few personal details I've been able to glean from her, and I tuck away the fact. Why, I don't know, other than some bizarre desire to know the woman hiding behind those professional walls.

"My late grandmother had quite a collection. One of the largest in the DC metro area."

"You take over as the family orchid expert?"

Her smile disappears. "No. I tried, but . . . they take time I don't have, attention I couldn't give them. I learned the hard way it was the flowers or the job, and . . ."

She shrugs as if it's no big deal, but I'd bet serious money it's a bluff. She may *think* she's okay giving 100 percent to the job, but it clearly eats at her.

She inhales, as though to gather herself, and motions to the chair by my desk. "May I? I have some questions regarding my case."

Her crisp tone leaves me feeling like a fool. Here I am, musing about her love of flowers, and she's viewing me as "her case."

I give a curt nod and sit across from her, but before she launches into her questions, I fire off one of my own. "What the hell were you thinking, following me to lunch on Friday?"

If she's taken aback by my candor, she doesn't show it. "I'd hoped you were eating alone, and that I might get a moment of your time—since you've been avoiding me." She gives me a pointed look.

"And once you realized I wasn't alone?"

Her cheeks color, just a bit—so subtle I wouldn't notice if I hadn't been watching her so closely. "I thought she might be a source. Someone who could prove helpful to my case."

I grin and call her bluff. "Bullshit. You thought she was my girlfriend."

"Actually, no," she says calmly. "I figured you and she were trying not to be seen together."

"Why the hell would I want that?"

She shrugs. "Perhaps she's involved with someone else."

"Jesus Christ," I snap. "It's bad enough you accuse me of being a criminal, now I'm stealing other men's women?"

"You forget I've been spending an entire week researching every facet of your life. The women you're romantically connected to take up an entire legal pad."

"But none of them is married!" I explode. I may be a son of a bitch, but I've got morals. I don't take what's not mine.

"So she's not a girlfriend, nor a source."

"No," I growl. "She's a friend, and she's got nothing to do with your BS case, so leave her the hell out of it."

"A friend," Lara says, her voice skeptical. "When she looks like that, and you look like *that* . . ." She breaks off, her eyes widening in horror as she realizes what she's said.

I don't bother to hide my grin as I lace my fingers behind my head and lean back in my chair. "I look like what, Ms. McKenzie?"

This time her blush is unmistakable. She uncrosses her legs, then crosses them again, and I grin wider.

"I've got to say, seeing you uncomfortable is the most gratifying thing I've seen in days."

"I'm not uncomfortable."

I lift my eyebrows. "You're practically twitching."

"Maybe it's because you're killing your orchid," she snaps.

"Nice evasion, but some of us can manage the job *and* the flower."

I mean it flippantly, but I regret it as soon as I say it, because if her cheeks were flushed before, now they're white.

Shit. I'm an ass.

"Ms. McKenzie—"

"Save it," she snaps, holding up a hand. "You know, I think we'd better save this meeting for another time."

"Look, I'm sorry about the flower comment—"

"It's not that," she says too quickly. "I just don't have anything to take notes on."

"Horseshit. I hurt your feelings—"

"Please stop," she says, standing. "That's what I've been trying to make clear to you since the beginning. None of this is about feelings. It's *business*. I'm on your calendar for next Thursday. If you can fit me in sooner, I'd appreciate it. I'm sure we both want to get this wrapped up—"

A knock at the door interrupts her.

"Yeah," I say, my voice rough with irritation.

Kate pokes her head in, ignoring Lara altogether. "Mr. Bradley, Vanessa Lewis is here to see you."

Lara whirls around, eyes wide and shocked.

It's the moment I've been waiting for, and though I force a cocky grin, it feels hollow. I want to win this, obviously, to have the allegations disproven and my name cleared. But my winning means Lara losing. For the first time since this all started, the idea doesn't fill me with victory.

"Vanessa Lewis is your attorney," Lara says, her voice stunned.

It's not just us on Wall Street who know Vanessa's reputation for only taking clients she believes to be innocent. The SEC knows it, too.

I turn my attention back to Kate. "Send Ms. Lewis in. Ms. McKenzie was just leaving."

"I was," Lara says, lifting her chin, confidence restored as she turns on her heel and walks toward the door. When she's shoulder to shoulder with Kate, she stops. "By the way, he's overwatering it. Congratulations, it should be dead in no time."

Kate gives a startled look toward the orchid, then an assessing look after Lara, who doesn't turn back as she heads down the hall. "Is it weird that I might like her?" Kate asks.

No, I think.

What's weird is that I know *I* like her.

10

LARA

Week 2: Wednesday Morning

"Lara, hi!" Steve Ennis looks up from his desk, blinking in surprise to see me standing in his doorway. "Thought you were at Wolfe today."

"I'm headed there next. I just needed to pick up a couple things from my desk." *And was hoping to catch you.*

I keep telling myself I'm paranoid, but I'm fairly certain my boss is avoiding me. I've sent him three e-mails in as many days, and he hasn't replied to any. Nor has he returned my two voice mails.

"You got a minute?" I ask when he doesn't invite me in.

"Sure. Sure, come on in," he says, closing the folder he was perusing. "Shut the door."

The difference between Steve's office and Ian's is almost comical. Both are fancy but generic office settings, but one's from lack of budget, the other from lack of caring.

The SEC is the first category. For starters, the office is on the twelfth floor instead of the millionth. Steve's got a corner office, but instead of looking at New York landmarks, we've got a grade-A view of another office and an apartment building with residents who decline to close their blinds more often than not.

The inside aesthetic is different, too. Fluorescent lights, scattered paper clips, a tired chair, and the perpetual smell of stale coffee.

My boss fits right in. He's not a bad-looking man, but the ill-fitted *don't give a shit* suit does nothing to flatter his ever-expanding middle, and his thick head of salt-and-pepper hair could do well with a haircut that costs more than twelve dollars on his lunch break.

That, or maybe I've spent too much time with the polish of Wolfe Investments.

"What can I do you for?" he asks as I sit and cross my legs. Is it just me, or does his voice seem too booming, too upbeat?

"You got my status report on the J-Conn/Bradley case?"

He nods enthusiastically. "Yeah. Sounds like a real toughie we lobbed at you."

A real toughie? Not being able to find any evidence after more than a week of looking isn't a *toughie*. It's called not having a case.

"He let you at his personal files?" Steve asks. "Guy like that won't put anything on the company servers."

"He did. And his e-mail. I'm only about halfway through, but the chances of there being any useful information in there are slim."

"You saying you think he destroyed something?"

"No," I say carefully. It's not like Steve to put words in my mouth. "I think in the six years I've been doing this, nobody has been stupid enough to leave evidence in their personal files. You know as well as I do that requesting the files is a stalling technique."

His gaze sharpens a bit, his smile slipping.

I'm not insubordinate—I'm known as much for being easy to work with as I am for being tenacious and thorough. But something is going on here that I'm not fully informed on, and it's starting to piss me off. At first I thought it was just some weird gut reaction messing with my head, and I don't put much stock in instinct. However, the facts aren't lining up, either. There's nothing, and I mean nothing, connecting Ian Bradley to J-Conn.

Yet, I remind myself. Nothing *yet*.

"Look, Steve, you put me on this case because you trust me. I was at your wedding, for goodness' sake," I say, gesturing to the family photo on his desk taken a couple of years ago.

His third wedding, but who's counting.

"I need to know why you think our source is reliable," I say. "I need to know what you know. Who gave us the tip? What specifics did he tell you?"

He's already shaking his head. "No can do."

"Why?" I say, dangerously close to throwing my arms up in the air in complete exasperation.

"I've already told you, this is a confidential informant. It was part of the deal when he came to me. I am the only one to know his identity until it comes time for testimony."

"Steve." I gentle my voice and try for the soothing tone I use with nervous witnesses. "If the informant is too squirrelly to come forward now, what makes you think he'll testify? You know how often witnesses lose their nerve when it's time to put their name on paper. Being labeled as a whistle-blower is just as damaging to a reputation as being the criminal."

If not more so. Wall Street disdains a cheater.

But they loathe a whistle-blower.

Though I'm never privy to the actual conversations, it's not unheard of for big players to take matters into their own hands. Rather than come to the SEC with their information, they'll go directly to the offender with a blistering *do it again, and I'll cut you off at the knees.*

It's considered a sign of respect among peers.

Steve's source is either significantly beneath Ian in status and has zero authority to go toe to toe with him directly or he's hiding behind the SEC.

I don't mind. It's what we're here for. But it tells me we're not dealing with someone with much brass. And those sources are the most likely to back out when it comes time to testify.

And if that happens, guess who's stuck holding a broken case . . . Me.

"It's my reputation on the line, too," I say quietly to Steve. I'm not going to beg, but I'm not going to be a pawn, either.

Steve gives an emphatic shake of his head and stands, indicating that the conversation is over. "You don't need to worry about that."

I stand and meet my boss's gaze head-on. "You essentially told me that this case could be my high-profile win to warrant Quantico's attention. If the investigation never gets past the informal stage, it's not going to be high profile. It'll be dead in the water."

"It'll get to the formal stage," he says dismissively, going around the desk to the door.

"But that's what I'm trying to tell you," I say, following him to the door and trying to hide my impatience. "So far, it's not warranting a formal investigation. I can't find a single piece of evidence linking Ian Bradley to J-Conn or anyone with inside knowledge of J-Conn's impending doom."

Steve opens the door, my dismissal clear, but not without a parting shot. "Lara, you still want the FBI recommendation?"

"Of course."

"Then find some damn evidence."

11

IAN

Week 2: Wednesday Afternoon

Vanessa Lewis is the spitting image of Beyoncé, has the confidence to match, and thus is the hottest woman I know.

And one I'll never hit on.

Why? One doesn't hit on his lawyer. Even I know that.

Also, she's not the one I want.

"Ian. Are you listening?"

I stop strumming my fingers against the mahogany wood of my desk as I realize I've been staring blankly at her the entire time she's been speaking. It's our second meeting. The one on Monday had been to take care of logistics—discussing her fee, signing her retainer, etc. This meeting is about my case, and I'm . . . not paying attention.

"Sorry." I sit up straighter. "What?"

Her brown eyes narrow just slightly, full lips pursing as she sits back in the chair across the desk and studies me.

"Ian," she says finally. "What do you know about me?"

"Uh . . ." My brain scrambles. Is this a trick question? It *feels* like a trick question.

"Why do you think I took your case?" she amends, apparently reading my panic.

I relax. I got this. "Because you believe I'm innocent."

It's the other reason I'm damn impressed by the woman. In addition to having a near-flawless record, she's got something rarer than her legal brass: integrity.

It's an interesting quirk that's earned her as much disdain as it has admiration.

I'm in the latter category.

Being cleared of all allegations is my top priority, obviously, but I don't want it to be at the hands of some snake who doesn't care one way or the other whether I'm a criminal douchebag.

"I do believe you're innocent," Vanessa says, bringing my attention back to her. "And I'm glad I was able to take on your case. But just as I expect my clients to be honest with me, I believe in being honest with them."

"And?"

"Your case isn't looking good, Ian."

I tense, my fingers resuming their tapping on the desk. "You know this already?"

She lifts a shoulder. "I have more research to do, obviously. But here's what's bothering me . . . typically, when the SEC gets some sort of tip about insider trading, they'll launch an informal investigation to vet their source and determine the potential legitimacy of the accusation. Which they have. But so far, I've seen what they've seen from the files, and there's not much there. There's zero connection between you and J-Conn that I've found, which means they haven't found it, either."

I try to follow. "Isn't that a good thing?"

She shakes her head. "Not even a little bit. With the lack of concrete evidence I'm seeing, Lara McKenzie should have packed her bags by now. Instead, she's still camped out in that conference room pushing papers around."

"Meaning?"

"Whatever tip they received, whatever evidence they think they can find, they're damn sure they can win with it," she says matter-of-factly. *Shit.*

"Nor do I love that it's Lara McKenzie working your case," Vanessa continues. "She looks like a lamb but thinks like a fox. What are your impressions of her?"

Well, hell. I can't tell her the truth—that Lara and her hot glasses are playing on repeat in my dirtiest fantasies. Beneath me, above me, in front of me bent over my desk . . .

But I can't lie to her, either. Or rather, I could, but Vanessa made it clear in our first meeting that if she ever found out I was lying, she'd drop my case faster than a bad oyster. Her words.

"She seems by the book," I evade. "Follows the rules."

Vanessa nods. "That's precisely why she's so good and, I fear, is *exactly* why they put her on your case. McKenzie's reputation is nearly as good as mine. She doesn't power play, doesn't grandstand. She gathers and recites facts, and judges love her for it."

"She can't recite facts she doesn't have, though. So unless she's making them up . . ."

"Okay, let's back up," Vanessa says, her tone switching to soothing. "We need to figure out why you're in their crosshairs. They're here because they got a tip, but we don't know who's accusing you of insider trading or why."

"I already told you—"

"I know, I know, no mortal enemies, no archrival out to take you down," she interrupts. "But look, Ian, this isn't a movie. The person behind this isn't going to be lurking in your peripheral vision making overt threats with a sinister laugh. The answer will be in the subtleties."

"I don't really do subtleties," I say honestly. "In anything."

She surprises me by laughing. "So I've heard. But it's time to start, at least for this."

Vanessa stands and pushes a blank yellow legal pad across the desk to me. "I want you to make a list of every person you've crossed paths with in the last year. Hell, make it the last two years. Anyone who might be jealous, resentful, pissed, write their name down. Don't discount people you think are friends. Anyone who you've toasted Pappy with, write it down."

"I don't drink bourbon," I mutter.

"Negronis, then, whatever."

I glance up in surprise that she knows my favorite drink.

She lifts her eyebrows. "I told you I'd do my homework. If we want to win this thing, I'm going to need to learn every little detail about you. I need to know every secret, every birthmark on your balls—"

I hold up my finger. "Don't have one of those." I'm pretty sure.

She taps a coral-painted nail against the legal pad. "Names, Ian. Write them down, and do it today. Time's against us here. Their persistence makes me think they're damn determined to turn this into a formal investigation, and if they do, our chances of winning get lopped off at the knees."

I swallow, a lot less confident now than I was at the beginning of the meeting.

She stands and gives me a perfunctory nod. "I'll be in touch," she says, punching something on her phone.

I pick up a pen as Vanessa strolls out the door, phone already glued to her ear.

Pivoting my chair, I turn to take in the overcast afternoon, tapping my pen against the pad. I know I should be thinking about myself, trying to figure out who might be looking to take me down, but I can't stop thinking about how Lara and I are quite possibly looking for the exact same thing: what the hell is tying me to J-Conn.

The irony is, I don't have a fucking clue.

I've just started the process of naming all the jackasses on Wall Street when Matt enters my office without knocking.

"How'd it go with the lawyer?"

I glance up, grateful for the distraction. "The good news is she believes I'm innocent."

"And the bad?"

I drop my pen and rub my hands through my hair. "The SEC still doesn't."

He grunts and drops into the chair across from me. "We're still sure it's J-Conn they're sniffing after?"

I shrug. "Lara more or less confirmed it."

His eyebrows go up. "Lara?"

"Ms. McKenzie. Whatever." I wave my hand in the air. "We need to figure out who would lie to the SEC about me and why."

Matt looks at the pad on my desk. "That your list?"

"Start of it. You got anyone?"

"Fuck the list. It's a shot in the dark. If you want to know who contacted the SEC, you've got to go straight to the source."

I shake my head. "I already tried that, remember? She won't say shit."

"That was last week. Try again."

"What do you want me to do, interrogate her?"

"Whatever it takes, man. Your charm didn't work before, so use your other ace up the sleeve."

"I'm better with the ace in my pants."

He rolls his eyes. "Keep it zipped. What I meant was wear her down. In everything else, you're relentless about getting what you want, but you're pulling your punches with her. Why?"

I glance down at the notepad. He's right. I hate that he's right. Hate even more that I don't have an answer for him. Not one I'm ready to admit out loud, anyway.

"She's not pulling her punches with you," Matt says quietly. "She followed you the other day to get the information she wanted."

"So?"

"So maybe it's time she got a little taste of her own medicine."

12

LARA

Week 2: Friday Night

My best friend has a lot of good qualities, quite a few useful skills.

Her matchmaking abilities?

Not among her virtues.

I pull my phone out of my purse and check the time again.

7:20.

Either my blind date is twenty minutes late or he's standing me up.

And I suppose it says a lot about me that I can't decide which is worse: the prospect of enduring a bad date or no date at all.

My love life's not exactly what you'd call *thriving*. My longest relationship was last year, lasted five months, and ended with about as much excitement as it started, which isn't saying much.

Let's just say life as an SEC agent doesn't seem to spark much chemistry on the romantic front. Even when I do manage to put work out of my mind, I think guys *smell* the workaholic on me.

Best I can tell, guys want the fun party girl or the soft, marriageable girl. I'm neither. I'm not sure I'm even the "hot career woman," because even she is supposed to know how to relax at the end of the night, and, well . . . it's not a skill I've mastered.

Most of the time I'm okay with that. I've learned that at this stage in my life, I can focus on my career or guys, but not both.

See: my dead orchids.

I cringe, still hating that I let Ian's jab get to me the other day. They're flowers, for God's sake. It's just . . . if I can't keep a flower alive, how the heck am I supposed to figure out how to make a relationship work long-term?

A server approaches, and bless him for having perfected his nonjudgmental look as I sit alone at a table set for two. "Something from the bar while you wait?"

I smile, grateful that we're both pretending this isn't the second time he's asked. "Yes, please." Anything. "I'll take a glass of white wine. Something fresh, not too sweet. Surprise me."

He nods. "I know just the thing."

If it's alcoholic, I'm sure it'll be fine.

I text Gabby. No sign of your guy. He say anything?

She responds immediately. Shit, really? No, let me text him.

The server drops off my wine, and I smile in thanks as another text message comes through, this one from my mother.

Hey sweetie, up for a phone chat tomorrow? Sorry I've been so busy.

No prob, I text back. Been nuts here, too. Would lunchtime work?

Got a working lunch with my team. How about five? I'll call you.

Sounds great.

Actually, that might be pushing it. Is seven okay?

I take a sip of wine and try not to let it sting that my fiftysomething mother has a busier schedule than me.

Sure.

Perfect. How are things?

Oh gosh, how are things? Let's review . . .
I'm at the first date I've had in months—alone.
I'm the closest I've ever been to the FBI, but the case that is supposed to get my foot in the door at Quantico is a nonstarter because I can't find a single piece of evidence—after nearly two weeks of looking.
And I kill flowers for a hobby.
I text her back. **Things are great!**

I take a deep breath, feeling a little guilty about the lie but knowing even if I did lay it all out there, my mom wouldn't know what to do with it. I love my mom—I adore both my parents—but they're not the type of parents who believe in being their kid's best friends. Which is fine, it's just . . .

I wish they would have noticed that nobody wanted to be my best friend. I mean, I have Gabby now, but up until I lucked out with her as a roommate, my friendship life was about as thriving as my romantic life.

People respect me. Most even like me. But it's all surface level. I'm never the one people call in the middle of the night with guy problems. And as a result, I have no one to call with my guy problems. Not that I've had a relationship long enough to even have a guy problem . . .

I scan the room again, looking for the guy Gabby described. *Reddish-brown hair, great jaw, glasses. Not super tall but not awkwardly short, either.*

I don't see anyone matching that description.

You know who I do see?

Ian Bradley.

At first I think it's a dream. Sorry, did I say dream? I meant nightmare.

This isn't happening to me. I am not sitting alone at a table, clearly getting stood up, while the one person who'd like nothing more than to see me while I'm down sits at the bar sipping a cocktail.

Either this is some sort of hideous coincidence, or . . .

He looks over right then, his gaze colliding with mine with such deliberate purpose that I know immediately this is no chance encounter.

It's revenge for last week when I followed him.

I close my eyes just for a moment, opening them only when my phone buzzes with another incoming text. It's Gabby.

So sorry, babe. His boss offered him tickets to the Yankees tonight. He's a huge baseball fan, forgot all about the date.

Fannnnn-tastic.

I'm texting her back when a shadow appears over my table.

Bracing, I look up, keeping my face composed. "Hello, Mr. Bradley."

His eyes flick over me, then the table. "Ms. McKenzie. Enjoying your evening?"

"Very much."

His smirk calls my bluff.

"You here for dinner?" I ask, my voice never wavering in politeness even as the back of my neck's hot with embarrassment to be caught in a vulnerable moment.

"Nope, just grabbing a drink on my way home."

"This isn't exactly near your apartment or office."

The smirk disappears, and his eyes narrow. "How do you know where my apartment is?"

"I know everything," I say, seeing no reason to hide the fact that I know just about every possible detail on Ian that's public record.

"Yeah? How's that evidence collecting going?" he asks, his voice deceptively casual.

I'm not in the mood to play games, so I ignore his question and cut to the chase. "Did you know I'd be here?"

"Kate may have overheard you setting up your *date*," he says with a pointed glance at the empty chair.

I sigh. "I knew it. This *is* revenge for last week."

"*Revenge* is a strong word, Ms. McKenzie. Let's merely call this a lesson."

"In what, stalking?"

"You want to talk about stalking?" he asks, dropping into the empty chair across from me, his blue gaze intense. "Try going to a casual lunch with your oldest friend, wanting a brief break from the shitstorm that your life's become, and the very woman causing said shitstorm follows you."

I feel a little stab of guilt. "It's not personal, Mr. Bradley."

"Bullshit," he snaps. "Does this moment feel personal to you, when *you're* the one being followed?"

"Yes, but you—"

"Crashed your date? Infiltrated your life? Does it feel *personal*, Ms. McKenzie?"

Both of our tempers are simmering, and I take a sip of water to cool my own. "You're trying to make me feel guilty for doing my job."

"No, I'm trying to show you that the impact of your job isn't as clean and impersonal as you pretend."

"Fine," I say calmly. "Noted."

"Are you saying that because you feel bad about intruding on my lunch the other day or because you want me to leave?"

"Both?"

He studies me for a moment, then nods. "All right, then. Apology accepted."

"I don't know that it was an apology."

His eyebrows lift.

I sigh. "Okay, fine. I'm sorry I didn't leave the restaurant after I saw you were there on personal business. *Now* will you leave?"

He surprises me by grinning. "Nope." He winks and reaches for my wineglass, lifting it in question. "What are we drinking?"

"*We* aren't drinking anything. I'm having a glass of white wine. You were just leaving."

He glances at his watch and takes a sip of the wine—my wine. "Seven thirty-four. Your date is four minutes late."

Actually, my date is thirty-four minutes late, and that's if he were coming, which he's not.

I don't say this, obviously. The last thing I need is to be even a tiny bit vulnerable in front of someone who'd love nothing better than to see me humiliated.

"Yes, I'm sure he'll be here any minute, so if you don't mind . . . ," I say, wiggling my fingers in a shooing motion.

Ian sets my wineglass down in front of me.

I try not to sag in relief that he's leaving, his little demonstration over. "Enjoy your evening, Mr. Brad—Wait, what are you doing?" I ask in panic as he picks up the neatly folded napkin and places it on his suited lap.

"Joining you for dinner."

"But—"

"Your date's not coming, Ms. McKenzie. Now, have you or have you not been bugging my assistant to get some time on my calendar?"

"Yes, but she's playing hardball and won't put me on your calendar until next week. I have some questions I need answers to before then—"

"About J-Conn, sure. And I'll answer them, but only if you give me something in return." His gaze drops to my mouth, just for a moment.

I narrow my eyes. "I'm not sleeping with you."

His smile is slow and cocky as hell. "Famous last words. But that's actually not what I was angling for. I was thinking a question for a question. For every question I answer, you have to answer one of mine."

"That's not how this works, Mr. Bradley."

He shrugs and starts to set his napkin back on the table. "Good luck getting your subpoena, then, because that's the only other way—"

"Fine," I say, a little desperate. "A question for a question."

He grins and drops the napkin back into his lap. "Perfect. But first things first . . . we're going to need more drinks."

13

IAN

Week 2: Friday Night

My lawyer's going to kill me.

I'm pretty sure when the bosses told me to cooperate with the SEC, this isn't what they'd meant.

Having a dinner in a cozy East Village French bistro's not exactly what I had planned, either. Hell, I can't even remember my plan. It all went out the window the second I came in and saw Lara sitting all alone, looking so unexpectedly vulnerable my chest had ached.

I should have turned around and walked out the front door.

Instead, the completely foreign urge to distract her from the embarrassment of being stood up had taken over. I gave the guy half an hour to show up and make her smile.

He hadn't.

Moron.

Or maybe I'm the moron. Because while Lara may be the pain in my ass right now, even as I want to strangle her, I can admit she looks good. More than good.

Her hair's in its usual ponytail, but it's pulled to one side to drape over her shoulder—a bare shoulder, courtesy of a strapless dress that's not low-cut enough to torture me but is tight enough to make me wonder things I shouldn't be wondering.

A server makes his way toward us. "Can I get you something to drink, sir?"

"I'll have what she's having," I say, nodding at the wine.

"Very good. Shall I put in any appetizers, or are we taking our time?"

Lara opens her mouth, but I beat her to it. "*Definitely* taking our time."

She rolls her eyes as the server gives a deferential nod and backs away. "Very good, sir."

"So," I say, leaning forward. "I'll start. Who were you supposed to be meeting tonight?"

"I don't think so," she says coolly, taking a sip of wine. "I'll start the questions. You said you didn't know Arnold Maverick. You're *positive* the two of you never crossed paths?"

"Yes, one hundred percent positive. I didn't know the man. Now is this a boyfriend you were planning to meet, or—"

"What about a mutual acquaintance of Mr. Maverick's?" she presses. "Someone you both knew?"

"Question for question, Ms. McKenzie. That's the deal."

She blows out a frustrated breath but relents. "It was a blind date."

"Who set you up?"

"My best friend, Gabby. She can be a little . . . pushy. She's a serial dater and doesn't understand why I'm not the same."

"But you agreed."

Lara twists the stem of her wineglass between her fingers, watching as the wine swishes lightly from side to side. "Yes, it's been a while since—" Her head snaps up. "Hold on. That was more than one question."

"Whoops." I grin.

Her eyes narrow behind her glasses, and she leans forward. "So you didn't know Maverick. But you must've known someone from J-Conn. It was a huge company, and—"

"Christ, woman, you're like a dog with a bone."

She studies me. "If you're not going to take this seriously, Mr. Bradley—"

"*Nobody*," I snap. "I don't know a damn person from J-Conn, Ms. McKenzie. I didn't have any inside scoop. You can believe me or not believe me, but it's the damn truth."

I sit back in my chair, nodding in thanks as the server brings my wine and moves away again.

"Favorite food."

She blinks. "What?"

"What's your favorite food?"

"Why do you want to know that?"

"Jesus, you're ornery. Fine, why the SEC?"

She studies me for a moment. "Pizza."

I'm trying so hard not to check out her body in that dress that it takes a moment to register she's said something. "What?"

"My favorite food is pizza. How'd you get Vanessa Lewis as your lawyer?" she asks.

For a half second, I'm tempted to gloat—my getting the best attorney in the business is a win, and she and I both know it. But for reasons I don't feel like analyzing, I don't feel like gloating. I don't feel like working against Lara.

I want her to see me as something other than the fucking case.

"Charm?" I say teasingly, answering her question.

"It takes more than charm to get someone like Ms. Lewis on your side," Lara says, watching me carefully.

"Damn straight. She's got to believe she can get a nonguilty verdict. Because you know as well as I do that Vanessa Lewis only takes on clients she knows are innocent."

"*Thinks* are innocent," she corrects. "So if you didn't know anyone at J-Conn, how'd you luck out when they went under?"

Technically it's not her turn for a question, but I answer anyway because it's something she needs to hear, even if she doesn't believe me. "Good old-fashioned gut instinct," I say. "It bugged me that J-Conn had been sitting on a supposed big announcement for so long. Everyone else took the claims that they were releasing some game-changing product at face value. I didn't. My gut told me they didn't have the next Facebook or iPhone waiting in the wings, so I sold when everyone bought high."

"So a *gut feeling* saved you and your clients millions of dollars," she says, shaking her head. She takes another sip of her wine, frowns when she sees the glass is nearly empty.

"You don't believe in intuition?"

"I believe in facts, Mr. Bradley. Intuition is nothing more than your subconscious remembering something your consciousness forgot and attributing it to some outside source."

Aha. I study her for a moment as a crucial piece of the Lara McKenzie puzzle clicks into place. Here I've been approaching this thing like a game: winner, loser, hunter, prey.

For Lara, it's different. It's true or false, right or wrong.

"Why are you looking at me like that?" She shifts uncomfortably.

"The world's not black and white, Ms. McKenzie."

"Maybe not to you," she says.

And there it is, the root of this mess: we don't live in the same world. Or, at least, we don't look at the world through the same lens.

The sudden realization that our very realities might be incompatible feels . . . unacceptable.

The server comes over, interrupting my thoughts. "Another glass of wine, miss?"

She looks at me, and as our eyes lock and hold, something passes between us—a silent acknowledgment of . . .

Hell, I don't know. Wanting? Wishing things could be different?

"Yeah, okay," she says slowly. "Another glass of wine."

I lift my glass and take a sip to hide my smile as the server moves away. "So, why the SEC?"

"How long does this game go on?"

"We each get one more question after you answer this one."

She rolls her eyes. "Fine. I'm with the SEC because it gets me closer to my dream job."

"Which is . . . ?"

She points at me and smiles. "That's your last question."

I shrug. "'Kay." I'm a little surprised that I really do want to know more about what motivates this complex woman who's driven by structure and rules. I know it's not money. The SEC pays shit.

"FBI," she says.

I choke on my drink. "What?"

"You asked what my dream job is—it's the FBI."

"Jesus," I mutter, wiping my face with my napkin. "I'm starting to rethink this dinner . . ."

She smiles. "Don't worry. I haven't been to Quantico. Yet."

"Admittedly this isn't my area, but how does the SEC lead to a job with the Federal Bureau of Investigation?"

"Well, specifically, I want to be in their white-collar division. They work closely with the SEC, so there's a lot of overlap."

"Then why transition at all?"

She bites her lip, then looks up. "My parents are FBI."

"Both of them?" I ask, not able to hide my surprise.

"Yep. I was born and raised in DC. They both still live there, both still active in the bureau."

Damn. "I bet you had zero boyfriends growing up."

Her head snaps back a little, and I realize I've struck a nerve. *Shit.* I'm usually smoother than this.

"I just meant that had to be intimidating," I clarify. "Every kid picking up a girl for prom secretly fears her dad's got a gun. Both your parents had one."

She looks at me over the top of her glass. "Did you?"

"Did I what?"

"Go to prom."

It's her turn to strike a nerve, my turn to flinch. "No. But then, you probably already knew that."

"I didn't, actually. My research into your past is limited to details that might be pertinent to the case—relatives at J-Conn, etc."

"So you know that I don't have any relatives," I say, taking a healthy swallow of wine.

"I'm sorry about your parents," she says quietly.

"Eh. I was young. I don't remember them much."

"Which makes losing them in a car accident that much more tragic," she says, leaning forward.

"Is this the good-cop portion of your routine?"

She sits back and gives me a look. "Nice, Mr. Bradley. Being a jerk is a solid, mature way to deal with your pain."

I bite the inside of my cheek, hating that she's right. Caustic humor's my knee-jerk reaction to references to my childhood—both my parents' deaths and the aimless foster-kid stigma that followed.

"I asked a girl to prom," I say. "She said yes; her parents said no."

Shit. Why had I gone and done that? I haven't told anyone that . . . ever.

"Why'd they say no?"

A sarcastic deflection nearly rolls off my tongue, but I bite it back, feeling the strangest urge to be . . . open. Honest. I want Lara to know me like I want to know her.

So I give it to her straight, if a bit brief. "Even for the rough neighborhood I grew up in, I was still on the wrong side of the tracks.

Nice girls didn't go to dances with foster kids from the trailer park." I force a smile. "But look at me now and all that."

She smiles back, but it's a faint one, and her watchful gaze makes me think she sees something that nobody else sees—not even Sabrina.

"I got stood up tonight," she says after a long moment of silence.

"I know."

She winces. "Did you know the whole time?"

"I put the pieces together. He's a fool."

"Nah." She gives another of those slight smiles and finishes the last of her wine. "Just a baseball fan."

"Mets or Yankees?"

"Yankees."

"There you go," I say, spreading my hands. "You're better off without him."

"You're a Mets fan?"

"What, that wasn't in my file?" I tease.

"Lots of things weren't in your file."

"Such as?"

She hesitates. "The woman I saw you with at lunch . . ."

"Sabrina Cross, friend from Philly."

"You guys are . . . close?"

I lean toward her with a slow smile. "Is that professional curiosity at work there, Ms. McKenzie, or something else?"

Her only response is to open her menu and glance down at it, which is the most telling answer of all.

Obviously I'm not the only one warring with a forbidden, unwanted attraction here.

I'm torn between regret and relief, because she's SEC, I'm Wall Street—we're about as compatible as a wolf and a lamb.

Though, for the life of me, I'm not sure who's who in this scenario.

14

LARA

Week 3: Friday Morning

I'm going half-blind reading boring-ass e-mails when an enormous Frappuccino appears in front of my nose.

I have to look from the frothy Starbucks drink to the person delivering it twice before I register that she's brought it for me.

Kate drops into the chair on the opposite side of the conference room table, taking a sip of her own drink. "It's a peace offering, Ms. McKenzie."

"That or diabetes in a plastic cup," I say, picking it up and pointing at the mound of whipped cream. "Are those chocolate shavings?"

"They are indeed. And don't pretend you don't want it. Ian let the cat out of the bag."

My head snaps up, not entirely sure I want to know what Ian told his assistant. On the one hand, I hope it's nothing so I can maintain some semblance of professionalism. On the other hand, I want to know if he's as off-balance after our dinner last week as I am.

"About the coffee?" Kate prompts, giving me a curious look. "He said he brought you one a few weeks ago?"

"Oh. Right. *Right*."

I take a sip of the drink to try and cover up my awkwardness. It's even more amazing this time around. Cold and sweet and caffeinated.

"Do you think this is what heaven tastes like?" I ask, more to myself than her.

Kate considers my question seriously. "That or cheese fries. Or that place in the Village that makes ice cream out of cookie dough."

"Or a really good croissant. The kind that are buttery, flaky on the outside and then chewy on the inside."

She points her straw in my direction. "*Yes.* Like they have in Paris."

I feel a little twinge of longing. "I've never been, but yeah . . . I can imagine."

She shrugs. "New York does a pretty good version, too. But if you love croissants, you need to go to Paris."

I take another sip of my drink. "Someday." *After I get into the FBI and work my butt off to move up the food chain to earn vacation time and enough money for said vacation . . .*

Kate takes a long sip from the straw, cheeks sucking in as she watches me. "No Paris for you, huh? Is it time or money you're short on?"

I let out a little laugh at her bluntness. "Both. And you certainly don't mince words."

"Not so much, no. Five years of babysitting my boys"—she gestures out toward the office—"has evaporated any ounce of tact I once had, which wasn't much."

"They send you in here?"

She sets her cup on the table, rolls it back and forth between her hands. "It *may* have been suggested that you might be more likely to lower your guard around a female."

"Mmm, right. Because all we girls secretly want to do is consume chocolate and gossip about boys."

She laughs. "That's exactly what I told Kennedy, that he insulted us both by the suggestion. But since he paid for these drinks at six bucks a pop, I told him I'd get the scoop."

"Which I won't be telling you," I say, smiling to soften it.

"No, I know. But I'm going to sit here for a second anyway." She leans back in her chair. "I just . . ." She breathes out. "You ever just need a break? Like you maybe get the sense you live for your job, only to wake up and realize you're barely living?"

Not until recently. Not until Ian.

The thought is so foreign, so out there, I blink in surprise. Surely I haven't let a guy I've known less than three weeks get under my skin.

"You don't like your job?" I ask, to avoid saying something I shouldn't.

"No, I love it. I can't think of anything I'd rather do more. It's just"—she stabs the straw at the frozen liquid—"lonely, I guess."

"No boyfriend? Girlfriend?" I ask, not wanting to assume.

"Nope." She says it in a clipped little voice that tells me there's more to the story.

"Anyone you're interested in?" I ask. I keep the question casual, even though I've already got a good idea of who's holding a piece of Kate Henley's heart. The question is whether she even knows.

Her eyes shadow for a second. *Oh yeah, she knows.* But instead of answering my question, she shifts her gaze to me. "What about you? Involved with anyone?"

"Nope." I wrap my lips around my straw.

She studies me. "Ian's a good guy, you know."

I choke a little on the Frappuccino. "What does Mr. Bradley have to do with my love life?"

"Nothing," she says, eyes wide and innocent.

I feel a moment of panic at my mistake, then I see her slight smirk. *Busted.*

"You like him," she says with a teasing grin as she chews her straw. "Rumor has it you and Ian had a 'meeting' last Friday after hours." She adds air quotes around *meeting* for emphasis.

"We discussed his case, yes," I say, the professional in me warring rather obnoxiously with the newly discovered part of me that wants nothing more than to pick Kate's brain on everything there is to know about Ian . . . and not for reasons that have anything to do with the case.

Kate rolls her eyes. "*Riiiiight.* I'll pretend not to notice that you're blushing right now, and that every time you're standing at my desk, you look at Ian's office to see if he's in."

Oh, so that's how it's going to be.

"*Perfect*," I retort. "And I'll pretend not to notice the way you look at Kennedy Dawson when he's not looking."

Her eyes narrow at me. "Careful there, SEC."

I lift my cup in a truce. "No more boy talk?"

She taps her cup against mine. "Not until the case is over. Then I want details."

"Once the case is over, you might hate my guts," I say regretfully.

"Nah. I already know how this all ends, and I've got a pretty good feeling we're going to be friends."

"Even if I send one of your bosses to jail?"

I expect her to get pissed or upset, but she just shakes her head. "Look, I've known Ian a lot longer than you have. Ian's *good.*"

"Heart of gold and all that?" I say with a smile.

"Yes," Kate says, her tone dead serious. "Did you know he sets up college scholarships for high school foster kids? Or that he rents out entire theme parks for the younger ones once a year?"

I sit back, a little stunned. "I didn't."

"He paid for my master's in business administration. Even Matt and Kennedy don't know about that." She blows out a breath. "I'm worried that you've only researched the version of Ian you want to see—the one who's bought a car he doesn't need, whose black book's thicker than the Bible."

I keep myself from outwardly flinching, but inside, I feel like a jerk. A jerk for assuming that just because Ian makes a ton of money, looks like he does, flirts like he does, that he has no substance.

In some ways, though, knowing the truth makes it worse. After our spontaneous dinner date a week ago, I'd spent way too much time wondering *what if.*

What if I wasn't investigating him?

What if he were innocent?

"Ms. Henley . . ." I break off, not sure what I want to say. Not sure of anything anymore.

She gives me a knowing look. "How about you call me Kate, I call you Lara, and you listen very carefully when I tell you Ian's the last person who'd ever get ahead by cheating. This job is his entire identity—this world, the long hours, the fast pace, the parties, the money, all of it. It's all he's ever wanted, and I know he wouldn't jeopardize it by taking a shortcut. Ever."

"You care about him," I say quietly.

Kate shrugs and stands, finishing her drink and tossing it in the trash. "Sure. But more important, I respect him. He's one of the good ones." She points a finger. "Put that in your weekly report."

I feel strangely regretful after she leaves, like the room's too quiet, my thoughts too loud. I find myself wishing that Kate could be right—that we could be friends after this is over.

An e-mail comes through from Steve, and I half-heartedly open it, figuring it'll be yet another request for evidence I haven't found, information that I'm not sure even exists.

The e-mail's not what I expect.

> L-
> Did you check social media re: Bradley case?
> -S

I set my drink aside and hit "Reply."

> Working on it. Most of my key players aren't on social media. Been slow going.

His reply's immediate.

Another tip just came through. Veronica Sperry.

"That's great, boss. Don't be cryptic or anything," I mutter.

I Google her name, straightening a bit when her LinkedIn profile indicates she's currently a technology consultant but she used to be a senior project manager at J-Conn.

Remembering Steve's social media prompt, I look her up on Facebook, rolling my eyes a bit when I see that her account has zero privacy settings configured. I don't get how people can leave every one of their personal photos open to any curious perv—or nosy SEC agent.

Then again, if I looked like Veronica Sperry, I might think differently. The woman's gorgeous. Long red hair, wide blue eyes, and a teeny-tiny waist.

I click through her photos, which are mostly a collection of pouty selfies and carefully posed nights out with her girl squad.

Then I see it.

Veronica's dressed to kill in a tight black dress at a glam party, judging from the gold balloons in the background and the glass of champagne in her hand. But it's not the balloons or the champagne that interest me. It's the man she's wrapped around.

I glance at the date of the photo, and my stomach sinks.

The same man who told me last Friday that he didn't know a single person from J-Conn had his tongue down the throat of Veronica Sperry the same month he sold his J-Conn stock.

Stunned, I slump back in my chair and take a sip of my coffee. But it no longer tastes so sweet.

15

IAN

Week 3: Friday Afternoon

"Dave, I'd do just about anything for you, but I'm not buying the Phillies."

"But they're for sale!" my foster father barks into the phone. "And you've got money."

"Not *that* kind of money," I say, spinning in my chair and flipping my pen in my fingers.

"They're pretty bad this year. You could probably get a deal."

I smile at the hope in his voice. The guy actually thinks I'm in a position to buy his favorite baseball team.

Even if I could afford to buy a damn MLB team (which I can't), he knows full well I'm a Mets guy now. It's a point of good-natured contention between us—he's pissed I didn't remain loyal to my "home team."

My stance? The fewer ties between my life in Philadelphia and me the better—Dave, a few charities, and Sabrina being the only exceptions.

"Well, think about it," Dave grumbles. "How's the case going? They send you to jail, you let me know. I've got some guys who can look out for you."

"Thanks, but I don't think it'll come to that." *I hope.*

"You take my suggestion to seduce the lady agent?"

I smile. *Lady agent.* I wonder how Lara would feel about the moniker.

"I tried. Didn't take. Trying to clear my name the old-fashioned way, though," I respond.

"Hiring someone to take out the witness?"

I bring the phone away from my ear and stare at it a second. "I'm not in the mob, Dave. What the hell kind of movies have you been watching?"

"Well, what did you mean?"

"I meant that I'm trying to figure out who's framing me."

I hear a knock at my open office door, spin around, and still in surprise when I see Lara standing there.

"Hey, Dave, I've gotta run."

"Sure, sure. Think about the Phillies, though, 'kay?"

"Yeah, will do," I lie, because I know I'll never get him off the line otherwise. I stand and slide my phone back in my pocket. "Ms. McKenzie, what can I—"

"You lied to me," she says, eyes blazing as she storms into my office, slamming the door behind her.

I blink, startled by her fury. I thought we were in a better place after our impromptu dinner last week, but apparently we're right back where we started.

No, we're *worse* than when we started, I realize as I take in the angry woman in front of me. She might have disdained me before, but whatever she's feeling for me right now goes well beyond that.

Well, that's just fucking fine by me, because I'm a little pissed, too. I'm tired of this woman acting like I'm shit on her shoe.

"I've never lied to you," I say, crossing my arms as she stops on the other side of my desk and sets a laptop in front of me.

"*Really*," she says scathingly, pointing at the screen.

I brace both hands on my desk, leaning down to see what's got her in a snit.

I recognize myself in a photo taken at a generic party I don't remember, making out with a woman . . . well, honestly, I don't remember her, either.

I glance back up at Lara. "You're pissed that I went to a party . . ." I glance back down at the screen to check the date. "Nearly a year ago?"

"I don't give a crap about the party," she says, pointing at the computer. "I care about the fact that you're making out with Veronica Sperry."

"Who?"

Her eyes narrow. "Playing dumb is beneath you."

"Well, *acting* dumb is beneath you," I say, rounding my desk to stand face-to-face with her. "I have no idea who the hell Veronica Sperry is and why you care."

"Veronica Sperry," she says in a barely restrained voice, "is a former J-Conn employee. You told me you didn't know anyone from J-Conn."

"I don't!" I shout, getting in her face. "I'm sorry I don't immediately recall the face of every woman I've kissed at a party, probably after a few drinks." I gesture back at the computer. "And from the looks of it, she was kissing me."

"Yeah, you look really victimized there, Mr. Bradley."

"There it is," I say, lifting a finger to point in her face. "You're not pissed because this woman's from J-Conn. You're pissed because I've got my hands on her."

Her mouth drops open. "Surely we're not back to that. You know, this *God's gift to women* act is getting really old."

I step closer so she has to tilt her head back to meet my eyes. "Tell me you're not a little bit jealous," I taunt. "That you haven't wondered what it would be like to be in her shoes."

"You're delusional."

"And you're reaching," I snap back. "I *barely* remember the party. I barely remember the woman!"

"Wow. I'd heard you collect women like trophies. I didn't realize you couldn't be bothered to even remember them."

Before I can think better of it, I reach out and pull her close. "I've never lied to you," I repeat. "Now it's your turn to tell me the truth. Why are you really pissed right now? Because you actually think this woman gave me the inside scoop on J-Conn? After fucking *weeks* of sniffing around without getting your precious evidence, I'd think you'd be thrilled. But you're not, and you know why? It's because this photo's proof that while some of us have been enjoying our lives, you've been too busy coloring inside the lines, judging others, and living a lonely shell of one."

Her mouth drops open, and I brace for a feisty retort, but instead, she blinks rapidly, almost as though she's trying to keep tears at bay.

I could apologize—I *should*. But I'm still too pissed, still too frustrated by this woman and her determination to push all my buttons. And for what? For an SEC case that we both know is bullshit?

She pulls away from me and calmly shuts her laptop, pulling it to her chest. "I think we're done here."

"Like hell." I reach out for her again, but she pulls her hand back.

"Don't," she says quietly. "Please don't."

I let her go, watching as she calmly leaves my office. I want her to slam the door. Hell, I probably deserve it. But she merely pulls it shut with a quiet *click* as she exits.

I stand still for a long time after she leaves, sucking in deep breaths in an effort to get my self-control back.

I'd accused her of being jealous, of wanting my hands on her, but the truth is, it's me who wants her. Me who wants nothing more than to strip off that fussy jacket, shove up that prim skirt, and see if she's as wet as I am hard from our sparring.

I swear and pull my phone out of my pocket, shooting off a message to Matt and Kennedy to make it a club night.

I need to get drunk.

And I need to get laid.

16

LARA

Week 3: Friday Night

"How about this?" I say, holding out a blue top.

Gabby looks up from where she's rummaging in my dresser with one hand, glass of wine in the other. She wrinkles her nose. "What is that? A poncho?"

"It's a flowy top," I say, holding it against me and looking in the full-length mirror. "It matches my eyes."

"Perfect, you can wear it to my aunt's birthday party next week and she'll love it, but you're not wearing it tonight." She holds up a tiny tank top. "What about this?"

"You're in my pajama drawer. I sleep in that."

"Yes, and if you wear it out tonight, you won't sleep alone," she says, giving the shirt an enticing little wiggle.

"Not all of us are models with taut, perfect skin," I say. I take a sip of my own wine as I pull a dress out of the closet. "How about this? It covers my arms."

"Oh, so it's perfect for a club!" she says sarcastically. She points to the bed. "Sit. You're wearing what I tell you to wear."

I do as she says, mainly because my thoughts are too jumbled to manage even the simple task of finding an outfit. She glances at my near-empty wineglass and makes a *tsk*ing noise, then goes to the kitchen and comes back with the bottle of Sauvignon Blanc.

"Okay, what's the *little black dress* situation?" she says after she's topped off my glass.

I sigh and sip the wine. "There are two on the far right."

She pulls them both out, then gives me an exasperated look. "These are funeral dresses."

"They're not!" I protest. "Well, okay, the one on the left is. But the lace one I got to wear to my holiday party my first year at—"

"Honey, no. I mean, good on you in that it looks like a *government holiday party* dress, with those long sleeves and flared skirt, but . . ."

"Wait, it has a V-cut back!"

"No. To both dresses," Gabs says decisively, putting them back in the closet. "Jackie O wore dresses more revealing than that, and I'm taking you to Pearl, which means you need to show some skin."

I groan and set my wine on the nightstand before flopping back on my bed.

She gives me a curious look over her shoulder. "Going out tonight was *your* idea."

"I know," I say, putting my arms over my eyes to block out the ugly fluorescent light. "But I'm rethinking."

"Well, don't," she says, coming to sit beside me, patting my knee. "You had a crappy day, and you're right to want to forget about it."

"You weren't there," I mumble into my arms, reliving the awfulness in Ian's office. "I humiliated myself."

"Well, from what you've told me, he was an ass."

"Yeah, but he was right," I say, dropping my arms back to my sides in exasperation. "I was acting like a weird, jealous girlfriend. I should have done my homework before going in there. I should have asked that woman first if she knew Ian."

Gabby gives me a sympathetic smile. "She got back to you?"

I stare at the ceiling and sigh. "Yes. She didn't remember that night, either. Apparently, it was her bestie's birthday, and they'd had martinis before even getting to that party. I showed her the picture, and she said, 'Hot. Who is he?'"

"So then, *not* his source," Gabby says.

"Nope."

"Did you tell him?"

I give her a look. "Wasn't quite ready for the *I told you so* lecture."

"Well, Monday will be soon enough for that," she says, clapping her hands and standing again. "Tonight, our only agenda involves vodka and flirting."

"Easy for you to say," I mutter. Gabby's one of those effortlessly charming women who makes every man feel like the center of her universe when she talks to him. It also doesn't hurt that she's five nine with perfect proportions and cheekbones you could slice a steak on.

She pulls out a pair of jeans. "These are tight-fitting, right?"

I give them a skeptical look. "Yeah."

She flings them at my chest. "Put 'em on. Now, where's that slinky strappy top you wear sometimes?"

"I don't think I own anything slinky."

"Yes you do. You just usually wear it under one of those ugly boxy things."

"A blazer?"

"Whatever." She waves her hand. "It's yellow and you look hot in it."

"You're thinking of my yellow silk shell, which is definitely meant to be worn under something."

"Not tonight. Tell me it's not at the dry cleaner's."

"It's not," I say. But the second she pulls it out of the closet, I wish I'd lied, because there's no way I'm wearing this out in public. It's got tiny spaghetti straps and a lace strip on both the top and bottom hemlines. It's not tight-fitting necessarily, but it's definitely low-cut. You don't notice so much when paired with a blazer and slacks, but . . .

"On. Now."

Arguing with her is pointless when she's in mama hen mode, so I do as she says. I spread my arms to the side and expect her to see that I was right.

Instead, she grins. "Perfect. Almost."

She walks toward me and gently pulls the band out of my hair. "Doesn't your head hurt from wearing all this heavy hair in a pony all the time?"

"Better than having it in my face."

"It's your best feature," she says, fluffing my hair a bit. "Now, let's talk shoes. That's one good thing about you spending all that time in fancy corporate offices. You've got nearly as many high heels as I do."

It's true. I do have a nice assortment of stilettos. I dress conservatively, but high heels are one area where sexy and business casual have plenty of overlap.

She selects a pair of strappy silver sandals and then practically wrestles me into a chair, where she applies a smoky-eye makeup look.

Gabby turns me toward the mirror. "Well?"

I wrinkle my nose. "I don't even look like myself."

"Sure you do. You just don't recognize this version, because she looks like she wants to have fun."

"I have fun," I protest.

She pats my cheek as she steps into her own platform heels. "No, sweetie, you don't. But tonight, you will."

17

Ian

Week 3: Friday Night, Late

"Remind me again why we're here?" Kennedy asks.

"Because we want to get laid," Matt says. "Well, I want to," he amends. "You and Ian *need* to."

It's nearly midnight on Friday, and though we're out at one of my favorite clubs, I . . . can't get into it. I used to come here a few times a week, but I haven't been out since before I met Lara, and now the whole thing feels wrong, like a suit that no longer fits quite right.

I take another sip of my drink, determined to get my life back, where things weren't so fucking complicated, where a certain blonde SEC investigator didn't have the power to hurt me.

Christ, is that right? Hurt?

Fuck this.

"He's right," I tell Kennedy, taking Matt's side. "I need a woman."

"Really?" Matt sounds surprised. "Because I've gotta tell ya, you don't look like a man on the prowl."

"More like Heathcliff," Kennedy says.

Matt and I both look at him, and he sighs in disgust. "Never mind. So, we all know why Ian needs to get laid—to get over Sassy SEC. Why do I need to?"

"Because you're a prig," Matt says.

"*Prig?*" Kennedy repeats, eyebrows raised.

"And here you thought your pretentious vocabulary would never rub off on us," I say, clinking my glass against Matt's with a smirk.

Kennedy rolls his eyes and nods toward the dance floor below. "This is really great," he says sarcastically. "What thirty-four-year-old adult *doesn't* enjoy listening to deafening, God-awful music in the dark while wasted twentysomethings rub all over each other?"

"Hey, it's not like anyone's making you endure that," Matt says. "We're in the VIP section. Can we just do what we used to do? Find three hot women and forget our troubles for a while?"

I want to. God, how I want to. I just need one night to forget that the carefree life I enjoyed just a month ago is turning to complete shit.

If only I could get a little excited about the prospect.

A waitress in a silver sequin bra and short skirt saunters over to us. "Another round?"

I hold up my empty cocktail glass in confirmation that I want another without taking my gaze off the scene below. Reserving a table requires bottle service, so there's Grey Goose and mixers on the table, but I'm enough of a regular for the staff to know to keep the Negronis coming.

"So, what's our plan?" Matt asks, dropping both arms around the back of the booth and studying me.

I turn my attention from the dancers to my friend. I'll give Matt credit. He's doing a damn good job acting like this is any other night out on the town. Like me, his shirtsleeves are rolled up to the elbow, tie loosened, suit jacket long gone. He's trying for casual, but he comes up short because his eyes are guarded and watchful as he studies me.

Still, at least he's better than Kennedy, who didn't even bother with casual. The man looks just as buttoned up at midnight as he did at noon.

"Well, we're never going to get anywhere with him looking like that," I say, gesturing at Kennedy.

"I want to agree, but we've seen too much to the contrary," Matt says. "One of life's great puzzles, why women dig a nerd."

"Indeed," Kennedy says. "Nearly as baffling as why they love boy wonders."

Matt flips Kennedy the bird, then shifts his attention to me. "Okay, let's have it. Spit out what's really bugging you so we can get on with our night."

"I'm frustrated," I admit, blowing out a breath. "McKenzie doesn't have shit on me. If she did, she'd have laid it out there already, escalated her case, and brought in a subpoena. Instead, she's just pushing papers around. It's like she's trying to manufacture something happening just by perseverance and stubbornness."

"Sounds like someone I know," Kennedy mutters.

I give him a look and open my mouth to snap back, but Matt interrupts.

"You said she's angling for FBI, right? Maybe this case is a make-or-break thing for her."

"Yeah, maybe," I muse.

"That why you made her cry?" Kennedy asks. "Kate said—"

"I didn't make her cry," I ground out. "Look, I wanted a night out to forget what's going on in my life, not rehash it. I appreciate the concern, but it's not what I need right now. Either back off or leave."

A moment of silence stretches across the table, and the relentless throb of the music does nothing to ease the tension.

Finally, Kennedy nods and tosses back the rest of his drink. "I get it."

I give him a wary look. "You do?"

"Yeah. If I were in your shoes, I'd be doing the same. Well, not this," he says, waving at the scene around us. "But I'd be trying to maintain some semblance of my normal life as well."

"So you'd be at home with some hideous philosophy tome?" Matt asks.

Kennedy flashes a quick grin. "You guys mind?"

"Go," I say, gesturing with my glass. "I need to get laid, and you'll only crash my game."

Kennedy leans forward. "Worried I might get the girl?"

I snort. "Get out of here, old man."

"Going," he says, pushing his empty glass toward the center of the table and standing. "See you Monday. Try not to get arrested or dead."

"I make zero promises," I call after his retreating back. "What about you?" I ask Matt after Kennedy leaves.

Matt cracks his knuckles and surveys the room. "I'm not going to leave you alone at a table for six. Let's get you some female company."

"I'm too old to need a wingman, dude. Besides, I thought you wanted to get laid, too."

He gives me an idle smile. "Who said I'm not?"

My eyebrows lift. "You work fast."

He holds up his iPhone. "Booty text."

"Anyone I know?"

Matt finishes the rest of his drink. "Lynnae."

I groan. Lynnae Silverton is one of Matt's many *blink and you'll miss her* ex-girlfriends. She's hotter than hell and twice as psycho.

She's also the least of my concerns. I can't manage my own love life these days, much less his, so I wave him away. "Go."

He stands but hesitates, running a hand over his neck. "Ian, if you want—"

"I'm fine," I say, meeting his gaze. "Really." And I mean it. The entire point of this evening was to escape the mess of my life. I need a break from the constant overanalysis, even if my friends mean well.

Matt studies me for a moment in a shrewd, assessing way that reminds me why he's so damn good at his job. "You're fine," he says.

I throw up my hands. "That's what I just said."

"Yeah, but I'm the genius." He smirks, patting my shoulder. "Means more when I say it."

I roll my eyes as he laughs and goes off to hook up with his ex.

A few minutes later, I'm all alone at my VIP table. Any other time I'd be on the move, looking for a lady—or three—to keep me company, but I'm not in a hurry tonight.

For the first time in weeks, I feel like I've got a moment of solitude that's not actually solitude. It gives me a second to catch my breath, a break from bullshitting, and yet the pulse of the music, the hundred people around me keep me from being alone with my thoughts.

I've never particularly been one for being by myself. Too much time to dwell on shit that shouldn't be dwelled on. But I like it even less with the SEC on my ass. My thoughts are split fifty-fifty between going to jail and Lara McKenzie, and I'm not sure which one is more troublesome. Especially since the latter is the one who wants to put me in the former.

I spin my cocktail glass idly without taking a drink. I came here tonight to get obliterated and laid, and I don't feel like doing either. There's something about having your life turned upside down that makes you stop and look at said life.

Honestly? I don't know if I like what I see. I won't say I have regrets, per se. It's pointless to dwell on what you can't change, and on principle, I'm still a fan of *work hard, play hard.*

But I always figured I could play as hard as I wanted until I didn't want it anymore. That I'd have a chance for the wife and kid and Disneyland vacations when the time felt right.

Now? I'm a little terrified I won't even get that chance. Not unless I can convince Lara that while I may be a womanizing bastard, I'm not a law-breaking one.

Shit.

I take another sip of my drink and shift to scan for the waitress and close out. I should be at home working on that damn list of people who might have framed me, not pretending I'm twenty-four without a care in the world.

The room's more crowded than it was just a few minutes ago, and I don't see my waitress through the tight asses in tiny dresses and bros unsubtly trying to make their move.

In the sea of bare female legs, a denim-clad pair catches my gaze—both because they're long and damn good legs and because they're unusual. Jeans in a club? Maybe in January. On a sticky summer evening, most of the women are wearing short skirts or dresses.

The woman stands up from her table, and my eyes travel from the sexy heels up the dark-blue of the tight jeans, lingering on a great ass. The yellow top's both slinky and a little bit prim, with a crisscross back and preppy lace.

The hair's long and blonde, the face . . . *Come on, darling, turn around.*

The woman heeds my silent command, bending to pick up her purse and turning so I can see her profile . . .

I spill my drink all over my shirt.

Worse, it's a *red* drink on a *white* shirt.

"Motherfucker," I growl, wiping stupidly at the stain, my mind reeling. *What is she doing here?*

Pearl is quite possibly the last place I'd ever expect to see Lara McKenzie. Maybe it isn't her, just a look-alike.

The waitress apparently decides to take pity on me, because a wad of small square cocktail napkins is dropped onto the table in front of me.

"Thanks," I mutter, grabbing a couple of napkins and swiping futilely at the red blotch on my chest.

"I've heard club soda works for red-wine stains. Not sure about the fruit punch thing you've got going."

My hand goes still. That's not the waitress's voice.

I lift my head, and my gaze collides with familiar blue eyes, fears confirmed. Not the waitress. Lara.

"It's not fruit punch." My tone's just a touch childish, but I don't care. This is not what I need right now.

Lara's eyes drift down to my shirt and back up. Her lifted eyebrows say it all: *Looks like fruit punch.*

"It's a Negroni," I explain, as though that's what matters at the moment.

"Oh right," she says. "My grandmother used to drink those."

Fantastic, I think as I rub at the shirt. Now I remind her of her grandmother twice over—first with the orchid, now with my cocktail of choice.

I glance up again, and Lara's gone. I'm torn between disappointment and relief that she didn't stick around to witness more of the train wreck that my evening's becoming.

I pull out my wallet, hoping I have enough cash to cover everything so I can get the hell out of here without having to wait for the waitress to find her way back to me.

"Holy crap, that's a lot of cash," Lara says, returning to my table.

I blink in surprise, first at the cup of clear liquid that's set in front of me, then at the woman who slides into the booth across from me.

"Club soda," Lara says, nodding her chin at the cup. "Let's see if it works."

I give it a skeptical glance. She reaches across the table and pushes the glass closer.

Reluctantly I pick up a clean napkin, dunk it unceremoniously into the soda, and then rub at my shirt.

The result is a wet ring around the red stain that fades . . . not at all. Now my shirt's red *and* wet.

I look up and see that she's withholding a laugh. Barely.

Crumpling the napkin into a ball, I throw it across the table at her, and she bats it away before it hits her chin, the laugh slipping out.

No, not laugh. Giggle. The SEC investigator is giggling. And not an annoying, high-pitched girlie giggle, either. Just a feminine sound of enjoyment . . . at my expense.

"Sorry," she says, still smiling.

I raise an eyebrow. "Are you?"

Her gaze drops to the stain, then meets mine again. "Not really. How much is it bothering you to look less than perfect right now?"

I grin. "Are you saying I look perfect other times?"

Her smile disappears, and I realize I pushed too far, was too flirty, especially after our argument earlier.

"I should go," she says, scooting toward the edge of the booth.

I reach out a hand to stop her, almost touching her arm but not quite. "No, stay. You can point and laugh. I'll even let you take pictures." I soften my voice. "Just . . . don't leave."

She hesitates, and my stomach clenches with the realization that she's going to walk away.

I should be used to it. Most of my life's been spent braced for the moment where I'm shipped off to the next home, or told that *scholarship kids* aren't welcome, or that I need a sponsor to get into whatever bullshit club only takes people related to the Rockefellers.

I thought I'd grown used to it—that rejection or dismissal no longer has the power to hurt me like it did my nine-year-old self or even my nineteen-year-old self.

But I've never wanted—needed—anything like I want her to stay. To want me back.

Lara sighs, and then tosses her purse onto the seat beside her. "Okay, I'll stay. But no pictures." She holds up a warning finger. "I shouldn't be seen with you out on a Friday night, and there definitely shouldn't be any photo evidence of it."

Slowly, the tightness in my chest loosens, the tension replaced by something even more dangerous. I clear my throat to hide my reaction.

"So, I, um . . ." She takes a deep breath. "I owe you an apology."

I look up in surprise. "What?"

"I should have done my research before I came barging into your office today," she says, holding my gaze. "I should have contacted Veronica Sperry first, seen if it was even a valid piece of evidence. I've looked into it since then, and I was . . . wrong. She laughed it off as a drunken moment, said she doesn't even remember that night, much less the kiss."

I feel a surge of hope. "Does this mean you're dropping the case?"

She hesitates, and I deflate slightly.

"Never mind," I mutter.

"Mr. Bradley—"

To change the topic from whatever SEC line she's going to feed me, I nod in the direction of the table she left, where a very hot woman is talking to a guy with dark hair. "Friends of yours?"

She glances over her shoulder, her eyes assessing. "Gabby. That's her ex."

"Ah. Explains the intense conversation," I say, noting the way the woman's hands move furiously as she talks. Even from across the room, everything about both of their body languages screams unfinished business.

"I'm giving them space. They dated for a year. She was crazy about him, and she thought he felt the same. But he got a job offer in Amsterdam and took it."

"She didn't go with?"

"She wasn't asked."

I study her for a moment, trying to assess her mood. She seems nervous, but I don't think it's me. In fact, I get the distinct sense that it's the club that has her slightly on edge, and I'm the familiar safe space in the room.

The theory pleases me more than I care to admit.

"Drink?" I ask, gesturing at the bottles of vodka and mixers on the table.

"Oh, I shouldn't."

I reach for one of the clean glasses and pour a splash of Grey Goose into it, as well as a scoop of rapidly melting ice from the bucket. "Tonic? Soda?"

"Mr. Bradley—"

"Lara," I interrupt, and her gaze collides with mine at my use of her first name. "Have a drink with me," I say, my voice a little gruff.

She swallows before her gaze darts to her friend's table. Finally, she sighs. "Tonic. Please."

I fill the glass with the tonic and slide it toward her.

She looks up. "You're not having one?"

"I only like Negronis."

"Perhaps you should reconsider," she says, her gaze dropping to my shirt. "To something clear."

I pretend to think this over. "Valid point."

I make myself a vodka tonic as well, not because I particularly want it but because I want her to feel more at ease.

I lift my glass in a toast. "To . . . Well, hell. I don't know that I've got a damn thing in my life to toast to right now."

"That's not true," she says softly, putting her glass down. "You've got great friends. Your assistant would die for you. You probably make more money in a month than I will in my lifetime."

"And I've got the SEC just waiting to take it all away," I say. Not to punish her but to remind her—to remind both of us—just how much power she has over my life.

"Mr. Bradley—" She takes a breath. "Ian. I've told you since the very beginning that if you're guilty, I'll find the evidence. But if you're innocent, I'll find that, too."

I force a smile. "How long until you think you'll drop that *if*?"

"You're frustrated. I get that. It's a long process, and there are a lot of moving parts. A lot of them out of my control."

I frown. "Meaning?"

She sighs and rubs her fingers tiredly through her hair. "Meaning this case is wearing on me, too. And that's all I can say about it."

I stifle the urge to do what I usually do—push until I get my way.

It's different with her, and I haven't quite figured out how to navigate it—or if I even want to.

I gesture at her hair to change the topic. "You look different with your hair down. And without the glasses."

I bite back the urge to tell her she looks hot as hell. I've had many dirty thoughts wondering what Lara McKenzie's skin looks like, and though her top is modest for club standards, seeing her bare arms, shoulders, and a subtle amount of cleavage is enough for me to know it's every bit as smooth as I've imagined. Her hair, too, begs for a man's fingers to tangle in it, but . . .

I miss the glasses. Not just because they're my favorite fantasy material these days but because they're her. I'd bet anything the glasses are the real Lara, and this smoky-eyed, lip-gloss version is her way of trying to escape herself, just for a night.

Much like I am.

"Yeah, I'm a regular Clark Kent," she mutters.

I sip my drink and try not to wince at the sweetness of the tonic. "Come again?"

"Metropolis? You know, Superman? Clark Kent's glasses being his disguise?" She waves her hand. "Never mind. So, do you always buy bottles of vodka for yourself?"

"Nah, Kennedy and Matt were here earlier. Both bailed on me."

"Why?"

"They got sick of my company."

"Hmm." Lara nods behind my shoulder. "There's a group of women over there who I'm sure wouldn't mind taking their place. Or mine."

I don't turn around. Don't take my eyes off Lara. "I'm fine like this."

"Sitting in a club with an SEC investigator?"

I shrug. "She's a pain in the ass, but it turns out I find her a little compelling."

"I know how that goes," she says, running a finger around the rim of her glass in a gesture that shouldn't be erotic but has my body humming all the same. I want her to touch me like that.

"Do you?" I ask, my voice a little bit lower than usual.

She meets my eyes. "Hypothetically, I *may* know what it's like to be aware of someone who's completely off-limits."

"Sounds tricky. Do I know him?"

Lara takes a sip of her drink. "You know his type."

"Good-looking? Good in bed?"

She laughs. "More like arrogant, stubborn, and really accustomed to getting his way."

I nod. "Ah, yep. I do know him. I can assure you he's also good-looking and amazing in bed."

She rolls her eyes at my wink. "I'll plead the fifth on the first, ignore the second altogether."

"You don't have to," I say before I can think better of it.

Lara's head snaps up. "What?"

"Look, Lara . . ." I have the most annoying, unfamiliar urge to loosen my tie more. I can't remember the last time I've been this nervous. "This thing with us, I know it's complicated."

Her eyes are wide with panic. "There isn't a thing with us. There *can't* be."

"Why, damn it?" I snap. "Why, when this is all over, we can't—"

"Because you're you and I'm me," she says. "Even without the investigation, we're a mismatch. You're the life of every party, and I can't even keep a flower alive."

The damn orchid again.

"Lara—"

Before I can speak, I smell a wave of sweet perfume, then feel arms wind around my neck.

"Hey, Ian, baby. Haven't seen you around for a while."

I turn my head just as a woman who looks vaguely familiar but whose name I'm not sure I ever even knew presses her mouth to mine.

Shit. *Shit.*

I pull back. "Oh, hey . . ."

"Taya," she says, winding a lock of hair around her finger and not looking the least bit perturbed she just kissed someone who didn't remember her name.

Good God. Was that my life?

I look at Lara, braced for her disgust, but she merely looks resigned as she meets my eyes. "Point proven."

She stands, and my throat tightens in panicked frustration.

"Wait, Lara—" I make a grab for her wrist but miss.

And then she's gone.

18

LARA

Week 3: Friday Night, Later

"Lara! Damn it, would you hold up a sec?"

Out of the corner of my eye, I see Ian drop a wad of cash on the table and say something to Taya, but I'm already heading toward the exit.

I luck out. There's a huge group entering the VIP section. I slip out just before the mob moves in, but a dozen or so tipsy patrons block Ian.

You want to know what I was doing back there?

Great question.

I want to know what I was doing. I've been wondering for the past twenty minutes.

Here's what I do know . . . when I looked across the VIP lounge just in time to watch Ian spill a drink all over himself, I felt alive.

For the first time in a long time.

I don't know what it was exactly. Perhaps just sheer delight that someone so good-looking isn't perfect after all.

Or maybe it was the fact that after hours spent in front of a computer screen staring at names and numbers, I needed the visceral reminder that I'm dealing with real people in the real world.

I'd told myself that I'd just take a second to apologize for my unprofessional behavior that afternoon in his office, and then I went and topped that with a whole other layer of unprofessionalism.

If my boss found out . . . if *anyone* found out . . .

Bye-bye, FBI.

No recommendation letter from Steve, and I'd have to wait who knows how long for another opportunity like this one.

Not that I'm wishing for Ian to be guilty. Quite the opposite. It's just . . .

Well, I'm all jumbled, in case you couldn't tell.

I'm nearly to the door when fingers wrap around my arm, pulling me back around. I lose my balance a little bit and bump awkwardly into Ian's chest.

He keeps me from stumbling, but the contact only makes me feel more unsteady.

"You all right?" he asks.

Damn him. He seems genuinely concerned, and that makes it so much harder to walk away.

I mean, it's not like I want to have a fling with the guy. I'm not the kind of girl who hooks up with guys like Ian.

But . . . I like him. I like him a lot.

He makes me laugh, and he challenges me, and . . .

"I've got to go."

"I'll help you get a cab."

"Shit," I mutter. "I can't leave Gabby." I pull out my phone and text her.

"I'll walk you back to her table," he says as I type. "Or back to mine. Or we can talk here."

I push at his chest in exasperation. "Don't you get it? I'm SEC. You're suspected of insider trading. We can't do this."

His other hand comes up, catches my other elbow. "You don't have to cushion the blow, Lara. If you don't want to be seen with me because of the stain, you can just tell me. I can take it."

His voice is light and teasing, and a laugh bubbles out before I can stop it, my head dropping forward in defeat. Only he's right there, so my forehead rests on his chest. I mean to pull back, but his hand moves from my arm, slipping under my hair to cup the back of my neck. He squeezes lightly, as though wanting to take away some of my tension. And maybe he can, because I let myself stay still, just for a moment, and I know it's crazy, but when I pull away, I feel a little bit steadier.

"Thanks." My throat is dry, and I clear it, try again. "Thank you."

His hands fall away. "You're welcome."

Our gazes lock and hold for a long moment, and I find myself wishing so badly that things could be different. That I wasn't SEC. That he wasn't Wall Street. That there was no investigation. That the stakes weren't my dream career of the FBI versus his career and reputation on the line.

I wish he wasn't a notorious womanizer. I wish I knew how to flirt . . .

My phone buzzes, and I glance down. It's Gabby telling me that she's going home with her ex but that they're happy to share a cab back to the apartment to drop me off first.

Third wheel. Just what I don't need right now.

I text her to tell her I'm fine—that I'll get a cab on my own.

I drop my phone back in my purse and look up at Ian. He smiles, but it's a sad smile, like he knows what I'm thinking and he understands. Because he feels the same.

"You good?" he asks quietly.

"Better, yeah."

"You think people will recognize us."

I lift a shoulder. *Yeah.*

"Say no more." Ian beckons for my purse.

I reluctantly hand it over. "I might have a Tide pen in there, but it won't make a dent in your stain."

"You know, most women bring one of those small envelope-style purses to a club, not a suitcase," he says, rummaging through my stuff.

"Well, in case it wasn't terribly obvious, I'm not exactly experienced at the club thing. What are you doing?" I ask in a panic as he pushes aside a tampon.

He pulls out my sunglasses case and waggles it at me as he hands my bag back.

"If you're checking to see if they're designer, I assure you they're knockoff." I stop short of telling him that some of us make a five-figure salary, not a seven-figure one like him.

He ignores me and opens the case, pulling out the sunglasses. Then he slides them onto my face and grins, clearly pleased with himself. "There. A disguise."

I use one finger to pull the glasses down my nose an inch and give him a look over the top of them. "Seriously? It's almost one a.m."

"People will think you're famous and wonder who you are."

"Fantastic. Because I was really hoping they'd stare more."

He jerks his chin toward my purse. "So, about that Tide pen . . ."

I shake my head. "No chance. But if you're embarrassed . . ."

After a quick glance to see we're in the shadows near the emergency exit with no one around, I step closer and button the top button of his dress shirt.

Yes, that's right. I'm re-dressing Ian Bradley.

I try to keep it casual, almost maternal and businesslike. But then my fingers accidentally brush against his throat, and we both have to pretend not to notice. Or at least I pretend. Maybe he really doesn't notice.

I pull out his pocket square—because yes, the man's wearing one— and tuck the corner into the neck of his now buttoned-up shirt so it fans down over his chest in a ridiculous diagonal square.

Did I mention the pocket square is lavender?

"There," I say.

He looks down and smooths a hand over the purple silk. "This is nice. A really manly look."

I nod in agreement and push the sunglasses back on my face. "Like a man bib. Too bad you weren't wearing it earlier to catch the spill."

He looks at me expectantly. "All right. Are we disguised enough to Bonnie and Clyde our way out of here?"

I want to. So badly. But . . . "Ian."

He sighs. "I'm thrilled we're on a first-name basis, but I'm not digging that tone."

I lift my eyebrows. "Do you even *know* that tone?"

"I've heard *of* it once. Rejection, is it? Never happened to me. Till now."

I open my mouth, wanting to tell him that I've never felt the way he makes me feel before, but no words come out. I don't know if I'm smart or just a coward. But when he presses the pad of his thumb gently against my bottom lip, I know I'm a fool.

He gives a quick smile. "Come on. Let's get you a cab home. I'm pretty sure your friend's gonna be a while." A moment later, he ushers me out into the warm night air.

"How'd you know the alarm wouldn't sound?" I say, gesturing at the emergency door.

"They turned off the alarm a few months ago. Too many drunk couples stumbling outside to make out."

"Speaking from experience?"

He winks. "Wouldn't you like to know?"

"I think I already do," I grumble.

"Now, now, Ms. McKenzie," he teases. "Have we learned nothing today about making assumptions?"

"So you haven't come out that side door and made out with club bunnies?" I ask.

"Nah, I have," he says, stepping toward the sidewalk and lifting a hand to hail a cab.

"Right," I mutter, unable to keep the grumpiness out of my voice.

"For what it's worth," he says, not looking at me as a cab pulls to a stop in front of us. "When I make out with you, it won't be against the wall of a seedy club. And I will definitely remember it."

"What do you mean, *when*?" I say, staring at his profile. "I told you—"

He puts a hand over my mouth and opens the cab door with the other.

"Where do you live?" he asks, lifting his hand from my face so I can answer.

Too confused to think clearly, I give him my address, which he relays to the driver before motioning me inside.

I pull off my sunglasses as I climb into the back seat. "Ian—"

He puts a playful finger against my lips. "That's Mr. Bradley to you. For now." He winks and shuts the door.

I turn around as the cab pulls away from the curb and watch as he lifts his arm, hailing another cab for himself. When it stops, he turns toward me and grins, as though knowing I'm watching him.

He fades from view as my cab takes a right turn, and I flop back against the seat, shaking my head. "Unbelievable."

But I'm smiling.

19

Ian

Week 4: Monday Morning

I look up at the knock on my door, and though I love Kate Henley like a sister, I feel a stab of disappointment that it's not Lara. And *because* she's like a sister, Kate totally calls me on it.

"I saw that," she says, waggling a finger at me as she comes into my office. "You sulked."

"I don't sulk."

"Not usually, no. Just apparently when your crush isn't here."

"Is this conversation optional?" I mutter, turning back to my computer screen.

She settles into the chair across from me. "You're sulking *and* grumpy. That's usually Kennedy's gig."

"I'm not grumpy."

"Little bit," she says, holding up her fingers.

"You know I can fire you, right?"

"Not without Matt's and Kennedy's agreement." She smiles sweetly as she crosses her legs and settles in. "Now, tell Kate *alllll* about what's bothering you. Relationship problems?"

"Go away."

"Oh, that's right," she muses, as though I haven't spoken. "You don't do relationships."

I look at her. "I do relationships."

"Um, no. Matt sometimes does. You, never. I don't think Kennedy even knows how to date." She furrows her brow.

"That's bullshit. I've had girlfriends." *One. Sort of.*

"You're thinking of Anne? That was four years ago. And it lasted for, what, two weeks? Barely counts." She looks down at her pale-pink manicure. "So, about Lara . . ."

My gaze sharpens. "Since when are you two on a first-name basis? You've been calling her 'the SEC' for weeks."

She waves this away. "Keep your enemies close and all that. Plus, she's one of the only females in this place, and ovaries bond with ovaries."

"Nope. Out," I say, pointing to the door.

Kate doesn't budge. "You can't be thinking of seducing her."

I sit back and allow myself to ask the question out loud that's been on my mind all weekend. "Why not?"

"Because she's not like one of your usual women," she says incredulously. "She's not some party girl out for a quick lay. Hell, Ian, she's not out for a lay at all. Not with you. Not as long as she's investigating you."

Just what I need, another person reminding me that Lara's off-limits.

"Was there something you needed from me, or were you just here to deliver the lecture?" I ask with a bit more bite than usual.

"It's Dave's birthday next week. Want me to get him something? Spare TV?"

"Nah, see if you can get season tickets to the Flyers. Best seats you can find."

"I thought he liked baseball," Kate says, making a note in her phone.

"He likes anything where yelling, beer, and junk food are encouraged."

"Hockey it is." She taps a few more times. "It's Lara's birthday next week, too," she says, not looking up from her phone.

I jerk to attention. "It is?"

She looks up and grins. "I have no idea. Just wanted to see if I was right about your interest in her, and I totally am. Ask her out."

I close my eyes. "Kate. You're giving me whiplash. You just said I *couldn't* ask her out."

"That's when I thought you just wanted to sleep with her. Now I know that you *like* her."

"Jesus," I mutter, running my hands through my hair.

"No wonder you've been moody," she says, leaning forward. "Have you kissed her yet?"

"Bye, Kate," I say, waving her toward the door.

She studies me. "Have you ever even been on a date, Ian?"

"Of course I've been on a date. I date all the time."

"Really." She sits back and crosses her legs. "When and where was the last date you went on?"

I mentally run through my recent encounters with women. The last being . . . well, hell. Now that I think about it, I haven't actually gotten laid in weeks.

That can't be right.

"And I'm not talking about sex," Kate drones on, reading my thoughts as she so often does. "I'm talking dinner. Drinks. Conversation. A date that wasn't just a stepping-stone to sex."

I think. And think. And realize that perhaps the closest I've come to anything remotely resembling a date in years happened at that restaurant with Lara after she got stood up. And again at the club.

I look at Kate. "You want to go out to dinner with me?"

She laughs. "Nope. I don't date my bosses."

That's definitely true. Kennedy, Matt, and I made a pact years ago that Kate was off-limits, little-sister territory. Not because she's that much younger than us, but because we adore her.

And all three of us know she deserves better than any of us can offer.

Still . . . I give her a playful look. "But if you did date bosses, it wouldn't be me, would it?"

Her laughter dies, and she gives me a warning look. "What's that supposed to mean?"

Right on cue, Kennedy strolls into my office, pausing briefly when he sees the back of Kate's head. "Am I interrupting?"

"Yes, and thank God for it," Kate says with a last warning glare for me.

Kennedy ambles toward my desk, dropping into the seat beside Kate. "What are we talking about?"

Kate leans toward him and loudly whispers, "Ian's trying to remember the last time he went on an actual date."

"That would be never," Kennedy says without hesitation.

Kate nods. "Exactly."

"Guys, my love life is not open for discussion."

"You don't have a love life," Kennedy says, flipping through e-mail on his phone.

"Well, neither do you," I say, thoroughly out of patience with this whole thing.

He doesn't look up from his phone. "I've had relationships."

I see Kate go slightly stiff at this announcement, though Kennedy doesn't seem to notice. Then again, he doesn't seem to notice much as far as Kate's concerned. It's like he's got a blind spot. He's fiercely protective of her—we all are—but he also keeps her at arm's length, almost as though he's wary of her. And it bugs her, I think.

"What relationships?" I ask him.

He shrugs. "I date women from my social circle."

Kate's mouth drops open. "Your *social circle?*"

"You know what I mean," he says, still distracted by his phone.

"Not really," she says.

"People . . ." He waves his hand. "People I grew up with. People I know through my parents and schooling."

I cover my mouth with my hand to disguise my laugh at the word *schooling.*

"Oh, *I* see," Kate says with a nod. "People you *summered* with."

My laugh slips out at the same time Kennedy says, "Yes, exactly—" He breaks off and looks up at Kate, then me. "You're mocking me."

"A little bit, Gatsby," I say.

He clicks off his phone and looks at me. "Why are we talking about relationships in the first place?"

"Ian's got it bad for Lara."

"I'm aware. What's that have to do with dating?"

"That's what I mean by 'has it bad,'" Kate says smugly. "He wants to date her, not just bone her."

I raise my eyebrows. "*Bone* her?"

She shrugs. "Or whatever. Insert the verb of your choice."

I wisely keep from sharing that I have many verbs in mind when it comes to Lara, each one dirtier than the last. Instead, I say, "I don't want to date her." The words are automatic, but I'm not at all sure they're true. Spending time with Lara is different from every other woman where I don't look past the one night.

Lara McKenzie isn't a one-night kind of woman. She's an all-the-nights kind of woman.

Surprisingly, the thought doesn't freak me out nearly as much as it should.

The question is—how the hell do I convince someone who doesn't want to be seen with me at a club to give me a goddamn chance?

I'm saved from my own thoughts by the arrival of Sabrina and Matt, along with the wave of sexual tension that they always seem to ride on.

"See," Sabrina says smugly, strutting into my office and gesturing at Kennedy, Kate, and me. "I told you they'd be in here."

Matt rolls his eyes. "I never said I disagreed. What I said was, *What the hell are you doing here?*"

"And *I* said I was looking for Ian and Kate," Sabrina says coolly.

I only have two guest chairs, so Kennedy stands to give his to Sabrina. "Hi, dear," he murmurs, kissing her cheek.

She pats his jaw affectionately. "Hey, love."

Kennedy and Sabrina have gotten along since day one. They're not as close as Sabrina and myself—they don't have our history. But like us, there's an easiness to their friendship thanks to a complete lack of chemistry that allows them to interact like normal humans.

"So . . ." Sabrina crosses her legs and sets her purse on the floor. "What are we talking about? I sense interesting topics at work."

"Ian wants to ask out the SEC," Kate says in a loud whisper.

"Oh, now that *is* interesting!" Sabrina says.

My entire net worth for a pistol right now.

"Interesting or not, he can't ask her out," Matt says, going to the window and shoving his hands in his pockets.

"Why not?" Sabrina demands.

"He can't ask her out *yet*," Kate clarifies. "Not until the case is over."

They're right. Lara cares too much about her career to date the guy she's investigating. Or sleep with him.

Ian wants to ask out the SEC . . .

Kate's words echo in my head. She'd said it teasingly but also . . . truthfully.

I *do* want to ask out the SEC. I want to date Lara.

And if there's anything I've learned from my time fighting out of the Philly slums, it's how to navigate the long game—how to take small but crucial steps to get what I want.

And Lara McKenzie's exactly what I want.

20

LARA

Week 4: Monday Night

I sip my wine and debate the delivery options on my Seamless app. "Thai or Chinese, Thai or Chinese," I muse to no one.

Regardless of what I end up with, I have every intention of ordering the greatest items. One of the downsides of living with a model is that there's a lot of kale and lean protein in the house. When she does agree to order takeout, it's usually with some God-awful special direction such as, "Don't cook in oil, please."

What, I ask you, is the point of delicious fried rice, if not for the oil part?

Tonight, Gabs is at her on-off-whatever boyfriend's place, so *I* get to order whatever the heck I want.

I take another sip of wine, then wrinkle my nose. I'm not a wine snob, but even I can tell it's awful. It was cheap to begin with, and the fact that it's been open for days has done nothing for it.

I reluctantly dump it down the drain. I'd really wanted an adult beverage to distract me from the fact that it's Monday and I haven't heard from Ian since Friday night.

I shouldn't care. I should be relieved.

Just like I should be relieved that I didn't see him at Wolfe today. Instead I feel a little . . . *blah*. Like colors are just a little less bright when he's not around.

There's a knock at my door, and I let out a quiet groan, because there's a 90 percent chance that it's Mrs. Peonta from across the street, who forgets her keys daily. We have a spare, and I wouldn't mind the interruption if she didn't use every encounter as a chance to tell me that in her day, women had three babies by the time they were my age.

I look through the peephole, then rear back. It's *so* not Mrs. Peonta.

To make sure I'm not hallucinating, I put my face back up to the door.

Nope, still there. I'm still looking at Ian Bradley standing in my hallway, a bottle of wine under one arm, takeout bag dangling from his fingers.

I put a hand over my pounding heart. All of this, just from seeing the guy through a peephole. When did I turn into *that* girl?

He rolls his eyes at my delay. "Open the door, Ms. McKenzie."

"What are you doing here?" I call through the door.

"Trying to feed you," he says, lifting the bag. "Also, to get in your pants," he says loudly, clearly for the benefit of my neighbors. "Maybe find out if your curtains match your—"

"Oh, for God's sake," I say, jerking the door open and pulling him inside. "How old are you?"

"Old enough to know what I want, clever enough to know how to get it," he says with a wink as he sets the bag and wine on my kitchen counter.

"Do you have any idea how much trouble we'd both be in if anyone knew that you were here?" I say. "The conflict of interest of us hanging out socially . . ."

I've been practicing this line all weekend, but I've forgotten the rest because Ian Bradley's in my apartment, and for something that's so unequivocally wrong, it feels . . .

Totally *right*.

Before I can register what's happening, Ian's opening all my kitchen drawers and rummaging around until he comes up with a corkscrew. "Wine? I know you ordered white at the restaurant, but this is a great red. Don't make me drink alone, Lara."

It's my first name that does it. I'd never realized how the simple use of someone's name can be used as foreplay, but ever since the night at the club, I've been thinking about the way my name rolls off Ian's tongue. It feels like seduction at its most effective.

He lifts his eyebrows. *Well?*

"Okay," I say slowly. "*One* glass of wine."

"Perfect," he says, opening the bottle.

"Ian. What are you doing here?"

He looks away, pouring us each a glass and handing me one. "We'll get to that." He takes a sip of the wine as he looks around, surveying my tiny apartment. "Nice."

"Yeah, I'm sure it puts your penthouse to shame," I say, looking at my home and seeing what he sees. Secondhand couch. TV perched on top of two wine crates Gabby nabbed from the liquor store trash. A kitchen table with an old issue of the *Wall Street Journal* rolled up beneath one of the legs so it doesn't wobble.

"I don't live in a penthouse," Ian says matter-of-factly. "Not yet. But it's on my forty-before-forty list."

"Naturally. And how are your chances looking?" I ask.

He turns back to me, his smile slow and seductive as he meets my gaze. "Haven't you heard? When I set my mind on something, I always get what I want."

The way he looks at me makes it clear what he wants: *me*.

And suddenly I'm warm and a little breathless for reasons that have nothing to do with the wine.

I look away, and he lets me off the hook, giving his wineglass a quick swirl and taking a sniff in that way rich people seem to do instinctively.

"You sure you don't want to drink that out of a sippy cup? Or wear a bib?" I ask.

He tilts his head and studies me. "I wondered if I was the only one thinking about that night at the club."

"I've been thinking about it," I admit. "And how it's inappropriate for us to be spending time together in a personal capacity."

"Agreed," he surprises me by saying, rummaging around in the bag of takeout and coming up with a spring roll. He takes a bite and offers the other half to me. "Which is why I'm here in a professional capacity."

I take the spring roll, telling myself it's because I'm hungry, not because he's the most gorgeous man alive, and if I don't put my mouth on something, I'll act like an idiot.

"How'd you even find my place?" I ask, trying to distract myself.

"You told me your address the other night when you got in the cab. Then I sweet-talked one of your neighbors outside, and she told me your unit. She also said to tell you your eggs are rotting."

I make a grunting noise. *Thanks, Mrs. Peonta.*

"Okay, I'll ask again," I say, swallowing the spring roll (fried, delicious). "Why are you here?"

"I told you. It's in a professional capacity."

I lift my wineglass and give a pointed look at the takeout bag.

"Doesn't the SEC have working dinners?"

"They do, it's just . . ." I take a breath and try to center myself. "This doesn't feel like one of those. I'm hyperaware that I'm in my yoga pants, that you're not wearing a tie for the first time ever. That you brought me food, and there's wine involved. That you're in my home, and I have bras draped over my shower rack—"

He turns away, already marching toward the bathroom.

"Hey!" I say, realizing his plan. "I didn't mean—"

I'm too late. He's already stuck his head into the bathroom. "*Very* practical, Ms. McKenzie," he says from inside. Then he turns around and comes back down the hall, rolling his eyes. "Good Lord, woman, you're too young and hot for this frumpy shit. Haven't you ever heard of lace?"

I rub my temple. "So you've seen my underwear. I hope it was satisfying, because it's the only time you're going to see them."

"We'll see," he says, returning to the kitchen. "Grab a couple of plates. We can talk while we eat."

"Ian." I wait until he looks at me. "You really should leave. The case isn't wrapped yet."

His playful gaze turns serious. "I know. That's why I'm here."

"I can't—"

"Just hear me out. Please. If you still want me to leave after we're done eating, I'll go."

I open my mouth to protest, but he takes a step closer, his face earnest as he grabs my hands.

"Put yourself in my shoes. For one second, switch this around. Pretend that *you're* the one being accused of breaking the law. All you know is that you didn't do anything wrong, but it's your word against some mystery person who's lying. What do you do? Do you let someone ruin your life—either put you in jail or have the career that you love ripped out from under you—or would you do everything possible to try and stop it?"

He's breathing hard, his blue eyes urgent and pleading. And just like Friday night when he spilled his drink, I see him not as a spoiled, womanizing, amoral playboy but as a man—a person.

One who might very well be innocent.

"Let's work together on this, Lara, please. We'll get answers faster that way." He rests his forehead on mine, just for a moment, and it's his vulnerability that breaks me.

"Okay," I say quietly. "But Ian, if you stay, you can't tell anyone. Definitely not your lawyer. Not even your besties."

He pulls back, and one corner of his mouth lifts. "My besties?"

"Matt Cannon and Kennedy Dawson. Even Kate and Sabrina. No one can know."

"Can I tell Matt and Kennedy you called them my besties? They'll love it."

"I'm serious, Ian." I drop my gaze and give voice to my biggest fear. "I could lose my job."

He squeezes my hands. "Lara, you can trust me."

I risk lifting my gaze. It's a mistake because he's close—very close. And I've never wanted something as badly as I want to know if Ian's as good a kisser as I think he is.

I pull out of his grasp and take a quick step back, clearing my throat and turning to get us plates.

"Hope you like Thai food," he says, opening the rest of the cartons and acting as if nothing just happened. "I got a little of everything."

"Wow, literally everything," I say, hungrily taking in the multiple options. He takes both plates from me to bring to the table, and I grab a stack of paper napkins and the wine bottle.

He shrugs off his suit jacket, and we settle at the table, and though I'm braced for an intense wave of awkwardness, there's none. Well, other than the fact that I'm very aware that his suit probably costs more than my monthly rent.

"So, what did you want to talk about?" I spear a piece of chicken and plop it into my mouth.

Ian takes a deep breath, and instead of eating his food, he picks up his wineglass and leans back in his chair. "Evidence."

I pause midchew. "I really can't say—"

"You don't have any, do you?" he challenges.

My hand goes still in the process of shoveling in pad Thai, and the knot I've had in my stomach ever since my conversation with Steve tightens.

My boss has always been opinionated, but he's also seemed fair. In fact, he's the one who regularly reminds me that there are two sides to every story, and our job is to figure out which side is telling the truth.

The fact that Steve won't even consider the possibility that Ian is telling the truth bothers me. A lot. And yet, conceding that to Ian is a direct violation of my job as the investigator.

I put down my fork, take a deep breath, and meet his eyes. "You keep saying you don't have a connection to J-Conn, and the evidence backs you up on that, but it doesn't change the fact that *someone* thinks otherwise."

"But you don't know who that someone is, do you?"

I shake my head, and even as I know I'm stepping over a dangerous line, I'm also realizing that this case isn't black and white. There's a definite murky-gray area, and Ian and I are right in the middle of it. Together.

"No, I don't know," I say quietly. *My boss won't tell me.*

He rubs a hand down his face. "If we had the name of the source, this whole thing would be over," he says. "It's got to be someone with a vendetta against me."

I've been starting to think the same thing, but I can't tell Ian that. Not until I've looked at *everything*, until I've dotted every *i*, crossed every *t*. I'm close, but I'm not there yet.

Until then, I have to play by the rules.

"It's also possible the source is someone who needs the SEC's protection."

Ian raises his eyebrows.

"It's not uncommon," I say. "The system does what it can to protect whistle-blowers. Their reputations, sometimes even their lives, are at stake the moment they come forward. It's why we do the informal investigation first before escalating it to a formal one."

Ian snorts. "What, like a white-collar version of witness protection?"

His tone is sarcastic, but his jaw draws open when I don't say anything.

"Wait, really?" he asks. "They could be keeping a source confidential because they think he's in danger?"

I shrug. "That's how it's supposed to work."

He rolls his eyes. "Give me a fucking break. You really think this person is in danger? He's *lying*, Lara. And the longer he stays in the shadows, the less time my lawyer and I have to refute his claims."

"This isn't a John Grisham movie, Ian."

"Well, it's not a fucking Disney movie, either. You said yourself you haven't found any evidence, so why is there still a case?"

"Because I'm not done yet!" I shout. "I'm close. I haven't found any evidence yet, but I wouldn't respect myself, and you wouldn't respect me, either, if I quit now."

"Fine," he snaps, draining his wine and standing up with ill-concealed impatience. "Keep the food. Enjoy the wine," he says, shrugging his suit jacket back on.

"Ian, wait. I thought—"

"We're either on the same side or we're not, *Ms. McKenzie*. Either you think I'm innocent or you think I'm guilty of insider trading. You've had more than enough time to decide," he says grimly, turning to leave.

"That's not your call to make," I say, standing and reaching out reflexively but then dropping my hand before I can touch his sleeve. "I do this for a living, and I'm telling you I'm not done. I haven't been through all the archives yet; I still have a half dozen people to interview—"

"Forget all that!" he shouts, spinning back toward me and stepping so close my breath catches.

He closes his eyes for a moment, taking a deep breath as though fighting for control. When he opens them again, his gaze is gentler but no less intense. He reaches out, touching my chin lightly so my face is tilted up to his.

I'm not sure what unsettles me more, the desperate urgency in his voice or the feel of his fingers against my face.

"Do you think I'm guilty?"

I sigh. "It's not that easy—"

"Don't answer as Ms. McKenzie. Answer as Lara. *Do you think I'm guilty?*"

I close my eyes to avoid his piercing gaze. The SEC investigator in me knows exactly what I should do—show him to the door and tell him I can't discuss his case. But it's not that simple. For the first time in my life, my usual cool objectivity has abandoned me, and in its place is something complicated and scary—something I want more than I've ever wanted anything, even the FBI . . .

"Ian," I whisper, pleading. "*Please.*" I don't know what I'm asking for, but he does.

His hands gently cup my face, pulling me closer. The second his mouth closes over mine, I don't give a damn about right and wrong, or black and white, or rules and protocols.

I only give a damn about him, about the way he makes me feel.

His lips own mine with complete possession, his kiss as confident as it is skilled. But it's the need that undoes me piece by piece, the desperation in the way he holds me close . . .

He breaks the connection far too soon, breathing hard as his eyes lock on mine. "Figure it out," he says roughly, stepping back. "And let me know when *Ms. McKenzie* catches up with Lara."

"Ian, wait . . ."

But he doesn't. He walks out the door without another word.

I touch my fingers to my swollen lips, dimly registering that my phone's buzzing with an incoming message. I dive for it, hoping it's him.

It's not. In fact, come to think of it, he doesn't even have my phone number.

The text message is from my dad. Good news. Rumor has it white collar is expanding head count. I MAY have found a way to mention that a letter of recommendation was coming through for my favorite daughter in the near future . . .

The message is accompanied by a winky-face emoji.

It's a first from my dad, both the emoji and the show of support. I close my eyes and try to ward off the wave of frustration that I'm finally getting everything I want . . .

And yet I'm terrified that what I need just walked out my front door.

21

IAN

Week 4: Thursday Night

"Are my boobs lopsided? The new bra and tight dress don't seem to be getting along. Ian?"

"Nope," I say, refusing to look down at my friend's cleavage. "I don't know how many times I can say it—I refuse to analyze your breasts."

Sabrina huffs and turns to Matt. "Fine. Cannon, since Ian's a prude and I don't know where Kate and Kennedy wandered off to, help me out."

Matt has none of my hesitations and takes his time checking out Sabrina's chest. "Right one's kicked up a notch too high. Hope you didn't pay your plastic surgeon too much."

Sabrina doesn't bother to get offended as she hands him her champagne flute to hold, turns away from the crowd, and adjusts her boobs. "These are one hundred percent me," she informs Matt coolly. "I'd offer to let you find out for yourself, but oh wait . . . been there, done that. *Snore.*"

I wince and finish my drink. "No sharing whatever you two did to each other, remember?" I've been dodging the details for years. I'd like to keep it that way.

"But—"

"Nope," I tell Sabrina. "My party, my rules."

"It's one hell of a party," Matt says.

He's right, I guess. There's an unspoken rule on Wall Street that a party's not a party unless it's overly extravagant as hell. Caviar. Dom. Foie gras. Top-shelf everything.

Not that I take care of any of it personally. I have Kate make a couple of phone calls, and hours later, my apartment is transformed. The entire corner of my living room is a bar; I have one tuxedoed server to every five guests, the best caterers in New York.

It's a scene I've become plenty familiar with over the years, but tonight it feels . . . different. Stale.

And yet necessary.

Whoever set me up to take the fall for an imaginary J-Conn connection is someone in my world. This world. Maybe not someone here tonight, but someone's got to know something, and I'm determined to find it.

At least, that's the plan.

Once Sabrina's cleavage is restored to proper symmetry, she takes her champagne from Matt and turns to face the partygoers. "I'm loathe to agree with him, but this *is* an impressive turnout for the last-minute invite."

It is. Just a few weeks ago, I'd have been thrilled, half-drunk with both booze and the power my name commands on an invitation. Now, however, nothing feels quite right. Just like at Pearl last week, I feel like I'm looking at someone else's life, and not one I particularly envy.

I sigh, surveying the crowd. "I'm pretty sure half these people are just here for bragging rights. They want to be among the last to see my place before my new home is a jail cell."

"You're not going to prison," Sabrina says, linking her arm with mine. "Isn't that why we're having this party? To pump Wall Street elite for info?"

Matt catches my eye over her head and gives me a nod. The party plan was half his idea, a last-ditch effort to figure out who the hell's trying to torpedo me. I invited twenty-five guests—about as many as can fit comfortably in my small apartment. Instead, I've counted close to fifty. It's a tight fit, even with a few spilling onto my balcony, others chatting it up in my office. Many of them I don't even know. I'd only been half joking when I'd told Sabrina they were here to see me off before I serve two to five for insider trading.

Damn the SEC.

Damn Lara McKenzie and her process and her sweet little mouth.

And damn me for caring so much. For letting it get under my skin that she doesn't believe in me. That whatever's between us isn't enough to override her rigid rules and her blind adherence to a system that clearly isn't working.

She needed time, and I get that—or I've been trying to get that. I bombarded her that night at her apartment, so I've tried to respect she needed a moment to sort things out, but it's been *days*. Plenty of time to acknowledge my innocence.

I'm hurt, yes. But also . . . pissed.

Kennedy winds through the crowd, two drinks in hand—Manhattan for him, Negroni for me. "Kate saw you were empty."

I accept the drink gratefully. "We don't pay her enough. Where is she, anyway?"

"Last I saw, she was chatting up one of the juniors from Morris and Keale."

"I don't know any of the juniors from M and K."

He shrugs. "Since when has that mattered? You know how this goes. They catch a whisper of free booze and big names . . ."

"Yeah, I get it," I grumble. "Hell, that was me once."

He gives me an exasperated look. "Ian, that was you just weeks ago."

I grunt. He's right, and we both know what changed me. Who changed me.

I rub a hand over the back of my neck. "When did we start getting too old for this?"

"Speak for yourself," Matt says.

"Really?" Sabrina says to him. "I don't see you mingling with the young sprites. You're wallflowering with us old farts, too."

"We're not wallflowering because we're *actually* old. We're just . . ." I glance at Kennedy and Matt for help. "Well, what the hell *are* we doing over here in the corner?"

"Not getting any closer to figuring out who's running his mouth to the SEC about you, that's for sure," Matt points out.

Sabrina sighs. "Hell's frozen over, because I'm about to agree with him again. Boy Wonder is right. We've got the cream of the Wall Street crop all in one place, all on their way to drunk." She drains her drink. "Break to mingle?"

"Fantastic. Because I love small talk," Kennedy grumbles.

"Do it for Ian," Sabrina says, patting his arm.

"That's why I'm here. But I draw the line at talking about the weather," he says, with a thump on the back as he says it. The gesture's brief but telling.

I start to open my mouth to thank him. To thank *all* of them, but I don't know what to say.

Kennedy gives me a brief, rare smile. "You'd do it for me."

"Damn straight," I say, grateful that he understands what I'm not able to put into words. "But I'd talk about the weather for you!" I call after his retreating back.

Sabrina and Matt break off as well, Sabrina to charm an MD from a competing firm, Matt to flirt with a group of women dressed in nearly identical black dresses. I'm about to join Matt and the women, figuring female interaction with someone who's not an SEC investigator might be exactly what I need, when a hand clamps on my shoulder.

"Ian, man!" I turn and shake hands with . . . Shit, what's his name? A director from Green Garrison . . . Jacob. Jacob Houghton.

I don't think Kate invited him, but at this point I'm beyond caring. Maybe I'll add a new element to my plan for the night: drink until I stop thinking about Lara. But my chances of ridding her from my mind are slim. She's all I can think about.

"Good to see you," I force myself to say. "Glad you could make it."

"How you been?" Jacob asks, taking a drink of his whiskey soda.

I force a laugh. "Been better."

He winces. "Yeah, I heard. Rough break, man."

"Hey, the SEC's got to pay its employees' bills somehow, right?"

"Sure, sure." Jacob's barely looking at me, far more into the ass of the redhead behind me. "You think they got anything on you?"

"There's nothing to find." My voice has just the slightest edge, but he doesn't seem to notice.

"Good for you," he says absentmindedly as a server walks by with a plate of crab cakes. His attention's back on me, and he leans forward slightly. "Heard you've got Vanessa Lewis reppin' you. You must talk a damn good game if you've got her fooled."

Before I can reply to this jackass with something that's absolutely not cocktail-party appropriate, Kate appears by my side.

"Hey, Ian! Can I borrow you for a second?"

I glance down at her, seeing that her smile is wide and bright but there's a nervousness to it. At first, I think it's because she's overheard my conversation with Jacob and thinks I'm going to cause a scene, but a moment later, I realize she's nervous about something else entirely.

"You didn't," I say through clenched teeth at my assistant.

"Don't get mad." Kate sets a hand on my arm and pins me with a look. "Whatever this thing is, Ian, you need to deal with it."

Kate's right, as she usually is, but I barely hear her.

Because my brain—and my heart—can't quite figure out what to do with the fact that Lara McKenzie is standing in my living room.

22

LARA

Week 4: Thursday Night

When I dressed this morning, I confess I thought I was looking pretty good. The sleeveless blue turtleneck matches my eyes, the gray pencil skirt does a decent job of disguising the past few weeks' stress eating. The nude pumps are both classic and sexy.

So I thought.

Walking into Ian's apartment, I feel like an utter frump.

Who *are* these people who look better at six o'clock on a Thursday than I do after primping for a black-tie wedding?

The men in expensive suits, I can get. I'm used to that. It's the women who throw me a bit. The strappy high-heel sandals, the short cocktail dresses, the flawless makeup.

It's a good reminder that *this* is Ian Bradley's world—glamorous, expensive, and elite. A world to which I don't and will never belong.

That's never bothered me before. I'm not sure it bothers me now. I like who I am. I like that I own more pantsuits than cocktail dresses, that I work hard in a profession I believe in.

I'm okay not fitting in here. What I'm *less* okay with is what that means for Ian and me.

"Lara, hi. I wasn't sure you'd actually come," Kate says as I'm ordering a drink at the makeshift bar.

"I wasn't sure, either. I nearly chickened out," I admit, turning to face her. I quickly scan the room, but it's packed wall-to-wall, and I don't see Ian. "Is he here?"

She gives a slight smile. "It's his apartment. I should hope so."

"Okay, I'll rephrase. Does he know *I'm* here?"

She looks away and doesn't answer, the first time I've seen Kate anything less than forthright.

My heart sinks. "Maybe this wasn't a good idea."

"No. You stay," she says determinedly. "There are only so many places he can hide."

"Do you think anyone will know who I am?"

"Probably," she says. "Or they'll at least know *what* you are. They're all in Prada heels, and you look like a government worker."

"Um, ouch," I mutter, even though I know she's right.

"Just remember why you're here." Then she gives me a curious look. "Why are you here? You never said why you wanted to come."

I give her a steady look. "No, I didn't."

"A hint?"

"Kate," I say mildly. "If I wanted to go through a messenger, I would have done so already."

She sighs. "Fine. Can't blame a girl for trying. Okay, so look. He's a little pissed at me for telling you about the party, and he's a little pissed at you for . . . well, I don't know what. We need to figure out a way to get you two alone." She nibbles her lip. "I'm just not sure how. He's not as easy to handle as he was before."

"Before what?" I ask, taking a large sip of my wine.

Kate pats my arm. "Before you."

My head snaps up as I stare at her, my heart thumping. "Before me. What does that mean?"

Kate merely smiles enigmatically and scans the room, then points toward the sliding glass doors on the far side of the living room that lead to a balcony. "Go wait out there, just until I can be sure he won't cause a scene."

I laugh. "I'm being sent outside? Like a dog that destroyed a pillow?"

"Yes, but I'm getting you a refill first," she says, pulling my wineglass out of my hand and holding it up for the bartender. Then she thrusts it back at me and points. "Ten minutes. Max."

I do as I'm told, mostly because the thought of standing out on the balcony sounds vastly preferable to making small talk in here. Nobody is paying me any attention—yet. But that'll all change the second I get the *so, what do you do?* query and word spreads like wildfire that they have the enemy in their midst.

"Truffle arancini?" A slim woman in a black-and-white server's uniform presents a tray in front of my face.

"No, thanks," I say with a smile.

She pivots and presents the tray in her other hand. "Lobster toast?"

Damn. So this is how the other side parties.

"No, thank you. I'm good."

She moves on with her lavish snacks, and I step out onto the balcony. On my walk over here, it was sunny, but it's started to cloud over thanks to an approaching summer thunderstorm, so I've got the whole area to myself. Not that it's particularly large. It's not a *grill on the deck and sip beer* kind of space. But it's nice.

Who am I kidding, it's more than nice. The guy lives on the fifty-sixth floor of a fancy high-rise with a view of the Freedom Tower.

I take a sip of my wine and try to enjoy the view without thinking about how much it stings that Ian didn't so much as come over to say hello. Just a few nights ago he was kissing me. Now he won't even look at me, won't answer my calls, won't agree to a meeting.

Still, I get it. He needed something I couldn't give. Not then, not until I'd seen the case all the way through.

But I can now. It's why I'm here.

"May I join you?"

I turn and do a double take when I recognize the woman stepping out onto the balcony. She's the one I saw Ian with at lunch a few weeks ago, and she's even more gorgeous up close. She's got long, thick black hair that falls almost to her waist, piercing blue eyes, an angular but striking face, and if I'm going to be perfectly honest here . . . rather spectacular boobs.

"Sure," I say, resisting the urge to pull my hair out of my ponytail so I feel slightly less juvenile.

She gives a cool smile and extends a hand. "Sabrina Cross."

"Lara McKenzie."

Her smile cools even further. "I know."

I take a sip of wine, wondering what the heck that means. What does she know? Did Ian tell her about the kiss? "So, you also know . . ." I say it casually, fishing.

"That you're the SEC investigator looking into Ian? Yep." She tilts her head and studies me. "But you're not what I expected."

"You've already seen me. In the restaurant at lunch that day."

"True," she admits, taking a sip of her champagne. "But then I was more interested in Ian's reaction to you than I was you."

There's bait there, but I don't take it, much as I want to.

"I always picture SEC employees in boxy brown suits and clogs."

"Well, all my boxy suits were dirty, and the clogs hurt my bunions."

She laughs, and it's as low and sultry as I'd guessed when I'd seen her laugh at the restaurant with Ian. "I see why he likes you."

"Yes, men just love my combination of forthright and awkward."

"Men like the combination of witty and smart," she corrects.

"Assuming there was a compliment in there, thank you."

"You're welcome." She takes a sip of her drink and watches me for a moment. "Why are you here?"

I lift my eyebrows at the blunt question, but she merely shrugs. "I'm very protective of Ian."

"Ian told me you two are close."

"Did he?" Sabrina says thoughtfully. "Interesting. He doesn't often discuss our friendship. With anyone. But yes, we're close. As close as possible to siblings without sharing parents."

Siblings. I can't deny that her word choice gives me a fierce stab of relief that the relationship's as platonic as he'd claimed.

"Are you close with Matt and Kennedy as well?" I ask, both curious and determined not to look too interested in Ian specifically.

"Sure. Kennedy's a good guy. A little uptight but as loyal as they come. As for Matt . . ." She practically sneers his name. "We have . . . history."

"He's an ex?"

"Eh. More like . . ." She waves her champagne around, searching for the word. "A past fling. It ended badly, and I wish regular suffering upon him, and he me."

"Sounds *wonderfully* adult," I say, smiling to soften the sarcasm.

She laughs. "It keeps us entertained."

"What about Ian?"

Sabrina blinks. "What about him?"

"Does it bother him having two of his best friends at odds all the time?"

"Possibly. He doesn't hide the fact that we get on his nerves." Then she frowns. "I guess I've never thought about if it really bothers him, though." Sabrina tilts her head and studies me before continuing. "I've never thought about it, but it seems you have. You care about him."

I take a sip of wine and stay silent.

She doesn't. "Ian and I have never slept together."

I keep myself from choking on my wine. Barely. "I didn't ask."

Her smile is sly. "But you've wondered."

Most definitely.

"You two grew up together?" I ask, deciding to flip the tables. Ian's oldest friend clearly has me under a microscope right now, wanting to know who or what I am to Ian. But the exchange of information can go both ways. And I'm more than a little curious as to Sabrina and Ian's story.

"We did. We looked out for each other." She turns to watch the slowly setting sun. "Neither of us had a good run of it, but we had each other."

I want to know more, but it's not my place to ask, so I take another sip of my wine.

She turns to face me after a moment of silence. "He's on good terms with his foster father—the last one, the decent one. But I think it still stings that Dave never adopted him."

I give her a wary look. "I don't think he'd be overly fond of you sharing this with me."

"Oh, he totally wouldn't," she says with a quick laugh. "But that's too damn bad. For both of you."

"What's this have to do with me?"

"Ian likes you," she says, turning to face me full-on. "He likes you in a way I haven't seen in . . . Actually, I don't know that I've ever seen him act like this."

"What, ignoring me altogether?" I say, nodding back toward the party.

"What did you expect?" she asks. "You hurt him."

My heart squeezes a little. "How can I have hurt him? I don't even know him."

"I think you do," she says quietly.

Before I can reply, the balcony door opens, and Kennedy Dawson and Matt Cannon step out to join us.

Sabrina sighs. "Do you mind, boys? This is girl talk."

Matt drops an arm over her shoulder and nuzzles her ear. "You telling her about how you're still trying to get over me?"

"Well," Sabrina says, using her nails to pick his hand off her shoulder as though it were a piece of trash, "I do definitely remember being over you. I've never been with someone quite so content to just lie there on his back."

Kennedy leans down slightly toward me. "Don't worry, eventually you get used to them."

I smile, a little flustered at being surrounded by Ian's inner circle. I've spoken with both Matt and Kennedy over the course of the investigation, but it's always been formal to the point of borderline chilly. Not that they're giving me warm fuzzies right now. In fact, all three of them are watching me. Not glaring, but I have the distinct sense that they're trying to figure out what the hell I'm doing here.

I don't blame them. This isn't my scene—at all. Not only that, I've always made a point of separating my professional from my personal life, separating work from after work. Before this case, I'd never once blurred those lines. But as with everything having to do with Ian Bradley, I'm breaking my own rules. All of them.

I hope it's worth it.

I let my gaze sweep around the balcony, making eye contact with all three of them to let them know that while I'm not the enemy, I'm not a pushover, either. "I'm here to talk to Ian."

"At his cocktail party," Matt says dubiously.

"Yes, well, if your friend hadn't decided to play the game of *avoid the SEC* for three days straight, perhaps I wouldn't have had to crash his party."

"It's important?" Matt asks.

I nod. "It is."

"You think he's innocent."

This comes from Kennedy, and it's not a question. It gives me a good indication of why he's so good at what he does. Ian plays on wit and stubbornness, Matt on smiles and flattery, but Kennedy gets what he wants with quiet command and competence.

"Oh, for God's sake, let her talk to him," Sabrina says, waving at the two men.

"You say that like you're not his lead guard dog most of the time," Matt snaps.

"She thinks he's innocent," Sabrina insists.

"Actually," I interject, "all *she* said was that she needs to speak to him."

Matt cuts me a quick glance with his blue eyes. They're darker than Ian's and usually friendlier, although I suspect that's a deliberate effect. The man didn't take Wall Street by storm in his early twenties just by being cute.

Although he is that. Very.

"All right, then," Kennedy says, opening the door. "Matt, you're up."

"On it."

Matt hands his cocktail glass to Sabrina, who accepts it with an eye roll, and then walks back into Ian's living room.

"All right, everyone, time to clear out," he says in a commanding voice.

The noisy chatter of a successful cocktail party falters slightly as they all look toward him, trying to assess if he's serious.

"You heard the man," Sabrina says, sweeping into the room. "We're taking this party elsewhere."

"How about your place, darlin'—party for two? Or three, I'm game." A drunk, douchey-looking guy laughs as he says it, leering at Sabrina.

Out of the corner of my eye I see Ian step forward, his gaze ice-blue and murderous as he searches for the speaker.

Sabrina lifts a hand to halt her friend, then slaps her other hand against Matt's chest, who's also stepped forward. "What's your name, pet?" she purrs at the drunken guy.

"Sean."

"Sean . . . ?"

"Galen."

"Lovely to meet you," Sabrina says with a warm smile. Then she claps her hands like a mom at a soccer party. "Okay, boys and girls, we're moving this party to the Brandy Library. Drinks on Sean Galen. Be sure to get whatever you want; Sean's feeling *very* generous tonight."

"Hey!" the man exclaims, just sober enough to realize what's happening. "You can't just—"

"Oh, I'm so sorry." Sabrina puts a hand to her chest as though appalled by her faux pas. "Can you not afford it?"

I press my lips together to stifle my laughter. It's well played. The Brandy Library is a ridiculously expensive cocktail bar, with every top-shelf liquor a booze snob could dream of.

The bill will be unthinkable.

But not as unthinkable as a power player having to admit that he can't pay.

He swallows and forces a smile. "I got it. Everyone enjoy themselves. On me."

Sabrina gives him a condescending pat on the shoulder, and Kate buzzes around the room, plucking glasses out of hands and ushering everyone toward the door as Kennedy hands wads of cash to the servers and bartenders and sends them off as well.

He catches my eye and winks.

It all happens so fast, I barely register just how thoroughly the situation's been handled until Kennedy and Kate pause in the doorway of the now empty apartment.

Kate looks at Ian. "You good?"

He only glares.

Kennedy nods and puts his hand on Kate's back, ushering her into the hallway. "Yeah, he's good."

A moment later, the door closes.

And then it's just me, a bunch of empty glasses, and one very pissed-off-looking Ian Bradley.

23

Ian

Week 4: Thursday Night

"So. The SEC makes house calls now," I say, turning away from Lara and walking toward the now deserted bar.

Too irritated to make myself a proper cocktail, I pick up a bottle of open red and pour myself a glass.

"What are you drinking?" I snap at Lara.

"Pinot Grigio. But Ian, you don't have to—"

I've already pulled the bottle out of the ice bucket and am walking toward her. I top off her glass without looking at her. I can't. Not yet. I'm too afraid she'll see the real reason I've been avoiding her—the real reason I'm so damn mad at her.

Because I want her.

And my heart's terrified she won't want me back.

"I didn't come here for wine," Lara says softly.

I return the bottle to the bucket and pick up my glass of red. "No? What was the plan, then? Wait until everyone else drinks the wine in hopes they'd share some dirt on me?"

She sets her glass on the coffee table and crosses her arms. "You're angry with me. Why?"

The question pisses me off, because . . . I'm not even really sure.

I'm mad, yes, but I don't know if it's at her anymore. Mostly, I'm mad at myself for wanting a woman who could think even for a moment that I could be a criminal. I want her more than I've ever wanted anything or anyone, but she's still not sure if I belong in jail.

"Fine," she snaps when I don't answer. "Stew in silence. But I'm mad, too, Ian. You come to my apartment, you make me feel . . . and then you ignore that I exist—"

I spin around. "So you decide to crash a party at my house?"

"Kate invited me! It was the only chance I had, and I—"

"Well it's a chance you should have passed up. I have nothing to say to you."

Her eyes flicker with hurt, and I feel a stab of regret.

But before I can apologize, the hurt's replaced with anger again and she stalks toward me.

"I wouldn't have to chase you down after hours if you'd have made yourself available during the workday," she says. "How many voice mails did I leave you? How many messages with Kate that you ignored? How many e-mails did I send?"

I push her hand out of the way and step closer. "Oh, so sorry that I didn't clear my schedule to tell you for the *nine hundredth time* that I'm innocent when you had no intention of believing me."

"Reverse the situations, Ian."

I snort, and she shoves my shoulder.

"No, just shut up and listen. You played the *imagine-if* scenario the other night; now it's my turn. Pretend that you're an SEC agent, and your boss, whom you respect, who's going to write you a letter of recommendation for your dream job, tells you there's a reliable tip accusing an über-rich Wall Street investor of insider trading. As an SEC investigator for five-plus years, you know from experience that these tips are more often than not legit—you know that people really do cheat the system, and you get paid to find out the truth.

"What would you do, Ian? The entire reason you're so upset about this is because you take pride in your work and are insulted that someone would accuse you of cheating. Well, isn't that what you've been asking me to do? Just blindly take your word for it because you're charming?"

My conscience takes her speech right in the balls. I hadn't thought of it that way, and damn it, she's right.

My pride, however . . . the part of me that wants her to believe in me—no, *needs* her to believe in me . . .

That guy's the one who opens his mouth.

"If you've got something to say to me, you can leave a message with Kate."

Her lips part in outraged shock, but she recovers quickly, sidestepping around me and putting a chair between us. "Fine. I'll send an official memo to your office."

She stalks toward the side table where the lone purse remaining is hers, the same ugly brown one she carries with her everywhere. She snatches it up, shoves the straps over her shoulder as she heads to the front door, and wrenches open the door. But instead of marching through it and slamming it shut, she whirls back toward me, eyes blue and blazing behind her glasses.

"You know, I thought I had it wrong. I thought that first day when you were a total dick on the sidewalk . . . I thought—*hoped*—that was a shield, an act you put on to play the Wall Street game and to hide the fact that beneath it all you're actually a decent guy. But that wasn't the act, was it? The act was the rest of the time when you played nice. The nice Ian's the fake one."

The accusation stings, but I can't bring myself to deny it. I'm not sure who the real Ian is anymore. Not when she's around.

"I already told you what I want," I say quietly, turning away. "I want you to believe in me."

"Why the hell do you think I'm here, Ian? Why do you think I'm trying to chase you down? You tell me to let you know when the woman *and* the SEC believe you're innocent, but then you don't even give me the fucking chance."

I snap around, both at her temper and at the words themselves. "What?"

She lifts her chin. "I've finished my investigation. I wrapped it up yesterday and wrote my report this afternoon."

I'm a fucking idiot.

I've been so damn pissed at her for continuing the investigation after that kiss that I used all my willpower the past three days to avoid anything to do with her—seeing her, talking to her, letting myself care about her and want her.

"I'm recommending they close your case," she says quietly. "No formal investigation."

The roar in my ears dims to complete, eerie silence, and I'm certain that I've misheard her. "What?"

She looks me in the eyes and lifts her chin with confidence. "There's no evidence indicating you got a tip about J-Conn. I said as much in my report. I turn it in tomorrow."

I take a step closer. "What about your FBI recommendation letter? You don't get it without the formal investigation, right?"

This time she doesn't meet my eyes. "Not your problem, Ian."

Lara steps into the hall and closes the door behind her, and for a long moment—too long a moment—I stand perfectly still, untouched wine in my hand.

Like hell is this the way it ends.

I set my glass on the counter and yank open the door. "Lara."

She's in the elevator lobby, pushing the button, but I know she can hear me.

"Damn it, McKenzie." I walk toward her, cursing again when I hear the beep of the elevator arriving.

The doors open, and she steps in.

"Lara!" I run now, jamming my hand into the closing doors and hoping like hell my building's elevator sensors are up to snuff.

The doors open again, and I hold them back, glaring at her where she stands calmly. "What?"

I punch the emergency stop on the elevator. "Where the hell are you going?"

Her eyes start to fill, and I feel like an ass. I *am* an ass.

She shakes her head, her chin trembling. "I can't do this, Ian. I can't play your games. I don't know what to do when one day you want me, the next you're angry with me and don't."

"I've never stopped wanting you," I growl, putting my hands on her face and gently wiping away the twin tears that escaped her eyes. "Yes, I'm angry. You think I want to want you? You think I relish the fact that the woman who's occupied my every thought for the past month is the SEC? You think I like that this is the first time I've ever felt this way, but you—"

Lara leans forward, setting her hands to my chest, and presses her mouth to mine.

I groan in gratification, pulling her closer.

I've kissed my fair share of women—more than my fair share. But I've never *needed* to kiss one like I do this woman, never felt like I'll regret it the rest of my life if I don't take my chance.

My fingers wind around her ponytail.

Mine.

I want this frustrating, complex woman as my own.

I nip her lip. *Surrender.*

She does with a soft gasp, and I take shameless advantage, my tongue teasingly flitting across her bottom lip before slipping inside to deepen the kiss.

Her kiss is shy at first. Her tongue tentative as it touches mine. Then her hands slide up from my wrists to tangle in my hair, and I lose all control.

With a groan, I press her back against the elevator wall. The elevator is still on emergency stop and continues to beep at us in outraged warning, but I ignore it. Hell, I barely register it. There's only us, her hands in my hair, my hands on her back, her hips.

The kiss is breathless and frantic and so damn hot my fingers itch to slide beneath her skirt, find out if she's wet and soft and wanting.

Lara breaks away with a gasp. "Ian."

"Hmm." My lips find her neck, loving her involuntary moan.

She pushes at my shoulder. "Wait. Stop."

I go still and groan. "My two least favorite words."

Lara lets out a little laugh as she wiggles away, straightening her glasses and looking as dazed as I feel.

I want to unravel her. I want to unravel with her. My hand reaches out again, but she steps farther away.

"I . . . I need to slow down, just a little," she says, running a shaky hand over her long ponytail. "I haven't turned in my report yet. Officially I'm still investigating you."

I growl in frustration, even as I understand. Her job's as important to her as mine is to me. I haven't done a good job of supporting that, but I plan to start now.

"When do you turn it in?" I ask.

"I need to read it through once more, then I'll send it to my boss tomorrow before noon."

"Perfect. Have lunch with me after."

She laughs. "Ian."

"Too soon? I can do dinner instead. I'm nothing if not flexible," I say, letting a smile spread across my face.

She bites her lip. "I don't know if I can do this kind of thing as well as you do," she says quietly. "Actually, I know I can't."

"What sort of thing?"

"Casual . . . sex. Flings."

It wouldn't be casual. It wouldn't be a fling.

The thought catches me off guard, so jarring that I'm relieved I didn't say it out loud.

"It'd just be dinner. Two people sharing a meal." My tone is easy, careful not to betray just how unusual—and unfamiliar—the request is for me.

She may not do casual sex, but I don't do *this*. I don't ask women to dinner simply because I want to spend time with them. As Kate not so gently pointed out to me, I don't date. Not as a means for anything other than getting laid.

But I want to date Lara. I want to make her laugh, and hear about her life, and figure out how to get her to that FBI dream job, and I want to be there when she gets the call.

I want it all.

I'm in so much trouble over this woman.

"I'll think about it." She points to the elevator doors. "Out."

Damn it. This is not how I saw this going. "But—"

"I'm going down to the lobby. You're going back to your apartment."

I've done enough deals with stubborn, reluctant investors to know when it's time to pull back.

For now.

"All right," I say with an easy smile.

I move toward the open doors, stopping when I'm even with her. Her breath catches, and though I want to devour her mouth all over again, I want to surprise her even more.

I brush my lips against her cheek, smiling when her sigh is half relief, half disappointment. Then I step back into the hallway, still facing her.

"Goodbye, Ian."

"Good night, Lara. I'll see you tomorrow."

It's a promise. A guarantee that this isn't over.

I see her swallow as she pushes the emergency stop button back in, and when we lock eyes before the doors close, I know she knows it.

24

LARA

Week 4: Friday Morning

I'm packing up the Wolfe conference room that's served as my office for the past few weeks when Kate strolls in with two mugs.

She hands me one.

"Oh, thanks," I say, taking it. "But I already have—"

I glance down at the contents. Not the coffee I was expecting.

I look up. "Orange juice?"

"With a splash of something bubbly." She winks and clinks her mug with mine and takes a sip of her own clandestine mimosa.

I hesitate. Strictly speaking, it's drinking on the job.

"Oh, come on," she cajoles. "It's a Friday and we're celebrating. Plus, it's your last day here. What are they going to do, fire you?"

I try to hide my wince at the reference to my employment status. Not that I'm worried about being fired—none of the SEC higher-ups are going to give a shit about a sip of champagne-laced orange juice. They're never going to know about it.

But I am worried about the fallout of my report.

I sent it off this morning and haven't heard anything. I tried calling Steve—three times. He hasn't picked up. I don't know if he's just busy or . . .

If he's pissed.

Which is stupid. I did my job. I looked at everything—e-mails, files, social media, Internet searches on the company computers. I turned over every rock I normally turn over and came up empty. There is *zero* proof Ian is guilty of insider trading. There's no evidence. Nothing.

My weekly status reports have said this all along.

But while my ethics are firmly in place, my dreams are . . . hazy. I'll get to the FBI someday, I know that. But I need a high-profile case to get there.

This wasn't it, no matter how much Steve thought it would be.

For that, I've earned a sip of champagne. Besides, there's OJ in there! Fruit serving, right?

"There you go," Kate says when I take a drink.

She pokes through the cardboard box on the table. "It's going to be weird without you here."

"Good weird?"

"Well, everyone will be a lot less on edge without the SEC lurking, that's for sure."

"Par for the course," I say, dropping my stapler into the box. "We don't tend to make a lot of 'work friends.'"

"What about within the SEC? Surely you've got some friends there."

I shrug. "I'm friendly with everyone. But it's not like here, where people come to the same office every day. We have a home base, but we're on-site elsewhere more often than not. And even when I am in the office, it's mostly married men who've got no interest in befriending a twentysomething woman."

"Could be worse," Kate points out. "There could be a bunch of married men who are interested in a little somethin' somethin' with a twentysomething woman."

"True."

"Have you seen Ian yet this morning?"

My mug stops halfway to my mouth, and I hope it hides my blush. The way that man kisses . . .

Kate studies me. "You okay?"

A little hot-flashy, but yeah, fine.

"Yep!" It comes out too peppy, and Kate's eyes narrow.

"What happened after we all left last night?"

"I told him about my report. He was relieved. I left." *After we made out in the elevator.* Seriously, is the AC not working in here today?

Kate gives me a skeptical look. "You could have told him about the report in an e-mail."

"Actually, I always tell the people I'm investigating my findings in person."

It's true. It's not an SEC rule or anything. It's not even necessarily recommended. But it's a part of my own process. It feels like a human decency thing—whether I'm turning their life upside down or giving them their life back, it's the sort of thing I feel I should look a person in the eyes and say, you know?

Of course, it's never resulted in getting felt up before, not that his hands had wandered to any bikini areas. I'd just wished . . .

I take another gulp of the champagne, then set the mug down before I chug it.

"Well, thanks for taking the time," Kate says, dropping into a chair. "He's in a really good mood this morning. Like, I heard him whistle."

"Really?" The information causes a thrill to rush through me that has nothing to do with professional satisfaction.

Kate shrugs. "Wouldn't you if you'd just been told you weren't going to jail?"

"There was no guarantee he'd have gotten time. Sometimes it's just a hefty fine and job loss, though for some, that can be just as devastating."

"The fine wouldn't have bothered Ian."

"Some of these guys end up losing seven figures. Not to mention their jobs."

"I already told you he's not about the money," she says. "And I think you know that."

I look down at my drink. I do know.

The Ian I've gotten to know over the past several weeks wears expensive suits, drinks overpriced wine, and hosts parties with caviar, yes, but that's merely the top layer. Just like the flirtatious womanizer is just a layer. The man beneath that is kind, and generous, and maybe a little bit vulnerable.

"Lara." Kate's voice is softer than I'm used to, and I glance up. "Don't play games with him. Please."

I swallow and nod but say nothing. I've been so busy figuring out how to protect myself from Ian, it hasn't really occurred to me that Ian might need protecting from me.

That he might be just as out of his element as I am, albeit in a different way.

Kate looks down at her mug. "Damn, it's empty. I told myself I could only have one until I finish up the weekly reports. Guess it's back to work."

The sudden sting of sadness I feel at her words surprises me. I've been so focused on whatever the heck is going on between Ian and me, it hasn't hit me that this is goodbye. Kate's become a friend, or at least someone I would like to be friends with.

I'll miss Kennedy and Matt, too, even Sabrina in all her gorgeous prickliness. It's a group I wish I could be a part of . . .

If only things were different.

Kate stands. "Look, I know this might be weird, but if you ever want to grab lunch sometime . . ."

My smile is huge. "I'd like that."

"Good."

"Hey, Kate," I say when she's almost to the door. "Is Ian in his office?"

When she turns back, her grin is a little bit mischievous. "He had a meeting at nine, but it should be done by now. He's got a break till eleven." She leans against the door. "Whatcha need him for? I mean, the case is wrapped up, right? And you delivered that message last night. So—"

"Kate."

"Yeah?"

I pick up my mimosa and take a sip. "What's the deal with you and Kennedy?"

Her grin vanishes. "We're not *that* good of friends yet, SEC."

I smile. "Exactly."

Kate points at me. "I knew I was going to like you."

I'm still smiling when I walk down the hall toward Ian's office. It's just past ten, so assuming his nine o'clock didn't run over . . .

Ian's behind his desk, attention on his computer screen.

I watch him type for a moment. I'm used to seeing him in his charming people-person mode, but I'm realizing there's another side to his professional persona. The guy who gets things done is very intense, very focused, and . . . very hot.

He's wearing a dark-pink tie today, but it looks anything but feminine when paired with his dark-gray suit, broad shoulders, and sharp jawline.

The man's every woman's fantasy.

And he asked me to dinner.

Ian reaches for a pen and does a double take when he sees me in the doorway. "Hey there, Creeper. Come on in."

"Hey," I say, feeling a little flustered as I shut the door.

He starts to stand, but I hold up a hand to stop him. "Wait. If you could just . . . I need to say something, and I can't when you're all . . . close and stuff."

Ian gives a puzzled smirk. "All right. What's up?"

"You asked me to dinner."

His gaze is steady. "I did."

"Why?"

"Because I like to eat." He smiles.

"Ian, I'm serious."

He stands and comes toward me. "Because I like you, Lara. What the hell do I have to do to prove that? Get a skywriter? Tattoo? Take out a classified?"

My stomach flips at his words, and I can't hide my silly grin.

"Did you turn in your report?" he asks, reaching out and taking my hand.

"I did."

His eyes flicker in relief. "So I'm no longer under investigation for insider trading? *You're* no longer investigating me?"

"Correct."

He pulls me in for a kiss, and I'm ready for it. Hell, I meet him halfway, my hands on his waist, his cupping my face, pulling me close.

I can't remember ever feeling this hungry, this reckless. Yes, we're in his office. Yes, anyone could walk in. But right now, with his hands on me, I don't care. I don't care about anything but wanting more.

Without breaking contact, he reaches behind me and locks the door.

"My place," he says, dragging his mouth from mine and trailing it down my throat. My head falls back, and I let out a little moan as he kisses my neck. "Seven o'clock."

"I can't come to your place on a first date."

His mouth returns to mine. "Why not? You said you didn't want anyone to see us."

I huff in frustration. "I know, but—"

"I'm a *really* good cook," he says with a slow smile.

That gives me pause. "You are?"

"Not at all. But I'm very good at takeout."

"Ian . . ."

I can't remember what I was going to say. This entire conversation has taken place in between kisses, and with each brush of his mouth against mine, it gets harder to think. And a lot harder to say no. I came in here thinking maybe we could take this thing slow . . .

Then his hands slide over my hips as he deepens the kiss, and slow sounds impossible. And not at all what I want.

I want this. I want the way I feel when I'm around him, the way I feel when his hands are on me.

"You want to come over," he says, bending slightly to press a kiss to the V of my blouse.

"I do?" I manage as his palm slides down my thigh, his fingers wandering under my skirt.

"Mm-hmm." His fingers trail up the inside of my bare thigh.

"But—"

The tips of his fingers brush lightly over the front of my underwear, and I can't remember anything. Not what I've said in the past, not why I shouldn't be doing this . . .

Then his fingers slip beneath the elastic, and I can't even remember my own name.

He groans as he finds my wetness.

I gasp as I cling to him, trying not to let my knees buckle as his clever fingers find all the right places.

I don't know this girl, the one who lets a polished playboy back her against an office door and slide his hand under her skirt, but right now I want to be her, if only for this brief moment of heaven.

"Ian." I run my hands over his shoulders.

He pulls away with a groan.

"No, don't stop," I moan, pulling him close, too turned on to be embarrassed.

He lets out a tortured laugh, his forehead resting against mine. "I have to. I can't take you here like this."

Why the hell not?

I don't ask it out loud, but he seems to know, brushing his lips across mine. "You're different. Let me show you that you're different."

Frustrated as my body is, my heart soars. How could it not? Isn't this every woman's fantasy, to be the one who tames the untamable?

He eases his hand out from under my skirt, using his other hand to smooth it back to rights.

Ian kisses my cheek, his lips moving to my ear. "Seven o'clock. My place. *Please.*"

I look away just for a second, trying to gather my thoughts, and my eyes lock on the orchid on the table behind his desk. The damn thing is flourishing.

I swallow, my eyes unexpectedly watering with a feeling for this man that I'm nowhere near ready to name.

I nod. "Seven o'clock."

25

IAN

Week 4: Friday Night

"Where'd those come from?" I ask as Sabrina fans out fussy little square napkins I've never seen in my life.

"Stationery store up in Flatiron," she says, tilting her head to analyze the angle of her napkin arrangement. "Aren't they fabulous?"

I grunt in response. "And you're here because . . . ?"

"Well, imagine for a second if we both had better parents," she says, going to the sink to trim the ends off the flowers she brought with her. "They would have wanted to see us off to prom. Document it. Make sure you had the corsage." She holds up the flowers.

I look at Matt, who's sitting at the barstool in my kitchen. "What's she talking about?"

"Got me." Matt shrugs and digs his hand into a bowl of fancy cheese cracker things, yet another Sabrina addition. "I never speak her language."

Sabrina slaps the back of his hand. "Don't touch. Those are for Lara."

"Ouch!" He shakes his hand. "Since when do you like the SEC better than me?"

"Since always. I like everyone better than you."

"I'm still not following the prom reference," I interject, watching skeptically as Sabrina arranges flowers in a vase I didn't know I had.

"Prom is a big deal," she says, repositioning a flower whose name I definitely do not know. "So is your first date."

"Oh Jesus," I mutter. "That again?"

"They grow up so fast," Matt says, picking up one of Sabrina's napkins and dabbing at his eyes.

"Don't touch those, either," Sabrina tells Matt. "Do you have any idea how much those cost?"

"Like you can't afford it. How much are you charging these days to play God with other people's lives?"

"Oh, I'm sure I'm within your budget, Boy Wonder. So if you're looking to hire someone to help with your inadequate—"

"All right," I interrupt. "Out. Get out."

"But—"

"Nope." I pick up Sabrina's bag and push it against her chest, shoving her toward the door. "Bye."

Matt gives her a goodbye wave, using mostly his middle finger to do so.

"You too," I say to him.

He frowns as Sabrina gloats. "I think I should be here," he insists, even as he stands. "You know, to run interference."

"Yes, that's what every date needs."

"Ian, you can't seriously be thinking about seeing this woman—"

"Enough!"

I don't have a temper. I really don't. But there's a fine line between friends being friends, and friends being monotonous pains in my ass.

"Did I give you shit when you and Sabrina screwed, and then screwed each other over? Do I lecture Kennedy and Kate on whatever the hell is going on there? No. I let you guys do your thing, live your lives, so let me do the same. Please."

Matt stares at me for a moment, then glances at Sabrina, who shrugs.

"Fine," he grumbles finally. "Will you call me when she leaves?"

"No, because that would be weird," I say, putting my hand between his shoulder blades and shoving him none too gently toward my front door.

Sabrina's already there, opening it before reaching into her purse to apply her lipstick. "At least text us. We just want to be sure she's not playing you, that this isn't some trick—"

"I don't deal in tricks."

We all turn to see Lara standing in the doorway, clutching a bottle of wine to her chest and looking pissed. And maybe a little stung.

Sabrina has the decency to wince. "I didn't mean—"

"Yeah. You did," Lara interrupts.

She's not wearing her glasses tonight, and her hair's down, the same way it was that night at the club. But my favorite part is that she's wearing jeans and some sort of strappy top. How long has it been since I've spent Friday night with a woman in jeans? It's usually fancy dresses, uncomfortable shoes, and a shit-ton of hairspray.

Lara looks comfortable. And it's one of the sexiest things I've ever seen.

Well, that and the righteously furious look on her face.

"The case is closed. I think Ian's innocent, both professionally and personally. I wouldn't be here if I didn't," Lara says coolly.

Then the impossible happens. Sabrina flushes with embarrassment and says . . . nothing.

Both Matt and I stare at her in shock. Sabrina Cross doesn't do anything but bold confidence.

"And you," Lara says, shifting her attention to Matt. "You and Kennedy are good watchdogs. I can appreciate that. But you're also Ian's friends, and you need to know when to back off."

"Hey," Matt snaps. "You've known him for how long? The rest of us have been here for years—"

"Excellent," Lara says with a bright smile. "Then as a friend who's known him for years, you trust and respect his judgment, right?"

Matt's jaw works angrily, but he knows when he's been outmaneuvered. "Right."

"Wonderful." She steps to the side in a pointed command. *Leave.*

To my surprise, they do.

Matt and Sabrina, for the first time ever, leave docilely without so much as a backward glance.

Hell, they're not even arguing with each other.

I give Lara an awestruck look. "You have no idea how impressive that was."

She smiles and walks into the apartment. "Sorry if I overstepped. They really do care for you."

"They do. Doesn't make them right, though."

Lara looks up at me, her blue eyes unguarded without her glasses. "So you don't believe them? You don't think I'm here in hopes you'll admit something about J-Conn?"

I step closer, and, hooking a finger beneath her chin, I tilt her face up to mine. "I don't think we should even mention the word *J-Conn* for the rest of the night." I brush my mouth against hers. "Deal?"

In response, her hand winds around my neck, pulling me down, and what I'd intended to be a quick peck immediately becomes heated.

Normally I like to be in control, but I love the way Lara kisses me. I let her do it her way, both hungry and a little bit shy. It's perfect. Everything from the tentative brush of her tongue against mine to the way she cups my cheek makes me feel like this is the only kiss that's ever mattered.

She pulls back and shoves the wine bag at my chest. "Here. Never come to someone else's house empty-handed and all that."

I reach into the bag and pull out what I'd assumed was a bottle of wine. I grin when I see it's not. "Campari." It's one of the main ingredients in a Negroni.

"And . . ." She digs through her enormous purse until she comes up with a bottle of . . .

Stain remover.

"Just in case," she says, handing it to me and patting my chest before she walks all the way into my apartment. "It looks different from the other night."

"I rearranged to make room for the bar," I say, setting the Campari next to Sabrina's flowers. "This is how it normally looks."

"It's very . . . manly," she says, looking around.

I pull a bottle of champagne out of the fridge. "Did you not see the prissy little pillow on the couch?"

She leans forward to look at the generic pillow in question. "It's hardly homemade needlepoint."

"Needle-what?" I ask, coming toward her with a champagne glass.

"My point exactly." She accepts the glass, and I clink mine to hers in a wordless toast.

She drops her gaze to my shirt and tilts her head. "It's black."

I glance down at my black shirt. "So?"

"And there's no tie."

"Your observational skills are top-notch tonight, McKenzie," I say with a smirk.

"It's just . . . this is the first time I've seen you in anything other than a suit. I like it."

I touch her hair, running my fingers through the silky strands. "Hmm. All this time I've been trying to get you to not hate my guts, and I could have just ditched the dress shirt."

"I didn't hate your guts."

I give her a knowing look. "You wanted me to drop dead that first day on the sidewalk. Admit it."

"You were a jerk. Admit that."

"I was a jerk," I say without hesitation.

She gives an exasperated laugh. "You're very difficult to argue with, you know that?"

"So don't argue. Sit. Let's discuss what I should feed you," I say, gesturing toward the barstools.

She hops onto the sleek black seat and picks up a napkin from the counter. "Sabrina?"

I roll my eyes. "Obviously. Now . . . sushi, Italian, Chinese, or other?" I say, sliding my cell phone across the counter where I've pulled up the food-delivery app.

She bites her lip. "How do we feel about pizza?"

The woman shows up in jeans, carrying Campari, and wants to order pizza.

Where has she been all my life?

"I feel good about pizza," I say, pulling my phone back and typing in the name of a place around the corner.

I feel pretty damn good about you, too.

26

LARA

Week 4: Friday Night

"Okay, we've exhausted favorite color, favorite movies, fought over whether or not mushrooms should be banished from the world . . ." Ian tops off my wineglass. "There's only one more vital piece of information left to be exchanged."

I pick a piece of rogue pepperoni off my plate and nibble it. "Birthdays?" I say at the same time Ian says, "Worst lay you've ever had?"

I nearly choke on the pepperoni. "That is *not* a first-date conversation."

"Isn't it? Sorry, I'm new to this. I'll try again . . . worst lay you've ever had?"

I laugh. "I'm not answering that." *Mike Lanter, junior year of college.* "But—"

"Next question," I say with a smile, enjoying his cockiness.

"All right," he says, sitting back in his chair. "What's going to happen with the FBI application?"

My smile drops. "I'll answer the other question. My most awkward sexual encounter was—"

"Come on, Lara," he says, reaching out and grabbing my hands when I move to clear our empty plates. "We have to talk about this."

"There's nothing to talk about. My boss said he'd write me a letter of recommendation once I had a big win under my belt. You being guilty was supposed to be that win. You weren't. End of story."

"It's a pretty shitty story," he says, rubbing his thumb along the inside of my wrist. "You should get the letter of rec because you did a good job."

I shake my head. "Actually, I shouldn't. Getting into Quantico's competitive. A junior investigator who does a thorough job with an informal investigation on someone who was innocent isn't going to stand out. An investigator who just won a big formal investigation on someone who's guilty . . . that's got the wow factor."

I expect him to argue, but he nods, which I appreciate. He trusts me to know more about my job than he does, which is a refreshing break from other guys I've dated who liked to mansplain everything.

"I'm sorry," he says, still not releasing my hands.

I shrug. "Me too. But it's just a timing thing. The FBI's not now, but it's not never."

"Have you told your parents?"

"Not yet." I fiddle with my napkin. "I'm too afraid they'll be relieved." I look up. "Did you tell your foster father that we closed the case?"

His smile is faint. "Not yet."

"How close are you guys?" I ask softly.

He shrugs as though it doesn't matter, but his shuttered expression tells me it does. "Close enough to stay in touch. Not close enough for me to call him Dad."

"Do you want to?" I ask.

He looks up. "I did once, a long time ago. Hoped for the whole adoption fairy tale. It didn't work out, but I get it. Who the hell'd want to take on the hassle of a teen kid with a chip on his shoulder?"

He smiles, but it's strained, and my heart aches both for the kid who wanted so badly to be wanted enough to be adopted and for the man who still doesn't think he was worth the effort.

"How do you feel about dessert?" he asks abruptly, standing and picking up the plates.

I grab the wineglasses and follow him from the dining area to his kitchen. "I feel like I love the idea in theory, but I can't fathom eating another bite of anything."

"Good," Ian murmurs, pulling me close as soon as I set the glasses on the counter by the plates.

A little part of me thinks I should protest. That it's too soon, that I'm not ready . . .

They're lies. It feels like I've waited forever for someone to want me the way he does. And I've *definitely* waited forever for someone to make me feel the way he does.

I don't feel like playing shy. I don't want to be coy.

I want him.

The kiss starts slow and a little sweet. The kind of soft teasing of lips that's a deliberate, delicious buildup promising more to come.

It escalates in little, sexy ways. His fingers digging into my hips, a little desperate. My nails scraping at his shoulders through the shirt, a little greedy.

His tongue coaxes my lips apart, and the moment it brushes mine, the kiss turns from sweet to scorching.

I don't know if he moves first or if I do, but a second later I'm pinned against the counter, his palm cupping the back of my head, his mouth slanted over mine as we devour each other.

Without breaking contact with my mouth, Ian lifts me up on the counter, and my legs wind around his waist, pulling him close—needing him.

All of him.

I've never felt this way, never felt like all that really matters is within arm's reach, if only I'd be brave enough to take it.

I want to be brave.

My fingers slide under his shirt.

Ian goes still, pulling back just enough that I can still feel his warm breath on my mouth. "Lara."

My hands glide farther up his back. "Ian."

He presses his hand over mine. "I don't have a lot of control right now. If you touch me, *really* touch me, I'm going to have to touch you, and then—"

"So touch me."

He pulls back farther and pins me with that ridiculously attractive blue gaze. "You're sure?"

I take a deep breath, and before I can chicken out, I pull my shirt over my head. "I'm sure."

Ian makes a sound that's half prayer, half strangulation as he looks down at my black lace bra.

Hey, I'm not going to say I planned for this, but I prepared. Just in case.

He trails his fingers lightly across my chest as his eyes greedily take me in, as I shove the shirt farther up his abs. "Off."

He reaches down, pulls it over his head. He's not wearing an undershirt. It's just him, and holy hell, can you say *perfection*?

He's tan and toned, and everywhere I look, he just gets better and better.

I touch my hand to his stomach. "Abs. I've never been with someone with actual abs."

"Abs are boring," he says, reaching around to unclasp my bra. "These, though," he says reverently as my breasts fall free of the lace. "These are spectacular."

My boobs are average. I know this. But the way Ian worships them, first with his hands, then his mouth, makes me feel like the most beautiful woman in the world.

His tongue strokes wetly over the tip of one breast, then the other, until I can't catch my breath. Then his eyes flick up to mine at the exact moment he wraps his mouth around my nipple and sucks, an unapologetically wicked moment.

With every lick, every light scrape of his teeth, he seduces me a little further until I'm arching into him with unmistakable invitation.

Ian's hands skim down my calves, ensuring my feet are hooked securely around his waist before scooping me off the counter.

"Impressive," I murmur, skimming my lips over the hard plane of his cheek as he walks me toward the bedroom.

And it is. I don't have a lot of experience, but the scoop-up-and-carry routine has been the stuff of my dirty fantasies, not real life.

But Ian's real. He's real, and he makes me feel both feminine and powerful, and it's a delicious feeling.

At least until he lays me on his bed and reality sets in.

He's in the process of unbuckling his belt when I jolt upright and crab-walk backward for some distance.

He goes still. "Lara, I'm sorry. I thought—"

"No," I say, holding up a hand. "No, you thought right. It's just being here in your . . ." I look around at the unmistakably masculine room. "I'm just suddenly aware that you do this a lot. Maybe in this very bed. And I . . . don't."

His eyes light with understanding, and though he finishes removing his belt and kicks off his shoes, the pants are still very much on when he casually plops on the bed.

He pats the spot beside him. "C'mere."

I shake my head.

Ian rolls his eyes and reaches out, hauling me to him. I gasp a little when my bare breasts collide with his chest.

He tunnels his fingers in my hair, locking his gaze on mine. "Use that brilliant brain of yours to listen and listen good. You're the only woman I'm thinking about, the only woman I've thought about since I saw you that first day in the break room."

"Really?" I search his features but see only honesty there.

He brushes a kiss on my cheek. "Swear to God, woman, I've never wanted anyone like I want you. I've been waiting for it to pass, but something about you's got me wrapped around your sexy little finger."

"So it hasn't passed?" I ask, setting my hand on the center of his chest, watching as I spread my fingers wide.

He takes my hand and gently lowers it until it's resting against the unmistakable bulge in his slacks. "Definitely not."

I move my hand slightly, stroking him.

He squeezes his eyes shut. "Lara."

Emboldened by the huskiness of his voice, I unfasten his pants, and the rasp of the zipper as I pull it down electrifies the moment.

Sitting up, I wiggle out of my jeans before returning my attention to him, easing both pants and black briefs over his hips and down his legs, until I see Ian Bradley as he was meant to be . . .

Utterly naked and utterly mine.

Ian props himself up on his elbows, watching me with hot eyes as I run my hands over his perfect body.

I lick my lips. "I'm so out of my league."

His gaze drops to my chest. "Not from where I'm sitting."

Feeling bolder than I ever have in my life, I slowly wrap my fingers around him. The velvety steel leaps against my hand.

Ian's head drops back down onto the pillow, and the way he growls my name in needy desperation causes a relentless throbbing between my legs.

I caress him tentatively, then more surely as his groans urge me on.

Until this moment—until him—I had no idea that pleasuring someone else was the most potent form of foreplay . . . for *me*.

Addicted to the feeling, I shift slightly so I'm on my knees. Then I bend and touch my lips to his straining erection.

"God. Lara." His hand tentatively touches my hair.

I open my mouth and take him in. He tastes salty-sweet, and this time there's nothing tentative about the way he touches me. His fingers tangle in my hair now, holding it back as he unabashedly watches me suck him.

I alternate between fast and slow, teasing and sure, listening to his pants to learn what he likes.

My eyes fly open as I feel his free hand skim down the length of my back, over my hip and butt. Then I moan around him as his hand nudges my thighs apart, and he works his way beneath the lace of my thong. His fingers slide over me, in me, fingering me with such torturous skill that it takes every bit of focus to keep doing what I'm doing.

It's a wicked battle of wills, his fingers teasing me senseless, getting me close but never letting me go over the edge. I return the favor, finding the exact rhythm that makes his hips buck, only to ease back at the last minute.

Neither of us wins. Or maybe we both do, when Ian pulls me up and rolls me to my back.

His mouth captures mine, kissing me deep as his body pins mine to the bed.

I arch, and we both freeze when his cock nudges against the damp V of my underwear.

He gives me one last kiss before pulling away and opening the nightstand drawer. Ian tears the foil packet with his teeth and rolls on the condom. Then he eases my thong down my legs and tosses it to the ground.

His gaze drops between my thighs as he parts them. "Later," he says quietly, "I'm going to lick you here." He runs a single finger down my wet seam, and I cry out, both from the touch and his words. "But right now," he continues, slowly resting a palm on each side of my head as he raises himself above me. "Right now, I need to be inside you."

Ian eases forward slightly, his expression pure concentration as he watches my face. I'm tight and he's big, but the friction is delicious.

He's breathing hard as he withdraws, then pushes back in slowly. He's the picture of restraint, clearly trying to take his time, for me, for us. To make it last.

There will be time for that later. Right now, I don't want to be teased. I want to be taken.

Greedy, I reach down and cup his butt, urging him forward. "Hard."

He looks in my eyes first, making sure. Then he gives it to me. His hips drill into me hard, and I arch to take him in, my body providing soft give to his hard strength.

Can you die from pleasure? If you can, this is the way I want to go, with Ian pounding inside me, his hips circling with every thrust to rub in exactly the right place until I'm aching, needing . . .

"Come," he says when my vision starts to go blurry with passion. He nips my breast with his lips. "Come for me, Lara, just like this."

I cry out, arching my back, and he meets me there, his body jerking as he lets go with a low groan.

I've always thought orgasms were orgasms. Always good.

Wrong.

Sometimes they're so blisteringly good you're both terrified it'll never end and terrified that it will.

Ian drops beside me, still breathing hard, and I muster the energy to roll toward him.

He turns his head slightly, pressing an absent kiss to my forehead before gathering me close. "Well."

I smile. "Well."

Ian shifts to look down at me, his fingers finding a lock of my hair and stroking it with his thumb. "You never did answer my question."

"Which one?"

"Worst lay you've ever had."

I bite my bottom lip. "Oh. Gosh. I had a different answer before, but . . . wow, this is awkward. I feel like I should at least let you get dressed before I answer. You know, to save your pride."

He tilts his head back, then lets out a laugh of pure masculine confidence. "All right. What about the best lay you've ever had?"

I roll my eyes. "Do you put notches in your bedpost, too?"

"Maybe." He gives a quick wink.

He rolls toward me until I'm on my back once again, and his eyes return to mine. "Ask me."

"Ask you what? Worst lay you've ever had?"

"A gentleman never kisses and tells. Ask me the other one."

"Best lay you've ever had? You just said a gentleman never—"

"You." He stamps a kiss on my lips.

When he pulls back, I mean to roll my eyes again and call him out on the line. But then I see it . . .

Embarrassment. His cheeks are just the slightest bit pink, and he looks at me, and he's . . . fidgeting. There's a sweetness to his nervousness that undoes me.

I set both my hands on his face. "Ian."

"Yeah?"

I lift up slightly to brush a kiss across his mouth. "Me too."

27

IAN

Week 5: Sunday Morning

I'm halfway down the hallway to my apartment when I realize I'm humming.

For fuck's sake, get it together, man.

Stacking one Starbucks cup on top of the other, I dig my apartment key out of my running shorts and push open the door.

And smile even wider.

There's a woman in my kitchen wearing one of my T-shirts and tiny little sleep shorts.

No, not a woman. *The* woman.

Lara glances up from whatever she's whisking and adjusts her glasses, taking in my running clothes and slightly sweaty state.

"Is getting up at four a.m. a regular thing for you? To exercise? On a Sunday? If so, I have very serious doubts about our compatibility."

I grin. "That's crazy talk. My alarm goes off at four thirty on weekends."

"And on weekdays?"

I grin wider. "Four."

"Oh, Ian . . ."

"What? I've got a lot of shit to get done before the market opens."

"I would have thought you don't get home until four."

"Well, that, too," I say, kissing her as I hand her one of the coffees. "Not as much as I used to, though."

"Getting old?" she asks, taking a sip of the coffee.

I wrap an arm around her waist, pulling her back to my front and nuzzling her neck.

More like getting domesticated.

I don't say it out loud. It sounds absurd. I've known this woman for all of a month, had her in my bed only two consecutive nights.

Which is one night longer than my previous record.

After our Friday date night, she slept over (out of sexual exhaustion, I'd like to think). And as fantastic as Friday night was—and it *was* fantastic—Saturday was even better. It never occurred to me before that spending an entire day with a woman could be centering, but I can't remember ever enjoying a weekend day so much.

Or enjoying a woman as much as I enjoy her.

"You mentioned yesterday you had some work to do?"

"Mm. A little," she says, her head falling back onto my shoulder as my tongue finds a sensitive spot behind her ear.

"I'm behind on e-mail as well. How about we eat whatever you've got going on here, take a couple hours for work, then brunch? There's a place uptown near the park—"

She stiffens slightly and eases away before turning to face me. "Ian, we still can't be seen together. Not yet."

I tamp down a surge of frustration, even though I understand. The woman's already gotten a delay on her dream job. The last thing I want to do is threaten her day job as well.

It just fucking figures that the first time I actually want to spend time with a woman, I feel like her dirty little secret.

But if we've got to be dirty . . .

I set aside my coffee, then gently ease hers out of her hands and set that aside, too.

"Hey," she says in a warning tone. "Taking caffeine out of a woman's hand is very dangerous business."

"I'll give it back. Eventually." I settle my hands on her waist and hoist her up onto the counter, much as I did that first night.

"Okay, new plan," I say, nudging her knees apart and stepping between them. "We eat whatever deliciousness you're cooking up. I'll go get us some orange juice and champagne for mimosas later—we'll sip them on my balcony and pretend we're someplace exotic. But first . . ." I run my palms up her bare thighs. "I'm thinking an appetizer."

"There's no such thing as a breakfast appetizer," Lara says, adjusting her glasses in that way that makes me crazy with lust.

"I beg to differ," I murmur, capturing her mouth with mine as my hands continue their leisurely stroking over her thighs.

When my fingers find the top of her underwear and hook inside just slightly, Lara pulls back from the kiss with a narrowed gaze. "I don't mean to be prudish, but one of us just got back from what was probably an obscenely long run; the other is already showered."

"I don't need to be clean for what I have in mind," I say, raining kisses down her neck. I bunch my shirt up around her waist with my fist, then bend and lick just below her belly button.

She gasps, and I do it again.

"In fact," I murmur, easing the underwear over her hips and all the way down her legs. "One might even say it's a little bit dirty . . ."

Spreading her legs wide, I lower, hooking my forearms beneath her thighs.

I look up her body. "You may want to get comfortable."

"Ian—"

I flick my tongue over her.

She lets out a long breath, dropping back onto her elbows.

"You were saying?" I ask with another teasing lick.

This time when she says my name, it's a plea, not a protest.

I take my time with her, tasting her with languid strokes of my tongue. Having spent most of yesterday getting her naked and keeping her that way, I've learned she likes it slow and gentle right until the very end. I do exactly that, soft licks over her most sensitive areas as she writhes beneath me.

Her hand comes down to mine, and I link my fingers with hers with my right hand, my left hand spread low across her stomach to hold her still. It's intimate in a way I'm not used to. I don't often have women in my kitchen, and I certainly don't eat them out.

But it's more than the location and what I'm doing. It's the way I am with her, the way she is with me. As though we're just getting started, and the best is yet to come.

Her hips tilt up, her thighs tightening around my shoulders, and I know she's close.

I'm tempted to make it last, wanting to prolong every moment with her indefinitely, but her nails find my head, digging in in a way that tells me she needs release now.

I give it to her. Circling my tongue faster, I slide a finger inside. The second I do, she comes with a quiet cry, tightening around my finger as her body arches up in helpless release.

I stay with her to the end, not pulling back until she drops limply onto the counter, the perfect picture of a satiated woman.

My woman.

Straightening up, I ease her into a sitting position, smoothing her hair back with a tenderness that belies my next move. Bending down at the same time I pull her forward, I hitch Lara over my shoulder so she half-dangles over my back as I walk to the bathroom.

She shrieks in protest. "What are you doing?"

"Showering. With you."

"I already—"

"Yes. But "—I interrupt her with a quick smack on her bare butt—"you're about to be a *very* dirty girl."

28

LARA

Week 5: Monday Morning

Objectively, I know I don't look any different. Same ponytail. Same glasses. Same pink lipstick. Same basic pumps, same black skirt I've worn a million times before, same blue shirt that's been in my workday rotation for years.

But I *feel* different, and as I walk into the SEC elevator on Monday morning, I'm paranoid that someone will notice. That someone will look at me and not only think, *oh, she got some*, but that they'll know who I got some with, and they'll know I want more, and . . .

"You're being ridiculous," I mutter to myself, since there's nobody in the elevator to witness my lecture. "People have sex every day. It doesn't have to be a thing."

It is a thing, though, because sex with Ian wasn't just sex. It was lots of sex, definitely. But it was other stuff, too. Meals. Conversation. Laughter.

It's the other stuff that has me tangled in a knot of happiness and terror.

It's the fact that I like him, not just in the bedroom but out. It's the fact that he's funny and smart and considerate in ways I never expected. It's the way that even now I'm wondering when I'll see him next, wondering if he'll call.

"Pathetic," I mutter, stepping out of the elevator and into the lobby of the SEC offices. Although *lobby* is a strong word for the entry area. It's more like a couple of sad chairs and an ugly coffee table topped with a few magazines that are three months old, at best.

I smile and wave at Ida, the front-desk receptionist, and she gives me a tired wave back without stopping her conversation with whoever's on the other end of her phone call.

I've taken only about five steps when I realize that my worst nightmare about this morning is true. Everyone is looking at me. And there are more than a few whispers.

They know. They know that I hooked up with a suspect.

No, not a suspect, my brain screams. *He didn't do anything wrong, and you waited until after you'd determined that to let anything personal develop.*

That's the rational, black-and-white part of my brain. The other part, the part that deals in nuances, merely raises an eyebrow.

"Hey, McKenzie," one of the other investigators calls out, coming toward me with his hand outstretched. "Nice work."

I shake his hand, a little perplexed, because his tone is genuine; there's no trace of mockery. This isn't a *nice work for toeing the conflict-of-interest line*, it's a *nice work for . . .*

I don't know.

Generally, turning in findings on an informal investigation recommending against a formal investigation doesn't warrant more than a nod and a *what's next?* in the eleven o'clock status report meeting.

Even more puzzling, I get similar reactions on my walk to my cubicle, including a couple of thumbs-up from people on the phone.

What the . . . ?

"Morning, Lara!" I turn and see Evie Franklin, Steve's busybody assistant, coming toward me.

"Morning," I say with a smile. "Love the hair."

She lifts a hand to her halo of slightly frizzy blonde curls. "Some days just aren't worth fighting the humidity. Did you know, back in the eighties, women used to pay for hair like this? What I wouldn't give for a time machine."

"Totally," I say, trying to be agreeable.

She gives me a wry look. "With that straight hair? I don't think so, honey. And were you even alive in the eighties?"

"I was." Barely. "Plus, I watched lots of old music videos with my dad."

"Old?" She puts a hand on her hip in mock outrage.

I hold up my hands in laughing surrender. "Unless you have a shovel so I can really dig myself a hole, I'm going to bow out of this conversation."

"Yeah, yeah. I'll let you off the hook if you show me how to use Instagram later. It seems to be my best chance of seeing pictures of my grandbabies, and I don't get it."

"Of course. I'll swing by your desk at lunch."

"Perfect. Now, go on in and see Steve as soon as you're settled, 'kay? He's free till ten and wants to see you."

I feel a little stab of nervousness at the thought. I haven't heard from him since turning in my report on Friday, and . . . it's weird. The guy's always been borderline anal about prompt communication, but with Ian's case, Steve's been either dodgy or annoyed any time I try to get him to even talk about it.

"Will do," I say, setting my purse down and punching the power button on my computer.

"Nice work on the case, by the way," she calls over her shoulder.

"Hey, Evie?" I say before she can leave. "Is something going on?"

She blinks in confusion. "What do you mean?"

"Everyone seems under the impression that I've done something . . . exceptional," I say.

"Well sure, babe. You wrapped the case."

"Yeah, but—"

"Evie!"

We both turn to see one of the directors throwing his hands up in the air in impatience.

"Oh crap," she mutters. "I gotta run, hon."

I blow out a breath. "Okay."

But she doesn't even hear me; she's already gone.

I start to unpack my box from Wolfe but decide to wait. If Steve's got another case for me, I'll just have to pack up again anyway.

I stop in the break room for a cup of coffee on my way to his office. When I take a sip, I wince. Let's just say it's not quite the caliber of what was in the Wolfe offices. There you could choose from three different machines, each one with a hundred different milk options.

And sometimes people would bring you fancy drinks from Starbucks.

You did not join a government agency to get pampered, I remind myself. *It's not like the FBI is known for its great coffee, either.*

Shaking my head, I start toward Steve's office, giving a faint smile at the few thumbs-ups and *way to go*s, trying to ignore the premonition that something is seriously wrong. His door is closed and Evie's on the phone, but she motions for me to go in.

I knock and hear Steve's sharp "Yallow," which I've learned over the years means, "Hi, come on in."

I open the door but draw up short when I see he's not alone. "Oh! I'm so sorry."

"No worries, Ms. McKenzie, I was just leaving," the man says, standing and buttoning his suit jacket.

He looks familiar, and my brain scrambles to place him. Medium height, medium build, medium brown hair . . .

Nope, no chance.

He takes pity on me and extends a hand. "Jacob Houghton. I'm Steve's—"

"Brother-in-law," I say, shaking his hand as the pieces snap into place. "Of course. We met at Steve's wedding. I apologize. I seem to have a bit of Monday morning brain fog, and this is my first cup." I lift the mug of black tar.

He gives a good-natured laugh. "Understandable. You've had a busy few weeks."

I look at Steve for guidance, a little unsure why his brother-in-law knows anything about my workload. The guy's not SEC, he's . . . I can't remember, exactly. Something in finance, but not particularly high up any food chain, if memory serves.

My boss isn't paying our conversation any attention, though, his focus on a document in his hand.

"Good seeing you again, Ms. McKenzie. Steve, I'll call you later. Or Whitney will. One way or another we'll get you and Katherine over for dinner this week."

Steve gives a noncommittal grunt as Jacob closes the door.

Familiar with my boss's inability or disinclination to multitask, I take a seat and sip my wretched coffee as I wait for him to finish reading.

A couple of minutes later, he sets the paper inside a file folder on his desk, then blinks a little in surprise, as though forgetting I was there.

"Right. Lara. How are you? Good weekend?"

The best.

"Yeah, it was all right. Yours?"

"Busy," he murmurs. "Very busy."

Guess that explains why you couldn't reply to my e-mail on Friday.

Steve taps his fingers on the desk, then leans back in his chair, folding his hands over his belly and studying me.

I wait. I've learned that pushing people to speak before they're ready rarely leads to good things.

He leans forward and exhales. "I want you to hear this from me first."

My mug is halfway to my mouth, but I lower it again, dread uncurling in the pit of my stomach. "Okay . . ."

He riffles around the piles on his desk until he comes up with an envelope. He hands it to me. "I'm delivering this later."

I reach out and take the envelope, pulling out the paper within. I recognize it immediately. A run-of-the-mill subpoena, just like the ones we issue for formal investigations . . .

I go very still when I see the name.

I look up. "What is this?"

His expression is regretful but also resigned. "I told you from the very beginning how this was going to play out, Lara. Ian Bradley's guilty."

"You didn't see my report, then," I say, putting the paper back in the envelope and handing it to him with a calm that belies my clammy palms.

He holds my gaze. "I saw the report. Just because there's no evidence at Wolfe doesn't mean he isn't guilty."

"The United States judicial system says differently," I snap. "Hell, Steve, this office says differently. What do you know that you're not telling me? Why are you so convinced that he's guilty?"

"Why are you so convinced that he's not?"

"Because there's no—"

"Evidence. Yeah. I saw the report. I've also met this guy once or twice, so I've seen him in action."

I clench my teeth. "What's that supposed to mean?"

Steve sighs as though I'm being obtuse. "It means that from here on out, you're off the case. You did good work, I know you did your best, but—"

"No 'but,'" I interrupt. "I did good work, I did my best, and there's no evidence. You only have your anonymous source. To ensure the case goes our way, we'd need another witness. And that's if your source even agrees to testify—"

"He'll testify. Regardless, it's no longer your problem."

"But—"

"The conversation's over, Lara," Steve says, with more irritation than he's ever directed at me. "I'd have thought you'd be happy with this. Even though I'm taking over the case myself, your participation in the early stages means your name will be associated—"

"I don't want it to be associated."

"If you want into the FBI, you sure as hell better."

I sit back, stunned at the implication.

He stands. "If you care at all about your career, you'll drop this case."

I stand as well. "Or what?"

Steve blinks in surprise. "Excuse me?"

"I drop this case, or what?"

"Lara, you don't want to cross me on this."

"See, that's the thing, Steve. I think I do," I say, setting my palms on his desk. "I've played by the book every step of the way, and I expect the same from everyone I work with."

He laughs, a harsh, dismissive sound. "You're what, twenty-eight? You don't know shit about the way the world works."

"Then enlighten me," I say. "Explain to me why, without a shred of evidence, we're launching a formal investigation."

"Evidence can be . . . uncovered."

I've never understood the phrase *blood running cold* before, but I get it now, because that's absolutely what happens when he says those words.

"What are you not saying?" I ask, careful to keep my voice steady.

When he looks back at me, he seems defeated and completely unlike the man I thought I knew. "Just stay out of it, Lara. The world's not going to fall apart if we make an example out of a slick Wall Street suit."

"No. I'm not going to sit back and let you take down an innocent man."

He runs a tired hand over his face. "Please. I'm asking you to do me a favor. You don't have to lie. Just keep your mouth shut and bide your time until I can get you into the FBI."

I stare at my boss for a long moment, my heart sinking as I realize what I have to do.

29

IAN

Week 5: Monday Afternoon

"So, how was it?"

I don't look up from my computer. "I've been ignoring Matt. I can ignore you, too."

Matt grunts from where he's been sitting in the chair across from me, tossing and catching a baseball for fifteen minutes.

Kennedy reaches out, nabs the ball, studies it. "What's this?"

"I caught it at the game on Saturday."

Kennedy flicks it back at Matt. "Who won?"

He doesn't have to ask which game. All three of us are Mets fans, although Matt's the one who makes the most time to get up to Citi Field for a game. Kennedy's too busy doing whatever it is he does (visiting museums?), and I'm too busy barhopping.

Historically speaking.

"She put out?" Kennedy asks Matt unsubtly out of the corner of his mouth.

"Hard to say," Matt says, resuming his ball catch and release. "He's kinda grumpy, but then he'll suddenly have a dopey smile on his face. Interesting."

"You know what else would be interesting?" I say. "Kicking you two out if you continue to act like high school jackasses."

Without a word, Matt turns the direction of his wrist and flicks the ball to Kennedy, who, without flinching or turning his head, catches it easily. Throws it back.

It goes on like this for a solid three minutes (that feel like three hours) before the constant, rhythmic *smack smack smack* of the baseball against their palms accomplishes its goal.

I turn to them. "Okay, what?"

Matt holds on to the ball and grins in victory. "Tell us."

"You already know. She came over. We ordered in."

"Tell me more."

"This isn't a *Grease* song. I didn't take her bowling."

"In the arcade?" Kennedy says, deadpan.

I let out an incredulous laugh. "I did not see that coming. I thought you only watched shit like *Citizen Kane*."

"*Grease* is a classic. I like classic things."

"You like *old* things," Matt says.

"True. It's why I'm not too keen on you. Have you had your first shave yet?"

Matt studies Kennedy. "You know, you would make a pretty good Kenickie."

Kennedy smiles. "I know."

"And we've got Danny Zuko here, who won't tell us if Sandy put out under the dock."

"Made out under the dock," I correct, before I can think better of it. "The line is *made out* under the dock."

"Ooh! Did you stay out till ten o'clock?" Kate asks, entering the office and shutting the door behind her.

At my look, she waves her hand. "Never mind. I'll ask Sandy. I mean Lara. Can I be Rizzo? She's my favorite."

"No," Kennedy says.

She glares at him. "Why not?"

"Because I'm Kenickie."

She snorts. "Yeah. Okay."

Kennedy's glower grows darker. "Who do you think I'd be?"

She snaps her fingers and pretends to think. "What's the principal's name?"

"You're thinking of the gym teacher," Matt says. "The principal's a woman."

"No, no, I know," Kate says with a sweet smile. "I was definitely thinking of Kennedy as the principal. Uptight, a little prudish . . ."

Matt hides his mouth with his hand, and I roll my eyes to the ceiling to keep from laughing and, thus, earning Kennedy's full-on wrath.

"*Annnnyway*," Kate continues, shifting her attention back to me to dodge Kennedy's scowl. "You've got to give us something, Ian. You saw her on Friday, and then none of us heard from you. Not even Sabrina."

"I was busy."

"Did she—"

"No more *Grease* lyrics," I say, pointing a finger at Matt.

He resumes his baseball toss as punishment.

"Was it a date? Are you dating now?" Kennedy asks.

"It's a very crucial distinction," Kate says in agreement, coming and sitting on the arm of Matt's chair.

"Hell if I know," I mutter.

Lara left my place late last night, much to my displeasure, and I haven't heard from her all damn day. For the first time ever, I'm on the other side of the equation—the one waiting by the phone, rather than the one avoiding it.

I don't like it.

"Oh. My. Goodness," Kate says. She covers her mouth in a pathetic attempt to stifle her amusement on my behalf. "Are you guys seeing his face?"

"Whipped," Matt says in concurrence.

"Smitten," Kennedy agrees.

Kate points at him. "See? *Smitten.* He *is* like the principal in *Grease.* Old-fashioned and—"

"Oh, for God's sake, just because I'm not a childish—" He breaks off.

Kate crosses her arms and lifts her eyebrows. "Yes? By all means, Kennedy, *please* finish that sentence."

I scrub my hands over my face. "I need coffee."

"I already brought you a quad shot this morning," Kate points out.

"Okay fine, I need . . ."

My three friends await my answer, their expressions a combination of amusement and dismay. Because we all know what I need. Or at least what I want.

Lara.

I want to know where things stand with us, but how can I expect her to provide clarity when I'm not even sure what I'm looking for?

I don't do this. I don't even know that I want to do this. I know how people see me. I know because I've deliberately cultivated the image.

The consummate playboy. The overgrown frat boy. The *order the most expensive champagne just because I can* guy. The one who never calls the next day.

That's who I am. And it's by no means the kind of guy Lara McKenzie wants or needs. At least not for the long haul.

"You guys want to go out tonight?" I ask Matt and Kennedy. The invitation sounds hollow and forced even to my ears.

"Ian," Kate says in a disappointed tone.

Kennedy shakes his head, and Matt just looks at me.

"All right, you win," I say, throwing up my hands. "I don't know what the fuck I'm doing. You guys happy now?"

"Do you like her?" Kate asks.

"Obviously," Kennedy snipes.

"Ian knows what I mean," Kate says, not looking away from me.

I nod. "Yes. But I don't know how to tell her that I want to try for real. I don't even know how."

"Harry Winston," Kennedy suggests.

"Nah," Matt says. "Jewelry's too intense. Go with bags. Women like a good handbag. Louis Vuitton."

"Oh my gawd," Kate says in exasperation. "No wonder the lot of you are single. Hold on." She leaves my office, comes back a minute later, and slaps a business card in front of me. "Call this number. And no, I won't call it for you. There are some things a man ought to do for himself."

I pick up the card. "Flowers?"

She nods. "They're nice. Women like them. And they're more first-week-relationship appropriate than a thousand-dollar handbag or diamonds." Kate lightly slaps both Matt and Kennedy on the back of the head as she says it.

"Well, it's technically only been a weekend, but we've sort of had something going on longer than that," I say, tapping the card against my palm.

"So make it a really big bouquet." Kate glances at her watch. "It's nearly one. Kennedy, Matt, you both have investors coming in. Ian, you've got an open hour, but you should call Vanessa Lewis to let her know you won't be needing her services anymore, and—"

A knock at the door interrupts her. Kate goes to answer it while Matt and Kennedy stand, attention already on their phones as they mentally prep for their upcoming meetings.

I'm surprised to see it's our boss at the door. Along with his bosses, both of the Sams. I don't recognize the man with them, but he's the only one of the bunch who seems happy.

"Ian. You got a minute?" Joe asks quietly.

Kate shoots me an alarmed look, and Matt and Kennedy are stone-faced as they all file out of my office. None of them likes this any more than I do.

I stand and button my suit jacket. "Sure. What's up?"

The man I don't recognize walks toward me with a sneer disguised as a smile. "Ian Bradley, I'm Steve Ennis with the SEC. I believe you've met my employee Lara McKenzie."

I manage a nod, my heart pounding.

"You'll be working with me now," Steve says, holding out an envelope.

"Working on what?" I glance at my bosses, but their expressions betray nothing. I glance down at the envelope and pull out the paper.

I've read only the first sentence when the SEC dick breaks it down for me.

"Ian Bradley, you're suspected of receiving an inside tip regarding the dissolution of J-Conn. This is a subpoena notifying you of a formal investigation for insider trading."

My head snaps up. "What? This is bullshit. Lara found—"

"*Lara?*" His eyebrows go up. "Yes, well, Ms. McKenzie is no longer working this case."

I take a step forward, caveman tendencies I didn't even know I had roaring to life. "I swear to God, if you fired her . . ."

Steve gives an incredulous laugh. "Fire her. Why would I do that? She's one of my best." He gives me a sly wink and lowers his voice. "Rumor has it, she's on a fast track to the FBI."

It's not until they all file out of my office moments later with a firm warning not to leave town that I realize what Steve Ennis just implied.

Lara sold me out to get her dream job.

30

LARA

Week 5: Monday Afternoon

Unemployment sucks.

But not being able to get ahold of Ian sucks more.

He's not answering his calls. Or his text messages. I briefly got ahold of Kate, but she was on the other line and said she'd have to call me back.

She didn't.

I even tried to get ahold of Sabrina, but the woman's a ghost. I couldn't find her contact information anywhere.

I'd finally gone over to Wolfe Investments myself, but the place is like Fort Knox, and without my contractor badge, there was no getting past the security guard. I'd had them call Ian, Kate, Matt, and Kennedy, hoping one of them would let me up to explain.

I struck out all around. So, desperate times, desperate measures, and all that.

The doorman at Ian's apartment building still had my name on the "okay" list from Friday night, so he let me up after I'd smiled prettily and told him I was here to surprise Ian.

He'll be surprised all right. It just might not be one he wants.

I've been here twenty minutes, sitting with my back propped against his door. I'll wait as long as it takes, even if he decides to go clubbing, comes home with some other woman—

My gut wrenches. I can't think about that.

And yet, maybe I should. Maybe I should prepare for the fact that I'm falling *hard* for a guy who's known as the city's most prolific playboy and has yet to indicate he wants a relationship.

Yes, we ate pizza together, had epic sex, sipped mimosas over brunch, and I did my laundry at his place (because he has a washer and dryer in his unit and I don't), but none of those things is a proposal.

Not that I want a proposal, but . . .

I groan and drop my forehead to my knees, wrapping my arms around my shins. I'm a wreck.

All this time, I've done such a good job of following the rules, doing what I was supposed to be doing, putting one foot in front of the other to get to my goal: the FBI.

Which is now more out of reach than ever.

And for what? A guy I'm not sure even wants me past tomorrow?

I texted Gabby but haven't heard anything back yet.

It hits me that I have no one else to call. I've been so focused on my job I've neglected my life, and now I'm . . .

Alone. Utterly, heartbreakingly alone.

"Lara?"

My head snaps up. Ian's just stepped off the elevator, though his footsteps slow as he nears me.

At first glance, he looks the same as always—briefcase in hand, clean-shaven, suit and tie perfectly in place. But then I notice his expression's one I haven't seen before—somber, worried, and . . . hurt.

Oh God, what did Steve tell him?

"What are you doing here, other than flashing my neighbors?"

I glance down. My position on the floor has my skirt riding up a bit, but nothing scandalous.

"I've been waiting to talk to you," I say, starting to push to my feet. "I haven't been able to reach you all day."

He extends a hand to help me up. Just twenty-four hours ago, he'd have pulled me in for a kiss, too, or at least delivered some inappropriate quip. This time, he releases me the second I'm steady on my feet.

"Ian—" I touch his arm, but he shrugs me off.

My suspicions are confirmed. He's been served his subpoena, and he thinks I either knew or had something to do with it.

"Let's go inside," he mutters, digging his key out of his pocket and opening the door. He gestures for me to precede him, but the motion is slightly mocking.

I set my purse on the side table and turn toward him, hands clasped. "You've had a crap day. Can I make you a drink? Pour wine? Order foo—"

Ian lets out an incredulous laugh as he tosses his keys beside my purse, setting his briefcase on the ground. "Yeah, a drink will make it all okay."

"It may make it a little better," I mutter.

He shoots me a dark look over his shoulder. He totally reminds me of Kennedy right now, but this probably isn't the time to mention it.

He goes to the window, shoving his hands in his pockets as he stares at the skyline. He looks miserable, and though I want nothing more than to wrap my arms around him, I know he'll only shake me off.

So instead, I let him have his silence and quietly gather the supplies necessary for a Negroni. I wasn't joking when I'd told him my grandma used to drink them. I even made a couple for her back in the day.

I do a quick Google search on my phone to see if my memory of the recipe's close. It's not. So I follow the instructions, measuring equal parts of Campari, gin, and the sweet vermouth I find in the fridge.

The recipe says it can be served on the rocks or in a cocktail glass. I've seen Ian drink it both ways, so I opt for pouring it over ice. Easier.

The orange twist, however, isn't easy. I end up with a mangled, pube-looking thing, but it's the thought that counts, right?

I take a sip. Not bad. Bitter, and an acquired taste, but I can see how it grows on people.

Despite all the noise I'm making in the kitchen, Ian doesn't turn around. When I walk to him and hold the drink in front of his face, he blinks in surprise, and I realize he didn't even know I was still here, much less register that I was making him a cocktail.

"Thanks," he murmurs.

Our fingers brush when he takes the glass, and our eyes lock for a moment. I hold my breath, but then the connection is broken and he looks away.

I stifle my sigh. Pouring myself a glass of wine, I go to sit on the couch and wait.

It doesn't take him long. His expression is blank when he turns around. "You wanted the FBI that badly?"

I'm braced for the accusation, figured Steve would go there simply to be petty, but it still stings. A lot.

I take a sip of wine. "What happened today?" I ask, ignoring his question.

"Don't," he snaps. "Don't play dumb. Don't pretend you don't know about the subpoena for the formal investigation, that you didn't sell me out to get your dream job."

"Is that seriously what you think of me?"

He lets out a frustrated growl, running his hands through his hair. "What else am I supposed to think when you didn't so much as warn me about the shitstorm coming my way?"

"I would have," I say softly, "except I was with HR all morning. They don't allow phones during exit interviews."

He frowns. "Exit interviews. What—Hold on. He fired you? He said he didn't."

"Steve didn't fire me," I say. "I quit."

Ian stares at me, his expression unreadable. Then he reaches for me. "Oh, Lara . . ."

I didn't realize I wanted to be held until he wraps his arms around me. I let him absorb all the emotions I haven't even begun to process yet.

I quit my job. I'm unemployed.

It'd be a doozy for anyone. But for the girl who's *literally* lived for work for the past six years, it's shattering.

I don't know who I am without my job—without my dream of the FBI.

Not that the dream's changed, but it feels a hell of a long way off now.

Still, I don't cry. I suspect that will come later.

"I'd say thank you," he says against my hair. "But I know you didn't do it for me."

I shake my head. "They're framing you, Ian. I don't know why, but I couldn't sit by and be a complacent part of that happening to anyone."

"Did you tell HR?" he asks, pulling back slightly.

"Of course. They said they'd look into it, but it's his word against mine, and he's got twenty years' experience on me."

His hand slides over my hair, the gesture tender and comforting. "I'm sorry. For everything. The way I acted, that I assumed you stabbed me in the back when it was the complete opposite . . ."

I lift a shoulder, but he shakes his head. "No, don't act like it's nothing. You had a shit day, and you came here. It means . . . everything. Okay?"

I rest my head against his chest and let him hold me, giving in to the realization that I don't know what comes next—giving in to the fear of it.

He does for several moments before pulling back slightly. "Why the hell were you flitting around getting me a drink? Sit down. Let me take care of you."

I reach out and grab his tie, pulling him back to me, crushing my mouth to his. "Take care of me this way," I whisper against his mouth. "Please."

Distract me.

He hesitates only a moment before doing as I ask, pulling me close.

I meet him kiss for kiss, pouring all my frustration into him, letting him pour his into me.

I tear at his buttons, and by the time he walks me backward, tumbling us both onto the couch, we're already half-unclothed.

I go for his belt, and though his breathing is rough with desire, he grabs my hands, pinning them gently above my head. "Easy," he murmurs. "We have time."

No we don't, I want to scream. I'm afraid if I stop for even one second, my thoughts will catch up and consume me.

His mouth is gentle on mine, pulling back every time I try to speed up until I have no choice but to succumb to his leisurely pace.

"I've wanted you like this for so long," he says as his lips trail lazily down my neck. He slowly removes my bra and drops it beside the couch. "I want to unwrap you, unravel you . . ."

He palms my breast, lifting it to his mouth as his lips wrap around my nipple. He's sure but unhurried, hungry but savoring. With each flick of his tongue, each nip of his teeth, I spin out of control more, and I realize he's right.

There is time for this.

I lose track of everything except the way he makes me feel. I barely register the rest of my clothes hitting the floor, much less the looming threat of tomorrow.

Ian drops soft kisses down my rib cage, then back up the other side as his fingers slip beneath my legs.

I gasp and arch up. *More.*

But instead of obeying my silent command, he keeps his touch a whisper-light tease.

"Please," I moan when I arch up once again, only to have him deny me.

He smiles against my throat. "Please what?"

"Ian."

His fingers press just a bit more firmly. "Yes?"

"Touch me."

"Like this?" he asks, circling my clit with his index finger.

A moan is my only response.

"Like this?" he asks again, sliding a finger inside me. "Or . . ." He slowly moves down my body, setting one of my feet on the ground beside the couch and lifting the other so my leg's draped over his back. "Like this?" He holds my gaze as he presses his mouth to me.

I come a little further apart with each swipe of his tongue, surrendering to every delicious sensation as he pushes my leg higher, spreading me wider until I have no choice but to go crashing over the ledge.

Ian stays with me till the end, pressing a tender kiss to my inner thigh as I try to catch my breath. "Stay," he commands, pointing a finger at me and going to the bedroom.

As if I could move.

He proves me wrong, though.

He comes back from the bedroom naked, armed with a condom, and moments later, he's gently flipped me to my stomach, kneeling behind me on the couch as he pulls my hips back to him.

I gasp as he thrusts inside me, my hips reflexively moving back against him, my hands finding the arm of the couch for support.

I'm braced for a fierce, frenzied coupling, but with this, too, he takes his time. He has one hand on my hip, the other almost tenderly resting on my lower back, and his thrusts are slow and controlled, demanding that I respond to him.

He leans forward slightly, the hand on my back sliding around to my front, setting two fingers against me, circling. I gasp and look over my shoulder. The second our eyes meet, he finally, *finally* loses control.

He groans and quickens his pace, his fingers moving faster against me until I cry out with my second orgasm. Ian's release matches my own, his groan tortured, his hands just a little bit rough as he stiffens behind me, head bowed, his breath staccato as he empties inside me.

My shaking limbs demand I lower to the couch, and he follows me down, rolling me onto my side so my back is to his chest, his warm arms coming around me.

Once my heartbeat returns to normal and I remember how to breathe steadily again, I lift his hand and press my lips to his knuckles. "So, what now?"

Ian kisses the back of my neck. "We figure out what's next."

We.

The word's both dangerous and comforting.

I look back at him. "Can we deal with it a little bit later?"

Ian smiles in understanding, then, giving a mocking frown, reaches above me and jerks the pillow out from under my head.

He holds it in front of my face. "You smooshed my manly throw pillow."

I push back against him, relieved to have a reason to laugh. "Okay, Mr. Manly. Go get me my wine."

He sits up and hands me my glass before going into the bathroom. He comes back, tying the drawstring of sweatpants, and tosses me a T-shirt and pair of clean underwear I'd left at his place over the weekend.

He picks up his drink and sits beside me on the couch, watching as I pull the shirt over my head. "Have you ever seen *Grease*?"

I pause in the process of pulling my hair out from the neck of the shirt. "Like Sandra Dee *Grease*?"

"Yeah. So, fair warning . . . the next time we see my friends, there's a good chance there will be a sing-along. You're to tell them that I was sweet. Just turned eighteen."

"Do I have to? Because that's super weird," I say, looking to see if he's serious.

"It's either that or you tell them you're hopelessly devoted to me."

His voice is teasing, but I press my mouth to his rather than respond because I'm too afraid that I'll admit the truth . . .

That *hopelessly devoted's* not too far off base from what I'm feeling.

31

IAN

Week 5: Tuesday Morning

I may not know much about relationships, but I know this woman.

I know that she's a lot more devastated by her unemployment than she lets on.

I *also* know if I push her on it, she'll wriggle away.

I'm trying for patience—I really am—but it's never been a strong suit of mine. I fight for what I want, remember? And what I want is for Lara to have her job back. Hell, I want for her to have the FBI, but I'd settle for whatever makes the shadows in her eyes go away.

"Maybe we should bring in your lawyer," Lara says, picking up her coffee mug. She's dressed in little shorts and my T-shirt again, and it's alarming how much I've come to enjoy the sight.

Focus, Ian.

It's eight a.m. the morning after she quit her job and I got served my subpoena, and Lara and I are no closer to figuring out why her boss is so determined to take me down.

Or who his mysterious source is.

After being up half the night reviewing every single name, note, and connection that could possibly tie me to J-Conn, we agreed to give it fresh eyes in the morning.

A solid plan.

With no results.

"I'm meeting Vanessa at ten," I say, glancing at the clock on the stove. "I just hoped to have some good news for her. She's working her side, but we're both hitting dead ends."

Lara takes a deep breath, then pulls her hair into a messy knot with the hairband around her wrist. "Okay, let's go through this one more time. Maybe we're approaching it the wrong way."

"How so?"

"Well, we've been focusing on a J-Conn connection."

"Yeah . . ."

She chews her lip. "I can't believe I'm saying this, because it sounds like a B-movie plot, but what if the connection isn't you and J-Conn but you and Steve?"

I stand to get us both more coffee. "Explain."

"Well, we already know that you didn't get a tip about J-Conn . . ."

The casual confidence in how she says this has me closing my eyes with emotion, and I'm relieved my back is turned so she doesn't see it.

"And," she continues, "we already know that there isn't any circumstantial evidence tying you to J-Conn that could be misconstrued. Because if there were, I'd have found it."

This time the confidence in her tone is for herself, and it makes me smile as I top off her mug.

"So what if J-Conn's not the key? What if it's just the most convenient, believable way to set you up?"

"Makes sense." I drop back into my chair. "But why? I'm sure I've pissed off some people over the years, but I can't imagine I've done anything deserving of fucking jail time. And how the hell is your former boss involved?"

She shakes her head and fiddles with her earlobe, deep in thought. "I dunno, but my gut tells me he is. I've never seen him act like this. It feels . . . personal for him."

I give her a gentle smile. "Your gut, huh? You finally admitting intuition is a real thing?"

Lara blows out a frustrated breath. "Let's just say I've learned that just because I follow the rules, it doesn't mean everyone else does."

"Which would make sense if I knew Steve. But I don't."

Her gaze flicks to me. "Maybe you know someone he knows."

"I'm sure I do," I say, gesturing at the dozens of papers in front of us with hundreds of names. "But the guy's been with the SEC for decades. It could be anyone, right?"

She sighs. "I'm going to take a shower. See if inspiration strikes."

I reach out and grab her hand, pressing my lips to her inner wrist. "Want company?"

She smiles and steps toward me, kissing my forehead. "Can I just take a minute? Think on my own?"

I kiss her wrist again and try to stifle the panic that she might be pulling away before we've really started. "Sure."

She squeezes my hand and starts to move toward the bathroom.

But then she pauses. Backs up.

With one finger, she pulls a sheet of paper out of the stack piled on my kitchen table and studies it. Then she turns it around for me to see.

It's one of the profiles I'd printed from my LinkedIn page—people who I don't consider as friends but who are close enough to my circle to know about the J-Conn coup.

"Jacob Houghton?" I shrug. "He's an investment broker. I don't know him well, but from what I do know, he's . . . well, he's kind of a douche. Why?"

"I know him. And if Steve hasn't unfriended me on Facebook yet . . ." She sits at the table and opens her laptop, her fingers moving quickly across the keys.

"Aha!" she says triumphantly, adjusting her glasses and turning the computer around so I can see the screen.

I bend down to look. She's pulled up a wedding photo on Facebook.

My eyes go to the bride first, a middle-aged woman I've never seen in my life. I move to the groom next, and him I recognize—it's Steve Ennis, Lara's boss.

"I went to Steve's wedding. Heck, he even had me sit at the head table with his family, which is how I know . . ." She points at the picture.

"Jacob Houghton," I say. "Why's he at your boss's wedding?"

"He's Steve's brother-in-law, married to his sister. I wouldn't have thought anything of it, except I just saw him yesterday. Jacob's always been friendly, but yesterday he was sort of . . . weird."

"He was also at my cocktail party," I say distractedly, remembering that the dude was a little off when I talked to him. I'd assumed he was just bad at small talk, but . . . "You think that's our connection?"

"It's the only one we have," she says. "Although I can't think of how you and Jacob connect. You ever go after the same client?"

"Not that I'm aware of." I scroll through the rest of the wedding photos. Then I go totally still.

"Who's this?" I point at the woman beside Jacob in what looks to be a family photo.

"That's Jacob's wife, Steve's sister. I'm blanking on her name . . . Wendy?"

"How long have they been married?"

She blows out her breath. "I'm not sure. I didn't really talk to her much beyond the usual small talk about the centerpieces. But Steve's wedding was two years ago, so at least that long."

My blood feels like it's running cold. Then hot. Then cold again.

"Why?" She looks up at me, then touches my arm. "What's wrong, Ian?"

"Her name is Whitney. I slept with her," I say, my voice a little hoarse.

"When?"

I can't bring myself to answer.

"Ian, how long ago?"

I have one hand on the back of Lara's chair, the other on the table beside her. I force myself to look down and meet her eyes. "A few months ago, after a party. I don't think I ever got her last name."

She exhales.

"I had *no* idea she was married, Lara. You have to believe me."

"I do," she says, touching a hand lightly to mine. "But Jacob wouldn't. And if he's convinced Steve to help take you down . . ."

"It can't be that," I say, straightening and trying to clear my head. "This isn't a TV procedural with cliché villains."

"We're right," she whispers, pressing a fist to her stomach. "I feel it here. I know we're right."

I think so, too, and I've built my career trusting my gut feelings. It's what got me into this J-Conn mess in the first place. Maybe it can be what gets me out.

I reach for my phone. "I'll call Vanessa."

32

LARA

Week 5: Thursday, Lunchtime

"You nervous?" Sabrina asks, watching me in the mirror as she reapplies her lipstick.

I meet her gaze. "Not even a little bit."

She smiles, dropping the tube back into her purse. "I *knew* you had grit."

"Or a simmering vendetta," I mutter, giving myself one last look in the mirror. The usual Lara stares back. Wide blue eyes. Ponytail that's neither too high nor too low, just there—practical. Black-rim glasses, minimal makeup . . . and a score to settle.

"Yes, well, take it from someone who deals with revenge plots on a regular basis—this is a good one," Sabrina says, stepping toward me and opening a button on my blouse.

"Hey." I start to button it again, but she slaps my hand. "Nope. This'll go better if he's distracted by a bit of cleavage."

"I'm not showing any cleavage." *Am I?* I glance down.

"No, but there's the prospect of it, and that's even more enticing," she says. But then Sabrina frowns and unabashedly puts her hands beneath my boobs, pushing them upward. "Seriously, what bra are you wearing, your grandma's?"

This time it's me who bats her hands aside. "Sorry, I didn't realize this mission involved a push-up bra."

She gives me a knowing look. "Do you even own a push-up bra?"

"What does it matter? I don't have *those* to go with it," I say, gesturing at her slightly low-cut dress.

She looks down at her chest. "You mean day cleavage?"

"What the heck is day cleavage?"

She holds up her thumb and forefinger to her cleavage as though she's measuring something. "No more than a half inch or so, see?"

"What's night cleavage?"

She widens the gap between her fingers. "An inch, at least."

I shake my head in wonderment. "It's like you're from a different planet."

"Well, get used to it, because I have every intention of making you a regular lunch date," Sabrina says with a smile that's warmer than I've ever seen from her.

"Because I'm helping Ian?"

"Nah. I mean, sure, that'd get you a thank-you lunch. Maybe a thank-you coffee. But you're doing this for *you*. And that's enough to make you a regular in my life."

"Thank you," I say, feeling unexpectedly touched.

Sabrina holds up a warning finger. "No hugging. No crying, either. Save those tears for the table."

"Right," I say, shaking out my hands. "I've been practicing my fake crying on command like you instructed."

"Verdict?"

I waggle my hand. "Fifty-fifty chance of waterworks."

"Good enough. If all else fails, let your chin wobble so he thinks you're trying to hold back tears. That's nearly as good." Sabrina glances at her watch. "Okay. It's go time."

In the two days since we've hatched our plan to catch Jacob Houghton and Steve in whatever they're up to, I keep waiting for the nervousness to set in—keep waiting to lose my nerve.

Instead, I feel . . . determined.

These men cost me my job at the SEC, they cost me my opportunity at the FBI, they are trying to send someone I care about to jail. I never thought I'd say it, but the system isn't working. I could escalate above Steve's head, sure, but without proof . . .

"Thanks for meeting me here early," I say.

She smiles. "I would've, even if Ian hadn't demanded it."

"He did?"

"It's killing him that he can't be nearby, but if Jacob sees him, the plan goes to hell. Jacob doesn't know me, so"—she blows me a kiss—"I'll be at the table just behind you guys."

I nod. "Okay."

"You ready, then?"

I blow out a breath. "Yeah. Yeah, I am."

"Okay, you go out first. Our reservations are at the same time, but I'll be fashionably late to mine so you and Jacob get seated first. You need anything, I'm there. Matt and Kennedy, too."

"We're the Avengers," I say with a little smile.

She pats my cheek affectionately. "I love that you're such a dork."

A few moments later, I'm standing at the hostess desk, waiting in line to give them my name.

"Thanks for joining us today, Ms. McKenzie," says the willowy hostess. "Looks like you're the first to arrive. Would you like to wait for the other member of your party before being seated?"

"No need!" comes a jovial voice from behind me.

Had I not practiced this moment with Ian a dozen times this morning, I might have stiffened. Instead, I paste on a deliberately shy smile and turn to face him.

Jacob *Freaking* Houghton.

For some reason, I expect him to look different, knowing what I know. Or rather, suspecting what I suspect. But he's the same. Same bland grin. Bland features. Bland suit. Bland everything.

"Lara, how are you?" he asks, kissing my cheek. "Hanging in there?"

Well, that answers that question. He knows I'm no longer employed by the SEC.

I let my hands wring like a damsel. "Well, um . . ."

He sets a hand on my shoulder. "I know. Let's sit down. Get a drink and something extravagant for lunch. My treat."

"Thanks, Mr. Houghton," I say with obvious release.

"Anytime, Lara. And please, call me Jacob. I think we know each other well enough for that."

Sabrina's coming out of the bathroom as we head to our table, but she sails past both of us as though she's never seen us before. I'm pretty sure Jacob glances at her "day cleavage," but it's little more than a male heterosexual checking out great boobs. He certainly doesn't seem to recognize her as the notoriously elusive Sabrina Cross, which works well for the plan.

He holds out the chair for me, and we both settle with our napkins and menus. I'd deliberately picked a business-causal place for us to meet that's nice enough for him to accept but not so fancy he'll think it's an odd choice for an unemployed SEC investigator.

"I was glad to hear from you," he says after he's ordered a bottle of white wine for the two of us. "I was just telling Whitney last night that I was sorry to hear you were no longer with the SEC. She so enjoyed getting to know you at Steve's wedding. We both did. And Steve always spoke so highly of your work."

I fiddle with my napkin and look down at my plate, noting out of the corner of my eye as Sabrina sits at the table directly behind Jacob, along with a tall woman with a sharp nose and even sharper gaze. I'm careful not to let my attention linger on them, instead waiting quietly as Jacob does the whole taste-and-swirl routine with the wine.

After the waiter moves away, Jacob lifts his glass. "To new beginnings."

"I'll drink to that," I say, careful to infuse just a bit of desperation into the statement. I take a tiny sip of the wine. Jacob takes a drink as well—and not a small one. *Excellent.* Liquid lubrication is exactly what this conversation needs in order for the plan to work.

"So, Lara," he says, starting to set down the glass but taking another sip of the wine instead. "I'll admit, I was surprised to get your call. I've always enjoyed your company, but you've been so careful to keep a slight buffer—understandably so, considering what I do and what you do."

"Did," I correct. "What I *did*."

"Right." He gives a sympathetic smile.

I take a deep breath as though gathering my courage. "It's actually . . . Well, it's your relationship with Steve that made me think of contacting you."

He nods encouragingly. "My brother-in-law was your boss a long time. I don't think he'll mind my telling you he was sad to lose you, Lara."

"I'm hoping that's the case," I say with a small smile. "In fact, I was hoping you might be able to intervene on my behalf."

He sits back and studies me. "You want your job back."

Hell no. But what's one tiny lie on the quest for justice . . .

"I made a mistake," I say in a rush. "I acted rashly, and I'm worried he won't listen to me. But I thought maybe if you talked to him . . ."

Jacob gives me a friendly smile. "Why don't you tell me what happened—your side of it."

I set my elbows on the table, burying my face in my hands. "I was such an idiot. I can't even talk about it."

He reaches across the table to touch my arm. "Lara. Talk to me. Let's not forget you helped my wife safety-pin her dress after a few too many Pinot Grigios at Steve's wedding. Whatever is said here stays between us."

You wish, asshole.

I drop my hands back into my lap and take another deep breath. "Okay, it has to do with the case I've been working on."

"Ian Bradley's case."

I see Sabrina straighten just slightly behind Jacob at hearing Ian's name.

I nod. "It was . . . Well, I really shouldn't say, but . . ."

"I know it was high-level," he says dismissively, taking another sip of wine. The waiter swings by to refill it. "That's what made you quit?"

I bite my lip. "Okay, here comes the embarrassing part . . . While I was working on the case, I sort of . . . Well, Ian—I mean, Mr. Bradley . . . He's got this way about him, and even though I was investigating him . . ."

"You fell for him," Jacob says, his voice just a bit more careful than before.

I give a small smile, letting my shoulders rise and fall. "I thought I did. I couldn't find any dirt on him, and I told Steve as much. That's why I didn't recommend we move forward with a formal investigation. I didn't know Steve was going to take over and move forward with the case anyway."

Jacob sips more wine but says nothing, so I keep rambling.

"The thing is, I really thought I was doing the right thing. I wanted so badly to believe Ian was innocent. But now . . ." I close my eyes. "Now I wonder if I didn't find anything because I let myself get distracted. Let *him* distract me."

The irony is, most of what I've just said is true, even if it's part of a bigger lie. I really did worry Ian was trying to distract me. I really did worry that I was letting him get under my skin in the way a better SEC investigator wouldn't.

But I've also learned that's not the part that matters. What matters is that Ian is one of the good guys. He didn't break the law, and he didn't betray me.

He wouldn't. He's better than that.

Jacob leans forward, eating up my line as we knew he would. "What happened?"

Showtime.

I take a shaky breath as I summon forth watery eyes. "I just learned that Ian's cheating on me. I quit my job for him, and the bastard's a liar."

"Oh, Lara," he says with a sigh. "Guys like that are amoral trash. Let me talk to Steve. He'll understand when I tell him that Ian seduced you to trip up your case."

I give an embarrassed wince. "But I don't really want Steve to know that I slept with the guy I was investigating. Then he'll never hire me back."

"I wouldn't be so sure." He gives a small smile. "Let's just say he might be more aware of Ian Bradley's shortcomings than you think. How are things with you and Ian now? Have you broken things off?"

I shake my head and wipe my nose. "He doesn't know I know about the other woman yet. A friend saw him out last night, all over some girl. I know I need to confront him, but—"

"What if you didn't?"

I blink. "I can't keep dating a cheater."

"You could if you wanted to get back at him." Jacob lifts his eyebrows.

"I don't understand."

Jacob takes another sip of wine. "I told you that you could trust me. Can I trust you?"

"Sure, of course," I say, the picture of confusion.

"Ian Bradley isn't a good man, Lara. He's the worst kind of Wall Street cliché—arrogant, womanizing, filthy rich even by Wall Street standards . . ."

"Yes, but is he a criminal?"

"Guys like that don't get where they are by being innocent. Surely you're not that naive, no matter how good-looking the guy is." He smiles, as though to soften the chastisement, and takes yet another sip of wine.

"You're right," I say with a self-deprecating slump. "The whole J-Conn thing felt dirty, but I couldn't get a single person to come forward to testify."

Jacob leans in with a smug expression. "Couldn't you?"

I give him a puzzled frown. "I don't understand. There's nobody except . . ." My eyes go wide. "Oh my gosh. You were Steve's confidential informant?"

He spreads his arms to the side with a rueful smile. "Guilty. I'm sorry Steve couldn't tell you. We thought it'd be best to keep it under wraps as long as possible, given his and my connection."

My mind is racing. Even though we knew—or at least had a darn good hunch—Jacob was the source, hearing him admit it makes me slightly nauseous. I glance at the back of Sabrina's head, her stillness telling me she heard everything. Even better, the woman she's with seems to be listening, too.

"Do you think it'll hold up?" I ask. "It's your word against his . . ."

"What if it wasn't just my word?" He takes a sip of wine. "What if it was *our* word?"

"But I never found anything. *You* actually have information."

"Eh." He gives what I'm sure he imagines is a charming, boyish grin and shrugs a shoulder. "I may have exaggerated the depth of my knowledge."

"Does Steve know?"

"Sure, he knows. He gets a fat check for playing along."

I fiddle with my napkin to hide my barely contained fury at the man across the table from me, as well as the man who was my boss. My *mentor.* "What would I do?"

He shrugs. "Maybe you heard him bragging about the whole thing to a friend. Maybe a former J-Conn exec mysteriously shows up in his list of contacts, which you find on his phone."

I stare at him wide-eyed. "I couldn't."

"Sure you could," he says, filling up my glass even though I've barely touched it. "You get your job back. Ian Bradley gets what's coming to him."

I sit back in my chair with a little laugh. "I can't believe it. All this time, I thought I was missing something, but you don't actually have anything tying him to J-Conn, do you? You and Steve set him up."

Jacob gives a cocky wink. "Sure did. The man's slick, but not nearly as smart as he thinks he is."

The moment is so quick, so subtle, I think maybe I've dreamed it, but the way Sabrina turns her head slightly tells me I haven't.

Jacob Houghton just confessed to framing Ian for insider trading—with Steve's help.

I shift my legs, purposely dropping my napkin.

A minute later, all hell breaks loose.

33

IAN

Week 5: Thursday, Lunchtime

Later, when I recall the look on Jacob Houghton's face when I approach his table, I'll laugh. In the moment, however, I only have eyes for Lara.

I reach for her immediately, my hand finding her back as she stands, turning to face me with obvious relief.

"What the hell?" Jacob sputters.

"No," Lara says with an angry hiss, lifting a finger to him. "You don't get to be outraged. *You set him up.*"

"He cheated on you!" Jacob says incredulously. "And you're defending him?"

"I don't cheat," I interrupt in a warning tone. "Not in my professional life or in my personal life."

Jacob makes a scoffing noise. "Right. You're a regular Boy Scout, I'm sure."

"You lied," Lara says, seething. "You and Steve *both* lied."

I press my palm more firmly against her back to steady her, even as a part of me would love to see her lunge at Jacob, as I sense she's itching to do.

Jacob laughs. "Oh, Lara. You're worse off than I imagined. He wound you around his finger, then sent you in here for a confession."

"This was my idea," she says, giving him a steady look.

"Huh," he says, looking surprised. "I can see why Steve always thought so highly of you. But, no matter." He picks up his glass and finishes the rest of his wine. "It's my word against yours, and nobody's going to believe a suspected criminal and his—"

I take a menacing step toward him, and his eyes go wary.

"Girlfriend," he says in a begrudging tone that tells me it wasn't his first word choice.

"Actually," Sabrina says, standing up from the table behind Jacob. "It's your word against *ours*."

Jacob whirls around. "Who the hell are you?"

She waves a hand. "Oh, *I* don't matter. But may I introduce Dana Keller? She's a journalist with the *Wall Street Journal*."

The story-hungry reporter stands with a gleeful smile. "You know, when Sabrina said she had a scoop for me, I thought it might be just another executive with pervy tendencies. But this is *so* much better."

Jacob pales and looks ready to puke. "I don't know what you think you heard, but—"

"Oh no, it's not what she *thinks* she heard," Sabrina purrs. She picks up a small black recording device from the table. "It's what she *knows* she heard."

"That little guy's state of the art," Dana says proudly, pointing at the recorder. "Picks up every whisper, even in a noisy restaurant like this."

As Jacob stares in disbelief at the device, Kennedy and Matt amble over from the other side of the restaurant. "Everything good over here, Lara? We noticed you dropped your napkin," Matt says in mock concern.

"All good," Lara says, waving the napkin like a white flag.

Jacob lets out a horrified laugh, turning to Lara. "You knew they were there. You had this all planned. What was the signal, drop your napkin and they call Ian?"

"Text, actually," Kennedy clarifies. "He was waiting outside."

"Hmm, maybe with a little less wine you might have checked your surroundings," Sabrina says, picking up and inspecting the half-empty bottle in the ice bucket.

"You set me up," Jacob snarls to all of us.

"Sucks, doesn't it?" I say, meeting the other man's gaze head-on. He's too much of a coward, though, and after a beat, he looks away.

"The only difference is, you deserved it," Lara says quietly to Jacob.

"It wasn't just me," Jacob says, obviously moving past denial and straight to bargaining. "Steve is just as guilty. The guy's up to his eyebrows in gambling debt and agreed to do just about anything for a price."

"Oh, we know," I say. "My attorney, Vanessa Lewis, marched into the SEC offices to notify Steve's boss of the situation within moments of Lara dropping that napkin."

He stares at us, aghast. "Just how many people were involved in this setup?"

"Just my lawyer and the people you see here," I say casually, picking up Lara's wine and starting to take a drink. "Oh, and my assistant and the SEC enforcement officers who should be here any—"

"There they are!" Matt says in a singsong tone.

We all turn to see Kate pointing two stone-faced suits in our direction.

"Wow, all sorts of things happened with that napkin drop," Dana Keller says admiringly.

Jacob ignores her, all his attention on me as the SEC agents approach the table. "You slept with my wife," he says, his voice quiet. Defeated. "My *wife*."

For a split second, I feel almost sorry for him. If I've learned anything through this whole ordeal, it's that a woman can turn one's life upside down. Then I remember he wanted to send me to jail because of it.

"I didn't know she was married," I say, meeting his gaze. "Something I'd have been glad to tell you if you'd just manned up and talked to me about it."

He frowns. "Whitney didn't—"

"No," I interrupt. "Whitney didn't mention you. Nor was she wearing a ring. I know because I'm not an asshole—I check. *She* knew she was having the affair, but I sure as hell didn't."

"Did she know about your plan?" Lara asks Jacob. "Or did you decide to take Ian down without bothering to get all the facts?"

His stubborn silence and angry scowl are answer enough.

"I hate him," Lara whispers as we all watch him get led away.

"I don't."

She looks up at me, eyes wide. "Really? He was going to perjure himself with the sole intent of sending you to jail."

"A dick move," I acknowledge, sliding my hand to her waist. "But I still don't hate him. I can't."

"Why not?"

I press my lips to her hair and tell her the truth. "Because he led you to me."

34

LARA

Week 5: Friday, Dinnertime

"Damn, Ms. Lewis. This is some good shit," Matt says, looking appreciatively at his champagne flute and then bending to look at the bottle.

"Call me Vanessa," Ian's lawyer says, handing a glass of champagne to Kate. "And I didn't buy this. Ian did."

Ian pauses in the process of sipping his champagne. "I did?"

"It'll be on your bill," Vanessa says with a wink.

Matt clinks his glass to mine and grins.

I smile back automatically. Even amid my own issues, it's hard not to feel jubilant at our victory over corruption. And yes, I realize that's very superhero-delusional of me, but, well . . . yesterday's win felt good.

Was our plan a bit outside the lines? Absolutely.

But if getting to know Ian and his friends has taught me anything, it's that fighting for what's right isn't always as simple as following the rules. Sometimes you've got to bend a couple to get the bad guy.

Sabrina sails through the front door of Ian's apartment, air-kisses Kate and me, then heads straight for the champagne bucket. "Dom! We really are celebrating."

Lauren Layne

"Hell yes, we are," Vanessa says as she and Sabrina air-kiss. "And may I just say, denying both those men a plea bargain? Highlight of my year."

"How'd they think they had a chance at that?" Kennedy asks.

"They figured they'd get brownie points for a written, tell-all confession," Vanessa says. "But since *both* were willing to sell out the other, neither had any bargaining power."

"You know the part of this that's killing me the most?" Matt drops into a chair at Ian's kitchen table. "How the hell didn't we think to look at Ian's hookups first? Should have known it'd be his dick that would get him into a mess."

Ian flinches, and I set a hand on his arm. He hasn't said much about it, but I can tell it bothers him to know that someone he thought was a harmless fling was not only married but that it came back to bite him in the worst way possible.

Ian pulls my hand up to his lips, presses a kiss there, while Sabrina swats Matt on the head.

"Right, because you're such a celibate monk. And Whitney was a long time ago," she says with a pointed look at me.

I smile, appreciating the sentiment, though it's not really necessary. I don't exactly love thinking about Ian's romantically prolific past, nor do I care to think about what it means for his future, our future . . .

But I've got bigger issues to deal with.

Ian's mess is cleaned up, and I'm grateful. Thrilled.

My own mess is just beginning.

Ian pulls me closer, pressing his lips just above my ear. "I'm glad you're here," he says quietly before he pulls away to head into the kitchen.

I'm glad, too. Not just because of him and us but because of everyone else here. I don't think he can possibly know just how starved I've been for friends. I have Gabby, of course, but if I'm being totally honest, I've always been aware that she and I probably wouldn't have ever been friends had we not ended up living together.

226

This group feels different. It feels like a group I could be a part of—a group I could truly belong to.

If things were different.

"Lara, your phone's buzzing," Ian calls from the kitchen.

I walk toward him, letting out a squeak when he tosses me my iPhone. "What are you doing? Do I look sporty?"

"Caught it, didn't you?" he says with a slow smile.

I did. But it probably won't happen again.

I glance at the phone, hating that I feel a pang of dread instead of my usual excitement at the name on the screen.

"Hey, you mind if I take this in your bedroom?"

Ian waves the gin bottle in a go-ahead gesture.

I step into his room and close the door. "Hey, Mom."

"Lara. I'm so sorry, sweetie. Dad and I just got your voice mail. You *quit*? Tell us everything. You're on speakerphone."

I lean against the door and slide all the way to the floor, blocking out the cheerful voices on the other side to bite the bullet and finally tell my parents about the utter mess I've made of my life.

35

Ian

Week 5: Friday, Dinnertime

After checking to see that Lara's still in the bedroom talking with her parents, I approach my lawyer.

"Vanessa, you got a sec?"

"Sure," she says, holding up a finger to Sabrina to indicate she'll be right back. "What's up?" she asks as we wander to the far side of the living room.

I scratch my cheek, a little out of my element here. I'm not in the habit of asking for favors—especially ones for my girlfriend.

Or the woman I hope will agree to be my girlfriend.

"It's about Lara."

"Ah, yes," Vanessa says, sipping her champagne and lifting her eyebrows. "You know, without her . . . Let's just say she was instrumental in this working out in your favor."

"I know." I'm grateful. Beyond grateful, and yet . . . hardly glad. Because I also know exactly how much this cost Lara.

I got exactly what I wanted. She got screwed.

"So, listen," I say, running a hand over the back of my neck, trying to figure out how to tell my attorney that I've been sleeping with the SEC investigator.

Vanessa takes pity on me and smiles. "It's okay, Ian. I went to Princeton. I think I can tell when two people are in love."

The word jolts me. Both because it's the first time I've heard it out loud and because I'm terrified that it feels . . .

True.

"We're not . . . we're just . . . *Shit*. I don't know what we are."

I only know what I want her to be—*mine*.

"Did you know she lost her job because of all this?" I ask Vanessa.

"Sabrina told me she quit."

"Yeah, because she has integrity," I snap, even though it's not Vanessa I'm mad at. It's those shitheads who set me up, who forced Lara to choose between her dream of the FBI and her morals.

"I know," Vanessa replies quietly. "What do you need from me, Ian?" She studies me. "Ah. You want your girl to get her job back."

"Yes!" I say a little too enthusiastically. "I mean, yeah, if it's a possibility . . ."

"It's not *im*possible," she says slowly. "But the SEC is scrambling right now. Even if Lara didn't actually do anything wrong, her boss did a damn good job of smearing her rep."

"But he's guilty for corruption of justice, accepting a bribe, and being an immense dick! His word doesn't mean shit."

"I know that. You know that. Everyone in this room knows that. But that's not how this world works, Ian. It's a perception thing. Investment brokers can come back from it. Hedge fund managers can come back from it. But SEC investigators suspected of sleeping with their suspect . . ."

I shake my head. "We waited—"

"Nobody's going to care about the timing," she says gently. "I suspect Lara knew that all along. It speaks highly of her feelings for you."

The words should make me elated. Instead, I've never been so miserable.

What's the point of clearing my name, of getting my life back, if she's not in it?

That's not even the worst possibility, though, I realize as I look at the closed door to my bedroom. Worse than no Lara in my life would be having her but her not having the SEC or the FBI because of her relationship with me.

I swallow, feeling the urge to throw my drink at the wall.

I remember now why I've never wanted to be in a relationship.

They fucking blow.

36

LARA

Week 6: Sunday Night

Of all the treks I've made to Ian's apartment over the past couple of weeks, this is without a doubt the hardest.

He opens the door at my knock, and it takes me a moment to register the sight of a wooden spoon in his hand, the smell of garlic permeating the apartment.

"Are you cooking right now?" I ask, a little bit stunned.

He gestures me in with the spoon and kisses my cheek. "I am. And you should be both flattered and worried that this is a first for me."

"Why worried?" I step inside and shut the door.

"Because I'm ninety percent sure I burned the garlic. I couldn't find shallots in the grocery store, so I subbed capers, which I later learned were not even close. And let's just say deboning a chicken is a hell of a lot harder than YouTube makes it look." He glances over his shoulder as he turns back to the stove. "Wine?"

"I'm good," I say, going to the counter and praying for courage to do what I came here to do.

He's already making it so hard. He's cooking, for God's sake. For the first time. For me.

I wouldn't have imagined there'd be a hotter sight than Ian in his suit or, better yet, Ian naked. But this Ian does something dangerous to my heart. This Ian has ditched the tie and jacket, rolled up his dress sleeves, and looks perfectly at ease.

No, not just at ease. *Happy.*

And for one brief moment, I wonder if maybe this could be our life . . . together.

But then I remember it's too soon, this happened too fast, and now we don't have the time we need.

"How'd the résumé updating go?" he asks, stirring whatever's on the stove.

I flinch. I'd told him I wanted to spend the day at the library updating my résumé, looking for jobs.

I'd lied.

"And are you sure you don't want wine? It's an excellent Malb—"

"Ian."

He turns toward me, and the second he sees my face, he flips off the burner and drops the spoon into the skillet. "What?" he asks, coming toward me and taking my hands. "Tell me."

"It's good news!" I say, forcing myself to smile.

He frowns, probably because my smile feels like a sad imitation of happiness.

"Just rip off the Band-Aid, Lara," he says squeezing my hands. "I can handle whatever you throw at me."

Not this.

"I got a new job," I say.

He furrows his eyebrows in confusion, then gives a tentative smile that breaks my heart. "That's great. Fantastic. Right?"

I nod enthusiastically, but like my smile, it doesn't feel right. "It's with the FBI. But—" I hold out my hand before he can get the wrong idea. "Not as an agent. As an analyst. It's a desk job. Bottom of the food chain, paper pushing, etc."

"Ah."

Yeah. *Ah.*

I have no issues with administration work. Hell, those people work harder than anyone I know and are some of the smartest.

But it's not what I wanted. It's not the dream. I know it. Ian knows it.

"With all that's happened, I'm no longer on the track to be an agent. My parents talked to some people, explained the situation, but . . . Well, like I said before, Quantico's competitive. My reputation right now? Mud."

He winces. "God, Lara. I'm so sorry—"

"No, it's okay," I interrupt, and this time my smile is a little more real, because it *will* be okay. I'm determined it will be. "It's still closer than I've ever been before. The job's in the white-collar division, so I'll get a ton of exposure and make connections. And every year, Quantico accepts analysts looking to become agents. It's not the way I thought I'd get in, but I'll get there."

"Then, hey, it is good news," he says softly. "But"—he bends slightly to look more closely at my face—"you're not happy. Why?"

I take a deep breath. "I wasn't updating my résumé today. I was packing." I say it quickly, directed at my feet.

His hands tense around mine. "Come again?"

I force myself to look up and meet his eyes. "I was packing. This FBI job . . . it's in DC."

His head snaps back in surprise. "Oh."

"Yeah."

He releases my hands and locks his behind his neck as he begins to pace, as though trying to work out a solution he likes better. "There's a branch of the FBI here, right? White collar, even."

"There is. But they're not the ones hiring analysts. And they're not the ones my dad has a connection with."

He stops pacing and drops his arms. "Your dad got you the job?"

I lift a shoulder. "My résumé got me the job. But yeah, he helped."

Ian smiles, and it's genuine. "That's great. Really great. It's taken him a while, but he's finally gotten behind your dream."

I study his face and see nothing but happiness. For me. Even as I walk away from him.

My eyes water, because it's in that moment that I know I love him. Because it takes a hell of a guy to put someone else's happiness above his own. To want something for me more than he wants something for himself.

He frowns when he sees my tears. "What's wrong?"

"Nothing," I lie. "Happy tears."

Happy about the job, sad to be leaving you.

"Hey," he says, pulling me in for a hug. "Don't cry. This is a good thing."

I nod, letting myself sink into his embrace, to absorb some of his strength and steadiness.

I hear him swallow, and his hand comes up to cup the back of my head. "Sucky for us, though."

I wrap my arms around his back. "Yeah. Sucky for us."

We hold each other for a long while. Not talking, not kissing. Just holding.

I wonder if he's doing what I've been doing for the past twenty-four hours, trying to figure out how to make it all work. His job. My job. *Us.*

If he is thinking that, he apparently doesn't come up with a solution, because he slowly eases me back. "What do you need from me? I can get a pizza. Help you pack."

I'm tempted—horribly tempted—just to have a little more time with him. But I don't think I can survive it.

I press the back of my hand to my nose to try and ward off the worst of the tears, but they come anyway. "I think I need a clean break," I manage.

His face crumbles for a second, and he shoves his hands in his pockets, looking at the floor then back up at me. "Right. Yeah. I get it."

We stand still in mute misery for a long moment.

Then he reaches for me, and I go to him, our mouths colliding in a kiss that's as hot as it is sad, a frantic melding of lips that's both a promise and a goodbye.

Don't go, his kiss says.

I have to, mine answers back.

When we pull away, we're both breathing hard, his hands on my face, his forehead resting on mine.

I have the fiercest urge to cling and an even more damaging urge to change my mind. To say the hell with the FBI and everything I've wanted and worked for my whole adult life for a guy who wants me but I think is still a long way off from loving me.

"I should go," I whisper. *I have to go.*

Ian nods and slowly releases me until his arms drop to his sides, letting me go.

I make it as far as the door before he says my name, the word both frantic and hesitant.

"Lara, what would you say . . . what would you do . . . if I asked you to stay?"

I could do it. The guy has more than enough money. I could ask him for a loan, and I know he'd give it to me in a heartbeat, though he'd be a pain in the ass about letting me pay him back.

And then what? I move in? Live off his salary? Become the kept woman known for trading her integrity for a man? It's not true, but the reputation would be there, and even if it weren't . . .

I need more than to be Ian Bradley's woman. I need to be Lara McKenzie, and Lara McKenzie still wants to be in the FBI.

"Don't," I whisper. "Please don't ask."

He nods and lets me go without another word.

I make it all the way to the back seat of a cab before I start crying for real.

37

IAN

Three Weeks Later: Thursday Afternoon

"You're doing it again," Kennedy says.

I look up at him in irritation. "Doing what?"

Matt is in the chair beside me and counts his fingers. "Grinding your teeth, muttering under your breath, glaring at anything that moves, snapping at anyone who looks your way . . ."

"So feel free to get out."

"It's my office," Kennedy says from the other side of the desk. "You get out."

"I thought we were debating who gets the other Mets ticket," I say.

Matt shakes his head and points at Kennedy. "I choose him. You're too much of a downer, man."

"Fine," I snap, standing.

Matt sighs. "Hold up. You need a distraction. Come to the game, but you have to promise to have a beer and at least try to have a good time."

"I don't want to go anymore," I say, knowing I sound like a petulant child and not giving a shit.

I haven't given a shit about much in the three weeks since Lara left New York.

And yeah, go ahead and accuse me of being the guy moping over a girl. I can take it because it's true.

I just don't know what to do about it. My job is here. Hers is there. I love my job. She loves her job.

I love her. She doesn't love me.

Damn it.

"Is this the end of my lecture?" I ask them. "If there's more, feel free to send me an e-mail with my flaws. I promise to read it never."

Kennedy and Matt exchange a look but wisely say nothing.

Kate sticks her head into the office to bark at me that I have a call on line two. She disappears without another word, and Kennedy and Matt stay silent, waiting for my explanation.

"She's still pissed at me," I explain. "Ever since . . ." I shake my head because I can't finish the sentence out loud. *Ever since Lara left.*

Kate's not the only one who's mad. Even Sabrina has been acting exasperated with me, as though I should be doing something about the situation.

But what can I do? It's not like I can call Lara and tell her to come back. I can't ask her to give up something she wants just because I can't stop thinking about her.

At my darkest hours, I want to. But I won't. I won't ask someone I care about to do something I can't bring myself to do:

Give up my work. Give up everything I've worked so fucking hard for.

This—Wall Street—is my life. This office, these people . . . they're everything I've wanted since I was fourteen, and I've *arrived*, damn it.

I've got the life I wanted.

Don't I?

I leave the guys and return to my own office, doing a double take when the orchid catches my eye. Fuck. When did it start to droop like that? Is there anything in my life not going to shit?

I drop into my chair, squeezing my eyes shut and pressing the heels of my hands to them for a moment.

Kate buzzes in on my intercom, and her voice is pure pissed-off female. "*Hello*? Line two!"

She hangs up again, and I pick up the line. "Ian Bradley."

"Hey, boy. My TV broke."

I let out an incredulous laugh. "Hey, Dave."

"This one wasn't my fault," he says defiantly. "My new girl brought her dog over, and the thing's as big as a horse. Knocked into the TV while chasing a damn tennis ball, sent the whole thing crashing down."

"Is the dog okay?"

"Yeah. You think I can get another TV before the weekend? Gotta see my boys beat the Cubs."

"Yeah, sure," I say, making a note.

He grunts in what I know is his version of a thank-you.

"So, how you doing? Saw those bastards who tried to take you down get sentenced next week."

"Yep." I tap my pen against the desk.

"Why ain't you gloatin' more?"

"Because I don't really give a shit what happens to two cowards. They've taken enough away from me."

Dave whistles. "You're good and pissed. If I didn't know better, I'd think they took more than your pride and a few weeks of your life."

"They took my girl," I mutter before I can think better of it.

"The SCT one?"

Close enough. "Yeah. She lost her job over this whole mess and had to take a new one in DC."

Dave grunts. "That sucks. The Nationals are pissing me off. Nothing but bad calls the last time they played the Phillies."

I say nothing, my mood too foul to feign interest in baseball.

"So, she didn't want ya?" he asks, cutting to the chase as he always does.

"I guess not." I rub my eyes. "Not enough, anyway."

He makes a spitting noise. "Ah, then who needs her?"

The unexpected show of loyalty makes me smile. It also makes me brave. Brave enough to ask something I've been wanting to for a long time.

"Dave . . ."

"Yeah?"

"Why didn't you ever adopt me?"

There's a long moment of silence, and when the answer comes, it's not what I expect.

"Hell, boy. You never asked."

I go still. "I was only fourteen when I came to stay with you."

"Maturity-wise, you were practically twenty. You always knew what you wanted, never made any secret 'bout it. Thought if you wanted me to adopt ya, you'd have said something."

My mind reels. It couldn't have been that simple. *Could it?*

"So, had I asked . . ." I clear my throat and break off.

"Well, yeah. Had you asked, I'd've adopted ya, son. You weren't much trouble."

Son. Not boy. *Son.*

I'm glad I'm alone in my own office, because my eyes water a little. All this time, and all I had to do was ask.

I go still, my tears drying immediately.

"Dave." My voice is a little rough, so I cough to clear it. "I've gotta go, but I'll get the TV there tomorrow."

"'Kay." He hangs up, and I smile, because apparently we've hit Dave's max capacity for affection.

We have not, however, reached mine. Not yet.

I pick up the phone again.

Kate's voice is clipped. "What?"

I blow out a breath. "Enough with the attitude, Henley. You should be happy. My orchid is almost dead, so you're going to win the bet. Congratulations."

"I didn't want to win like this," she grumbles.

"Meaning?"

"Meaning I didn't want to win because you died."

"I didn't die."

"You're acting like it. Dead on the inside."

I roll my eyes. "Are you going to spout hyperbole all afternoon, or can you do something for me?"

"What?" she asks suspiciously.

I grin. "Can you book me a flight to DC?"

I practically hear her sit up a little straighter. "For when?"

"As soon as possible."

38

LARA

One Day Later: Friday Night

"'Night, Lara. See you tomorrow."

I glance up from the filing cabinet and wave goodbye to Greg, one of the other analysts. "Have a good night."

I drop the rest of the files into their appropriate folders and head back to my desk.

My cubicle at the SEC was practically a mansion in comparison to the one I have here. The office lighting makes my hair look green, the coffee has a distinctly metallic taste, my desk smells like someone else's curry, and my chair has never even heard the phrase *ergonomically correct*. But . . . I love it.

I love it because it's in the FBI building.

I'll confess I was terrified it'd be a letdown. But I knew from the second I stepped through the front doors that it was right.

Or at least the right direction of right.

I'm still learning my way around, still learning who's who, what's what, who's helpful, and who will bite my head off when I ask a question. I almost love those interactions the most. I love telling myself that when I'm in that position of power, I'm going to be nice to the new kid.

And I am going to be in that position of power one day. I know it.

"Crap," I mutter, glancing at the clock. I'm supposed to meet my parents for dinner in fifteen minutes. The restaurant's nearby, but traffic is brutal.

Eventually I'll embrace the DC Metro system, but for now, I can only afford to live forty-five minutes from work and not particularly near any of the lines. My dad lent me his old car, and even with the constant maintenance on the damn thing, it's the easiest option.

I'm rushed for time, but I still take the long way to the elevator—the one that goes by the white-collar department. About half the agents are still in their offices. Agent Powers even lifts her hand in a friendly wave as I go by.

Someday. Someday one of these offices will be mine.

You see? I'm happy.

Well, I'm mostly happy.

A little sliver (okay, fine, a big sliver) misses Ian. A lot. I naively thought that it was just a proximity thing with him—that we had come together so fast, in such weird circumstances, that we'd gotten wrapped up in the idea of the romance rather than the romance itself.

Three weeks later?

I don't know. Three weeks later, it still feels like what we had was real.

He's called a couple of times, but I just . . . I can't. Not yet.

It's late enough in the evening that I have the building mostly to myself, so when I get off on my level of the parking garage, I'm able to do that awkward run/speed walk to my car without any witnesses.

Or not.

My footsteps slow as I approach my car. There's a man leaning against it, casual-like, feet crossed at the ankles.

Every woman's worst nightmare, right? Woman alone, dark parking lot, strange man.

Except he's not a strange man.

He's a familiar man in a really good suit. I hate to say it, but I miss Wall Street suits. The FBI does not give good suit.

Ian watches as I approach, arms crossed over his chest, bouquet of roses dangling from one hand.

"Ian?"

"She remembers my name. Good start." He flicks the flowers up and glances down at them. "I wanted to bring an orchid, but rumor has it they don't travel well. Kennedy and Matt assured me these are a solid substitute."

I smile and take them. "Tell Kennedy and Matt I'm impressed. I'm a fan of the classics."

"Thought you might be." He studies me. "How are you?"

I take a deep breath. Let it out. "I'm . . . confused. What are you doing here?"

He smiles and straightens. "We'll get to that. Tell me about your job first. Is it everything you dreamed of?"

I nod enthusiastically. "Yes. Absolutely. I mean, it's a lot of busywork but so fascinating. Today they asked me to revisit this cold case, and . . . well, I can't tell you about it, but the perp reminds me of you, and—"

He laughs. "The perp, huh? Maybe I should have brought two dozen roses."

I roll my eyes and smile. "You know what I mean. Too charming for his own good, great with the ladies."

"Hmm." He reaches out and grabs my hand, pulling me in. "You know this perp may have gotten it wrong. Turns out being great with the ladies isn't where it's at."

"No?"

"Nope. The smart ones zero in on one lady. Make her theirs."

"I see," I say, my heart pounding as I struggle to keep my voice playful. "However do they accomplish this? Bash her over the head with a stick and drag her back to the cave?"

"It's a thought. But I was thinking something more like . . ."

He reaches into his breast pocket.

Oh God! Oh God, he wouldn't. We are so not ready for that. I can't marry a man I barely know.

He pulls out . . . an envelope.

I don't know if I'm relieved or disappointed. Maybe a little of both.

He hands it to me.

I struggle to juggle the flowers, my purse, laptop bag, and envelope, so he takes my keys from my hand and relieves me of everything but the envelope.

I give him a curious look as I pull out . . . plane tickets. *Lots* of plane tickets.

The first one is a flight for next weekend—DC to New York.

The next is for the weekend after that—New York to DC.

I flip through the rest of them. There are three months' worth of plane tickets, alternating between New York and DC.

Between his city and mine.

"Ian?"

He lifts his eyebrows. "What do you say? Do long-distance with me?"

"Ian . . ." It's a sigh this time.

He reaches out and slides an arm around my back, the other cupping my neck, his thumb brushing along my jaw as though memorizing the shape. "I miss you, Lara. I miss you like crazy. I get you have to be here, and I have to be there. Though, for the record, I did contemplate the very impressive gesture of quitting my job and moving here. But I didn't think you'd respect me for it."

I shake my head. "You're supposed to be rich."

He laughs, and the sound makes my heart swell. "Damn straight. But I'm also supposed to be with you."

Ian touches his mouth lightly to mine, and when he pulls back to look down at me, his eyes are warm. "You thought I was going to whip out a ring, didn't you?"

I let out an embarrassed laugh. "Sort of."

He kisses me again, smiling against my mouth. "I thought about that grand gesture, too, but figured I'd better court you first."

I pull back. "Court me? Did you steal that from Kennedy's vocabulary—Wait. You *thought* about it? You thought about giving me a ring?" I nearly shriek.

He gives a little shrug. "It crossed my mind. After I realized I loved you."

My knees buckle, but he catches me.

"That was embarrassing for you," he teases.

I roll my eyes. "Give me a break. The guy I love surprised me with red roses, plane tickets, and vague chatter about marriage."

His eyes go bright. "The guy you love, huh?"

I tap the corner of the envelope to his chest. "Turns out I'm very impractical when it comes to you. You had me falling head over heels in love with you in just a few weeks."

"Just imagine what I can do in a few months," he says, wrapping both arms around me and lifting me off the ground.

I laugh and lower my mouth to his. "I can't wait to find out."

Epilogue

LARA

A Year-ish Later

"I'm late, I'm late. I'm so sorry I'm late," I say, dropping into the chair across from Ian. "Tell me you ordered me a drink."

As though on cue, a server appears with two glasses of champagne.

"Ooh, we're *fancy* tonight," I say, fluttering my eyelashes at the man who, after a year of dating, is still the best-looking thing I've ever seen.

"Yes, well, they were out of that terrible beer you loved so much at the dive bar near Quantico."

"Yeaaaaah, guess that was a situational thing. Who knew beer could taste totally different when it doesn't come after a long, grueling day of target practice?"

"God, I love it when you talk dirty to me," he says, winking and clinking his glass to mine. "So. How was your day, *Agent McKenzie*?"

I beam, because two months into my new job, it still doesn't get old.

"Didn't get to cuff anyone, but there's always tomorrow." I smile into my glass.

He leans forward and lowers his voice. "You can cuff me tonight, if you want."

"I think I'll take you up on that," I say with a mischievous grin. "How about you? Tell me about your day."

"Oh, you know, the usual. Kennedy pretends not to notice Kate; she continues to torture him. Matt and Sabrina got in a fight, so they might be dead."

"Same ol'."

He smiles. "Yep."

Except he's only partially right about the same ol'.

Some things *are* the same. Ian's still at the top of his game, still bringing in ridiculous amounts of money, plenty of which still goes to Ian's charity, another decent chunk to replacing Dave's TVs.

But some things are new, too. We managed to coax Dave out to New York for Thanksgiving last year. Ian looked so damn happy, I'm hoping Dave's holiday visit was merely the first in what will be a long-standing tradition.

As for me, I graduated from Quantico a few months back and was offered a job almost immediately. And brace yourself, people, because happily ever after doesn't get much happier than this . . .

The job's as an agent in the white-collar division. In New York. Headquartered just three blocks from Ian's apartment.

Well, now *our* apartment.

Told you. Happily ever after on steroids—my dream job *and* my dream guy.

Ian's studying me with a thoughtful look, and I glance up from my menu. "What?"

"You're smiling."

"Usually a good thing," I say, sipping my champagne.

He looks down, then back up. "You ever miss DC?"

"Nah. The pizza's better here."

"What about the men?"

"Toss-up." I shrug, glancing back at my menu. "My dad is still in DC, and he's pretty great."

Ian smiles. "Yeah, he is. Speaking of your dad, we had a little chat this afternoon."

My head snaps up. "You talked with my father? Without supervision? After the disastrous Christmas dinner discussion?" I'd never seen two men get so worked up over baseball versus hockey before. "What could you have possibly talked about?"

"You," he says matter-of-factly.

I narrow my eyes at him. "Me."

"Well, you and how he and I are going to have a lot more Christmases to settle that hockey argument," Ian says casually. *Too* casually.

My heart starts to pound. "Is that so?"

"I hope so. See, Lara . . ." Ian gets up from his chair and slowly starts to bend to one knee next to the table. "I called him with a question about his only daughter. An important one."

My eyes fill. "You did?"

Ian lowers all the way down in front of me and takes my hand as his other reaches into his pocket. "I did. He said yes, and I'm relieved. But what I really want to know is"—he flips open the ring box—"what will you say?"

I take a shaky breath, then pretend to be confused. "Hard to say. What's the question?"

Ian's eyes lose the teasing expression but none of the warmth. "Lara McKenzie, I love you more than any damn thing in this world. Will you marry me?"

I let out a hiccuping sob, even as the people around us make the requisite *awww* noises.

I set both hands on his face and press my lips to his. "You make me so happy," I whisper.

"That better be a yes," he says against my mouth.

I smile. "Yes. I can't wait to marry you, Ian Bradley."

So, I guess I lied before when I said happily ever after couldn't get any better.

It just did.

AUTHOR'S NOTE

Dear Friends,

Thank you so much for honoring me (and Ian and Lara!) with your hard-earned reading time. I know there are millions of books for you to choose from, and I'm so grateful *Hot Asset* made it onto your TBR list!

The 21 Wall Street series was originally conceived because of one simple author wish: to write about hot guys in suits. They're my favorite thing to read and thus . . . my favorite thing to write. ;-)

The series, however, quickly became so much more than that. Somewhere along the writing process, my "hot guys in suits" went from being stock photos in my mind to being real people—complex characters who came alive, not just through their relationships with the women who captured their hearts but through their friendships with one another. Soon I had not just the fantasy of the rich millionaires in their penthouses but characters whose vulnerability, banter, and loyalty to one another made me wish I could be part of their group. I hope you feel the same!

Next up in the series is Matt Cannon's story (*Hard Sell*, Fall 2018). As I'm sure many of you picked up on, he and Sabrina Cross have some serious chemistry . . . and major unfinished business. Ian and Lara will, of course, be making plenty of appearances, as will Kennedy and Kate.

Lastly, I need to take a quick minute to thank everyone who helped make this book possible. My agent, Nicole Resciniti, for knowing immediately what I was trying to do with the series the second I said the words *Wall Street*. For the amazing team at Montlake, especially Maria Gomez, for all their hard work in taking my beloved story and turning it into a polished book. For Kristi Yanta, my developmental editor, who put as much heart and soul into this story as I did. I know it was a long haul, but it was so worth it, and I'm so grateful! And lastly, a special shout-out to my Wall-Street-savvy father-in-law for pointing me toward the right resources for learning about the financial world!

Happy reading,
Lauren Layne

TURN THE PAGE FOR A SNEAK PEEK OF HARD SELL

21 Wall Street, Book Two
Available Fall 2018

Editor's Note: This is an early excerpt and may not reflect the finished book.

1

MATT

Monday Morning, September 18

"You're an angel, and I love you," I say with a reverence usually reserved for people in church.

My assistant lifts an eyebrow and holds out two aspirin. "Are you talking to me or the bagel sandwich?"

"Both," I say around a bite, holding out my free hand for the pills.

Kate waits until I swallow the sandwich, then holds out a venti Starbucks coffee that I use to wash down the pills.

"How'd you know?" I ask, picking up the egg and Swiss on sesame bagel once more.

"That you were hungover as crap? I get your flight change notifications. Taking an unplanned Sunday red-eye from Vegas to New York after a bachelor party pretty much says it all."

I wince. "Can we not say the word *Vegas*? Or *bachelor party*? And until further notice, all references to alcohol are hereby banned."

She smirks. "It sucks getting old, huh?"

"I'm not old," I say automatically. The very suggestion's an affront. After all, I'm Matt Cannon, Wall Street's legendary wunderkind.

And yeah, only douchebags would call themselves legendary, but in my case? It's kind of true. I graduated from high school when I was sixteen, college when I was nineteen, and got hired on at Wolfe Investments before I could drink. Legally. Because . . . this is Wall Street. Alcohol's as much a way of life as the money.

Whoops. I just remembered we're not talking about alcohol. Not until the aspirin, caffeine, and this sandwich work their sweet magic on my booze-fueled headache.

Anyway, the point is I'm only twenty-eight. Not exactly a boy wonder anymore, but to be one of the Wolfes before thirty is brag-worthy, and . . .

Oh hell, who am I kidding?

I can't drink like I could when I was twenty-two, and I am officially feeling the effects of the forty-eight-hour rager that was my big brother's bachelor party.

"How are you feeling, really?" Kate asks, giving me a critical once-over.

Kate Henley's one of those assistants who you guard more carefully than your wallet, Pappy Van Winkle, or bank account password.

Sure, she's got the petite, pretty, doe-eyed look of a 1950s debutante, but she's obscenely competent at her job. So competent, in fact, she works for not one demanding boss but *three*. A couple of years ago, I got promoted to director the same month as my two best friends and Wolfe colleagues, Ian Bradley and Kennedy Dawson. The promotion meant we each got our own assistant instead of sharing one. We couldn't decide who got Kate, so she took on all three of us and does it twice as well as any of the other assistants who support only one investment broker.

I smile. "Better. Thanks. Headache's already receding."

"Good. Because the Sams want to see you."

My smile disappears. "Now?" I check my Rolex. "It's barely eight on Monday morning."

"Yeah, well, this is Wall Street. Everyone's day started four hours ago. Speaking of which, I've called you, like, ten times."

I rub my forehead. "I lost my cell phone . . . somewhere. The Sams say what they wanted?"

"Nope," she says, bending to pull something out of a garment bag. "But they came by my desk themselves instead of sending Carla, which is never good. Put this on."

She hands me a skinny blue tie, and I obediently tug off the striped one I put on in the airport bathroom at baggage claim. At best it smells like the smoke of a Vegas casino. At worst . . .

The way Kate wrinkles her nose when she takes it tells me it's in the unnamed "worse" category.

I put the fresh tie around my neck, but she holds up a finger and waves it in a circle. "Hmm. You're worse off than I thought." She holds up a white dress shirt. "Wardrobe change. Where the hell'd you sleep last night, a barroom floor?"

"Didn't sleep at all," I mutter, unbuttoning my shirt.

It sort of sums up my and Kate's platonic relationship that I'm shirtless, but she doesn't so much as look at the six-pack I've earned through long gym hours as she hands me the shirt. "One day you really *are* going to be too old for this, you know."

"One day," I say with a grin as I put on the fresh shirt. "Not today."

A minute later, I've got a clean shirt, new tie, and feel slightly better as the aspirin and caffeine finally start to kick in.

"The guys in?" I ask, referring to Ian and Kennedy, as I straighten the knot of my tie. I don't have a mirror, so I spread my arms for Kate to assess.

She gives me a once-over. "Good as we're gonna get. Soon as you're done with the meeting, you need a shower. And no, the guys aren't in. Kennedy was grabbing an early coffee with a client, and Ian said he had an early meeting as well."

I lift my eyebrows. "Early meeting, meaning . . . he got distracted by Lara in the shower?"

"My thoughts exactly."

Ian is rather disgustingly in love with his fiancée, Lara McKenzie. And while their level of infatuation is nauseating, there's no woman I'd rather have lost my partner in playboy debauchery to than her. An agent with the white-collar division of the FBI, Lara's smart, funny, and, best of all, tolerates exactly none of Ian's bullshit, which is plentiful.

"Okay, let's do this," I mutter, taking one last bite of sandwich and a gulp of coffee. "Scale of one to ten, how intense were the Sams when they came by?"

"Eight," she says as we walk toward the elevators. "Here." Kate hands me a piece of gum as she punches the "Up" button.

I dutifully chew it until the elevator arrives, then spit it back into the wrapper so I'm not chomping gum like a sixteen-year-old cashier at the Gap when I meet with the CEOs of the company.

Kate holds out her hand, but I shake my head and step into the elevator. "I don't pay you enough to throw out my already-chewed gum."

"You don't pay me enough for *any* of this," she calls after me as the elevator doors close, separating us.

It's a short ride to the top floor of the building. Can't say I spend much time up here, thank God. It's not that I mind the bosses—or my boss's bosses in this case—I just tend to prefer drinking one vodka martini too many with them at the company holiday party.

Getting called up on a Monday morning when I'm hungover as hell? Not so much.

Carla, the CEOs' longtime assistant, gives me a smile that's friendly but a little sympathetic as well. That's not good. Either I look worse than I feel or she knows something I don't about what awaits me.

"Hey, Carla. Are they waiting for me?"

"Ohhh yes," she says with a low, nervous laugh. "They're waiting for you."

"Any hints?" I ask.

She blinks. "You read the paper today?"

"Uh, no. Not yet. Which one? The *Times*? The *Journal*?"

She sighs. "Oh honey . . ."

My heart beats a little faster because Carla's as unflappable as they come, and she looks . . . nervous.

I'm about to press her for more information when I hear my name. I glance up to see Sam Wolfe Jr. standing in the doorway of his office.

"Come on in, Matt." Shit. If Carla looks worried, Sam looks about thirty seconds away from an apoplexy.

"Sure thing," I say, forcing an easy grin as I amble into the small conference room where the *other* Sam is sitting at the end of the table.

Samuel and Samantha Wolfe, known as the Sams, are Wall Street's ultimate power couple. Sam inherited Wolfe Investments from his father around the same time that he married Samantha, a Wall Street powerhouse in her own right.

Neither smiles as I come in and greet them.

"Have a seat," Samantha says, gesturing at one of the available chairs.

I do as instructed, taking in the newspaper in front of her as I sit. I can see that it's the *Wall Street Journal* but not much else. I certainly can't figure out what the Financial District's favorite newspaper has to do with me personally.

Samantha takes charge, getting right down to business. "I assume you've read this." She sets a manicured hand on the paper.

"Ah, no. Not yet."

Sam's eyebrows go up, somewhere between disapproving and surprised. The *WSJ*'s required reading around here. I read it—I do. I just . . . Well, damn it. It's not even nine o'clock. I haven't gotten to it yet.

Samantha lets out a long sigh as she opens the paper, turns to the second page, and refolds it before sliding it toward me.

Still baffled, I reach out and pull the paper toward me, my eyes going straight to the photo. My stomach drops as I recognize the man in the picture.

Me.

And not *just* me. Me and a scantily clad woman draped across my lap, my hands on her bare waist.

The memories are hazy. This was Saturday night. Or was it Friday? The photo's in black and white, but the woman was blonde, the bra was red. Or was it pink? It was late by the time we got to that particular strip club, I remember that.

I drag my eyes away from the photo to the headline:

Have the Wolfes of Wall Street gone too far?

My stomach churns. I'm used to the Wolfes of Wall Street moniker—it's all any of us at Wolfe Investments heard after the Leonardo DiCaprio movie came out. But seeing it in print alongside my face in the *Wall Street Journal* of all places . . . this isn't good.

"You must have heard about it," Sam says, his voice a low, disapproving rumble.

"No." I resist the urge to run a hand over my neck, to see if I'm sweating. "I was on a red-eye." *And lost my phone somewhere in the weekend's debauchery.*

Sam grunts, then exchanges a long look with his wife. In my hungover state, I'm not at the top of my game, but I know that look doesn't mean good things.

Samantha's the one to give it to me straight. "You can read the full article later, but I'll give you the highlights: You stumbled into the same club as a *WSJ* reporter who was covering a story in Vegas. He was sober. You were not. You were seen tucking hundreds into G-strings, dropping *thousands* on a single round of expensive whiskey, and that wasn't even your last stop of the evening. He followed you to three other clubs, where members of your party unabashedly partook in illegal substances."

My head snaps up. "I don't touch drugs. Booze, that's it."

"Booze and women," Sam says with a pointed look at the paper.

"Lap dances aren't illegal. Neither's vodka or whiskey."

"No," Samantha grants. "And we're not here to act as your parents. You're one of our best, Matt, you know that. But this is bad. We've already received a half dozen calls from concerned clients, wondering just what the hell we're doing with their money."

"I spend *my* money," I say, stabbing a finger against the newsprint. "And I've earned every penny."

"We know that," Samantha says. "But you know as well as we do that perception often counts more than fact. Nobody's going to believe you didn't touch the cocaine. Nobody's going to believe the hundreds you threw at these women stopped at a harmless lap dance. Drugs, prostitution, reckless spending . . . those aren't accusations we can weather easily. Especially not after the insider-trading allegations against Ian last year. We're still doing damage control from that."

"He was found innocent," I snap, ever defensive of my friend, who may be a bit of a daredevil, but he plays by the book when it comes to his work.

"Yes. Officially," Sam says. "But as we said, there's the perception issue. And this . . ." He gestures at the paper and breaks off.

Samantha folds her hands on the table and meets my eyes. "Public relations and legal have been strongly suggesting that we let you go to ward off the worst of the reputation hit."

For a second, I think I've heard her wrong. "Excuse me?"

"We don't see the need to take it that far," Samantha says, pausing to let an unspoken *yet* linger in the silence. "We understand this was a bit of bad luck on your part, being in the same club as a reporter. But

Matt, we do have to do some damage control here. You've already had two clients request to be moved to another broker."

I manage to nod, even as my racing brain is in denial that this is happening. "Sure. Of course."

Samantha looks at her husband, who takes over. "We're thinking an image makeover."

"A what?"

"You know . . ." He waves his hand. "Cutting back on the booze. Limiting the late nights. Skipping the caviar at dinner. Keeping your bar bill under four figures. And for the love of God, avoiding the strip club and your cocaine-loving friends."

"Sure, of course," I say, already nodding.

"There's another thing," Samantha says. "All of this will help, but nothing signals a reformed man like a plus-one. I mean, look at Ian and Lara. He was even more wild than you, and now he's—"

"Domesticated, I know," I snap. "But he didn't plan for that, it just happened. I don't have a Lara McKenzie waiting in the wings. I'm single and happy to be."

"Well, get un-single," Samantha says, standing as though that's the end of the conversation. "Preferably in time for the Wolfe Annual Gala next month."

"Wait, what? What do you mean?"

Sam stands and moves so he's beside his wife. "She means that nothing cleans up a man's reputation like the right woman by his side."

"But—"

Samantha pins me with a look. "I'll spell it out for you, Matt. Get a girlfriend."

"Or?" I ask, sensing an ultimatum at play.

She gives a thin smile. "Or get a new job."

ABOUT THE AUTHOR

Photo © 2016 Anthony LeDonne

Lauren Layne, a former e-commerce and web marketing manager, moved from Seattle to New York City in 2011 to pursue a full-time writing career. Her first book was published in the summer of 2013, and since then, she's written more than two dozen romantic comedies, hitting the *New York Times*, *USA Today*, iBooks, and Amazon bestseller lists. She currently lives in New York City with her husband.

Made in the USA
Las Vegas, NV
17 November 2022